THE SENTINEL

THE SENTINEL

A Jane Harper Horror Novel

Jeremy Bishop

47NORTH

Text copyright © 2012 Jeremy Bishop

Published by 47North
P.O. Box 400818
Las Vegas, NV 89140

ISBN-13: 9781611099065
ISBN-10: 1611099064
Library of Congress Control Number: 2012951301

DEDICATION

For Kane Gilmour, for your unceasing support

1

Whales. What can I say about them? As an antiwhaling activist, I'm supposed to have this shtick memorized, supercharged, cocked, locked, and ready to fire across the bow of anyone who looks at a whale the wrong way. But here's the simple truth: while I share the same mild affection for the world's largest creatures that most people do, I sort of just fell into this job. I needed work when I got out of college and answered an ad in the paper. Turns out what I lacked in passion, I made up for by having an analytical mind and a knack for pretending to be someone I'm not; a lifetime of moving around the world and trying to fit in can do that to a girl.

So when I take the glass jar filled with red paint and lob it toward the *Bliksem*, one of Greenland's few whaling ships, I'm fairly indifferent to whether it hits the mark. But I'm currently incognito, so I need the effort to at least look genuine.

Red gore explodes across the *Bliksem*'s gray hull. I let out a genuine whoop. Some suppressed side of me finds this fun, and for a moment, I understand the appeal that has thirty, mostly college dropouts, heading out to sea to combat whaling for months at a time. It feels like when I egged Jimmy Sweedler's house after he left the prom with Susan Something. A part of me hopes he got her pregnant, was forced to marry her, and now lives in a trailer infested by rabid chipmunks. But the thirty-three-year-old, responsible part of me just feels bad for his parents, who had to clean up those two dozen eggs.

Yeah, *two dozen*.

I had anger issues.

Still do, actually, but I can keep it in check when I'm under-cover—or use it to fulfill the act.

"That's right, you whale-killing sons-a-bitches!" I shout, shaking my fist at the *Bliksem*, which is just a hundred feet away.

Cheers rise up from the deck crew (a.k.a., my fellow paint bombardiers) standing by my side. There are three men and two women on the deck with me—all at least ten years younger than me. In fact, other than Captain McAfee and his one-man "security" team, an Australian known only as Mr. Jackson, I am the oldest crew member on board. Much of the young volunteer crew sport dreadlocks, not simply as a fashion statement but also because freshwater showers are rationed while at sea. As a result, the *Sentinel*—the antiwhaling ship that's been my home for the past month—smells like it must have when it was an active-duty Norwegian whaling ship.

"Nice shot!" shouts Greg Chase, the scrawny first mate. He's got a big, awkward smile on his face, which is covered in patches of facial hair struggling to proclaim him a man. Complementing his shaggy face is a pair of glasses that sit askew on his nose. The kid—he's twenty-three, but I can't help thinking of him as a kid—looks like he should be in his parents' basement playing Dungeons & Dragons, not attacking whaling ships in the Arctic Ocean off the northern coast of Greenland. That said, his brown eyes absolutely gleam with excitement, and he's by far the smartest person on this ship, which makes him a threat. Because if anyone is going to figure out I'm not who I claim to be, it's him.

So when Chase hands me a second glass jar, I take it with a double flick of my eyebrows that says I'm getting my rocks off, too. Before my first attempt, the other deckhands had loosed a barrage of nearly fifteen paint jars, all of which fell short of the mark—so much so that the crew of the *Bliksem* had begun to laugh and mock us with an assortment of hand gestures that universally translates to "cocksuckers."

They're all frowns now. Dressed in thick sweaters and winter caps, some of the *Bliksem*'s crew leans over the rail to see my handiwork. The crimson stain, which looks eerily like blood, covers the ship's name stenciled on the side and runs in red rivulets toward the sea. It's a gruesome sight, which I suppose is the point. A dead and bled whale pulled into port doesn't do much to turn the stomach, but a ship covered in blood from the hunt might not be so kindly received. And the images being captured by the *Sentinel*'s crew will make great PR. Bold? Yes. Effective? I'm not convinced.

But judging the effectiveness of the *Sentinel*'s tactics isn't why I'm here. My job—my true job as an undercover investigator for the World Society for the Protection of Animals (WSPA)—is to observe and record the less noble actions, if any, of the *Sentinel* and her crew. The allegations leveled against the *Sentinel* and her captain are sullying the whaling debate and making the antiwhaling community look like zealots. So I'm here to either vindicate them or expose them as pirates, turn my evidence and testimony over to the international and Greenland authorities, and clear the good name of other antiwhaling organizations. On top of that, I'm tasked with the job of recording the effectiveness of the whaler's hunting techniques. Greenland only recently started hunting humpbacks again, and their whalers are out of practice. Many whales take a half hour to die—some as long as six hours. (Experienced whalers can put a whale out of its misery inside of one minute.) Given the dual nature of this mission, the WSPA needed someone with both undercover experience and a level head.

Translation: my lack of passion keeps me from freaking out at the sight of whale blood. Call me a cocksucker in sign language and I'll throw red paint at you—or worse if I can get my hands on you.

Kill a whale and I'll take notes. I believe in the cause—in a world full of cows, why hunt endangered or even threatened creatures? But I've lived all around the world, have eaten most meats imaginable, including—*gasp*—whale, and I've seen more than a few animals slaughtered.

It's the circle of life.

Hakuna matata.

Pass the A.1.

I haven't had a bite of meat since stepping foot on the *Sentinel*, which runs a vegetarian galley. I've lost five pounds and have more energy, but damn, I could go for a cheeseburger. I force the thought of cooked meat from my mind and focus on the task at hand.

With all eyes on me, I raise the jar over my head, take aim, and see a tall man with long blond hair on the deck of the *Bliksem*. He's pointing a video camera in my direction. I flinch away from the lens. "Shit!"

If my face is caught on camera while taking part in this act of high-seas vandalism, it could destroy the validity of my testimony. I can see it now: *The violence needs to stop, says the fist-shaking, paint-throwing, crazy lazy. But they called me a cocksucker by thrusting their hands toward their open mouths and pushing their cheeks out with their tongues! Like this! Sorry, that was rude. We were implying you needed to brush your teeth, say the whalers. Fresh breath is important to a seafood-eating culture.*

"What is it?" Chase asks. "You all right?"

His concern is nice but fades quickly when I say, "They're recording us."

"They *always* record us," he says. "This is what you signed up for, Harper. You're here to take a stand. To go on record against these murderers. If you go to jail, so be it. That's what we do. I've been in jail four times already."

How Chase could survive in jail is beyond me. I can think of ten raunchy inmate nicknames for the kid off the top of my head. He doesn't give me time to test them out in my mind.

"Look," he says. "I know this is your first time out. And it can be intimidating. You're not used to this kind of action. I get it. You can cover your face if you want, but eventually you'll have to make a stand and reveal yourself."

I contemplate making a joke about revealing myself, but that would either turn him on or piss him off—neither of which is something I want happening, so I hold my tongue.

He reaches past my head, pulls up the hood of my bright red jacket, and ties it tight so only my eyes can be seen. "These guys are amateurs. They've never had to face us before. This isn't like the Japanese. They have no LRAD, no flash-bangs, no water cannons. They don't even have a loudspeaker to shout at us! But you've got the best arm on board, and I want you to fuck their shit up!"

He's got a bigger smile now. Couple his grin with the goofy face and passion stolen from a *Braveheart* speech, and I can't help but laugh. He takes my chuckle for excitement, and I play the part. With my face concealed, I turn and send another jar sailing across the hundred-foot divide between the *Sentinel* and the *Bliksem*.

But I've put a little too much pepper on this pitch, and instead of striking the hull of the whaling ship, it soars toward the wheel-house. The tall blond man, who looks like some kind of modern Viking, ducks, and for a moment I think I've been saved. Then the distinctive sound of a breaking window fills the air. I cringe, thankful that the cinched hood hides my face from their crew and ours.

A battle cry rings out from all around me. Not just from the crew on deck but also from the *Sentinel*'s wheelhouse. The whole crew has seen what I just did.

Great.

Chase gives my shoulder a hearty shake like he's Captain Blackbeard and shouts, "They're not going to want to pilot that ship for weeks!"

"From paint?" I ask. I imagine that some of the instruments got splattered in red, but I can't see how a single bottle of red paint thrown through the wheelhouse window could disable a two-hundred-foot ship.

Chase's smile turns fiendish, and I know I've been duped.

I curse myself for not looking at the bottle before I threw it and ask, "What was it? What did I throw?"

"Butyric acid," he says.

"Acid!"

He's laughing now, and I suddenly wonder if he's sane. The FBI might have been a better choice for this undercover mission. Of course, we're in Greenland's waters, and the *Sentinel* is registered in the Netherlands, so I think this would actually be the CIA's jurisdiction. But the CIA is too busy keeping people from blowing up buildings. They probably don't think twice about whales, unless they can be weaponized, which I'm sure someone somewhere is working on. So that leaves me, Nancy Drew of the seven seas.

"Don't worry," he says. "It's no more acidic than orange juice. It's essentially rotten butter. Slippery as hell and smells worse than a point-blank blast from a skunk's ass. Worst thing you could ever smell."

Chase's nose must not work, because the people on board this ship are the worst thing I've ever smelled. I look to the *Bliksem* and see the wheelhouse crew stumbling and slipping out of the cabin. The tall Viking man with the camera catches an older, chubbier version of himself wearing a captain's cap and helps the man down the stairs leading toward the main deck. I'm thankful that the man is no longer recording, but my relief is short-lived. The old man I suspect is the captain of the *Bliksem* collapses at the bottom of the stairs.

The cheers around me grow louder still, and I feel sick to my stomach. Opposing the killing of whales does not justify harming people. It's just not the same. That's an opinion that could get me thrown off this ship, but the man could be having a heart attack. And it could be my fault! What if the jar hit him? What if he got a dose of the vile-smelling acid in his face? As panic grips me, I fear that Chase will ask me to throw more bottles. I feel so weak with worry that I doubt I could do it. Thankfully, the captain's voice booms from the wheelhouse window before more bottles can be thrown.

"Time to send the message home!" Captain McAfee shouts. The man is tall and skinny but has the voice of a baritone. He's all contradictions. Sixty-five, but full of energy. A full head of hair that's stark white. Went through knee surgery after an accident but walks like a middle-aged mom trying to regain her figure. Preaches love for the Earth's creatures, unless you include humans. "Get away from the rail, and hold on tight!"

The crew around me jump away from the rail like it's been electrified. But I stand dumbly in place.

"Harper!" Chase shouts. "Get away from the rail!"

"Why? I don't—" But then I see it. We've changed course and are closing the distance to the *Bliksem* at a sharp angle. The *Sentinel* was an ice-breaking whaling ship before it was bought and outfitted for antiwhaling missions. It sports multiple hulls, and its bow is strong enough to slice through icebergs. I imagine ship hulls aren't too dissimilar.

"McAfee's going to ram them?" I ask no one in particular.

But Chase has heard me and shouts, "Yes! Now get down here!" He takes hold of my jacket and yanks me back. I fall to the black deck and am pinned down by the malodorous Chase. A moment later, an impact shakes the ship. The groan of metal on metal drowns out the shouting voices of both crews and lingers for what feels like minutes.

When it ends, I'm pulled to my feet. The deck crew rushes back to the rail and lets out a cheer. I stumble up behind them and catch sight of the *Bliksem*. Its port side hull has a long dent that isn't nearly as bad as I expected, but that's probably only because it's also designed to take on icebergs. A lesser ship would have no doubt been sunk.

I marvel that the *Bliksem*'s crew hasn't taken aim with their harpoon or tried to ram us in return. At first I think they're incredibly patient people, but then I remember the captain. It's possible they're preoccupied with saving the man's life. In fact, as the *Bliksem* languishes behind, I wonder if anyone remains in the wheelhouse. The Arctic is a bad place to be on a boat without a pilot. But then I see the Viking man with a bandana wrapped around his face. He climbs the stairs to the wheelhouse and pauses at the top to look at us—at me. The *Sentinel*'s crew shouts obscenities at the man until he enters the wheelhouse.

As the voices fade and calm returns to the Arctic sea, I let slip my true feelings. "He's fucking insane."

It's just a whisper, but Chase hears me. He spins around, eyes ablaze, and says, "I know. He's amazing."

The fact that "fucking insane" is taken as a compliment is nearly the last straw, but I manage to swallow my revolt and say, "So what next? Is that it? Mission accomplished?"

"No, no, no," he says, licking his lips like a hungry dog. "We've only just begun."

2

I lie in my cot, hands clasped behind my head, and stare at the ceiling. I'm exhausted and emotionally drained from the day's excitement, but sleep is something I can only daydream about at the moment. The crew is having a party. It's not supposed to happen. Captain McAfee runs a dry ship. But the neo-hippie crew brews a tea that I think must be laced with something. Because after drinking it, the party starts, inhibitions go out the window, and the thump, thump, thump of drug-enhanced sex echoes through the ship.

The guys grunt like they're baboons with bright blue asses, each trying to upstage the other.

The girls put on an audio show worthy of any porno, filled with "Yes, yes!" and "Harder!" and squeaked-out *Oh my Gods*.

And all I can do is lie back and listen to a chorus of dry humping. Seriously, I doubt many of them are doing the deed. Maybe at first, but now, with so few opportunities to get clean? *The smell*—I laugh, thinking about it. I snuck a package of one hundred baby wipes on board. If it were discovered, I'm sure they'd be stolen or borrowed into extinction within a few days. I sneak a single wipe into the bathroom with me and wipe myself down twice a day in an effort to stay odor-free. The evidence gets flushed. My black hair is cut short, so it's easy to manage, and I keep it messy and spiky to help fit in.

But I'm also clean because I keep my pants on. Not that I've been tempted to do the nasty while on this trip. No one here, male or female, even closely resembles the kind of man I'd be interested in. Some of the guys are lookers, sure, and that's fine if you can get past the smell, but the true measure of a man is his heart, not his cock. That's what my father said. Lovely thing to teach a daughter, but the Colonel didn't censor himself for anyone. I swear he'd have been a general if he could've controlled that yap of his.

It also helps that no one has even approached me. A number of girls on board are pretty, but the guys seem to favor good humor over pretty eyes. In that category, Jenny Gillespie is queen, despite being a bit chubby. She's got a figure like some ancient revered fertility goddess. Apparently chunky women were hard to find a thousand years ago before Walmart gave them a place to congregate.

I like to think that I haven't been approached yet because they see the toughness in my eyes—a genetic trait inherited from my father—but that can't be it. If their hippie brew is enough to overcome their stench, it's certainly potent enough to blot out any fear of me.

Am I scorned? I wonder. *Am I a woman scorned?* Someone, somewhere climaxes loudly, and I burst out laughing.

A knock at the door silences me.

This is new.

The handle turns before I can respond. Light fills the room, forcing me to squint. "That you, Peach?"

Peach is my roommate—I have no idea what her actual name is. She's got long dreads, a short body, and a flat chest. Most of the guys here would pass her up if she weren't such a slut. When I see the silhouette of my visitor standing more than a foot taller than Peach, I know I've got my first caller. Must have made the brew extra potent tonight, because the only pheromone I'm putting off is unscented Seventh Generation baby wipes mixed with a strong dose of "get the fuck out."

"You awake, Harper?"

The voice is clear and unhindered by any mind-altering substances. As a result, my visitor is easy to identify.

Greg Chase.

"You'd have to be dead to sleep through this noise," I say.

"I witnessed a seal hunt once. Mothers and babies. None were spared the club."

Well, this is morbid, I think.

A rapid-fire banging issues from a neighboring cabin.

"This sounds worse."

His quick turnabout makes me laugh despite myself. "That's awful," I say.

"Mind if I turn on the light?" he asks.

"Go for it," I say, but then I'm filled with a fear that he'll be buck naked.

Yellow light blooms from a small desk lamp, lighting the small cabin in a gentle glow. I'm happy he didn't use the fluorescent overhead light. Those things make me wish I was blind. I'm even happier that he's dressed in shorts and a short-sleeve shirt. It's summer here in the Arctic, so the temperature bounces back and forth between forty and fifty degrees—warm enough to melt a crapload of ice but not really warm enough for beach attire.

He notes my attention to his clothing. "I don't mind a little chill. Helps me think."

I sit up a little, mindful to keep my blankets pulled up over my chest. I, too, don't mind a little chill. Helps me sleep. But my tank top could be misconstrued as suggestive, so I keep the comforter hiked up like a chastity cloak. He hasn't said anything else, so I break the silence with a simple, "What's up?"

He sits in the desk chair, which is free of Peach's mess mainly because I actually use the desk and clear it off on a daily basis. The rest of the room is pretty much a pile of worn clothes, odd supplies, antiwhaling literature, and rotting food.

I try to breathe through my mouth.

"You stepped up today," he says, looking down at me with what I think are kind eyes, but his glasses have made them small, like some kind of burrowing mammal, so I'm not entirely sure. "You know, I wasn't sure about you at first."

Uh-oh. "Why's that?" I ask.

"To be honest, you're not our typical volunteer."

I do my best to wave him off. "I'm not different from the—"

"Yes," he says, "you are. You're intelligent."

"There're a lot of smart people on board," I say, despite the words tasting like bullshit.

"Smart, yes," he says. "Intelligent, no. There's a difference." He motions to the messy cot behind him. "Peach is smart." He picks up an antiwhaling pamphlet with a Greenpeace logo on it. "She can absorb almost any subject and regurgitate the information in her own words. She's contributed a lot of great articles to Sea Sentinel's website."

I look at all the reading material strewn around the room. I'd never really noticed Peach reading it, but I suppose that's why it's there.

"But," he says, tossing the pamphlet away, "she can't think for herself. She can't plot, can't strategize, can't predict."

"And I can?" I ask.

"I suspect so."

"Why?"

"For starters, you're one of four people who won't leave this ship with an STD."

I laugh again but stop when I see that he's serious. I quickly identify the other three disease-free crew members: McAfee, who seems to have no interest in anything but whales; Mr. Jackson, whose obsession with order and cleanliness repels the ship's females like a force field; and Chase, who values clear thinking, is very responsible, and I now suspect is the mind behind McAfee's madness.

"Okay, busted, I'm smart *and* have opposable thumbs," I admit, but I need to end this conversation before he starts asking questions. I've got a cover story, but the WSPA isn't the CIA. I don't have fake IDs or the documents to back me up. A few calls from the ship's satellite phone and I'd be revealed. "But it's late, and I really should try to sleep despite the noise, so if this is going to be a 'way to go, champ,' speech, let's skip to the end."

I flash a smile that says I'm joking, but no one ever says something like that without at least being half-serious.

He grins and stands. "Fair enough. But that wasn't the only reason for my visit. Our cause needs more people like you. Like me. Committed people. I think we make a great team."

I'm tempted to say, "Me Tarzan, you Jane," which would be ironic because my first name *is* actually Jane, and it would be insulting because between the two of us, I'm clearly Tarzan and there is no doubt that he is Jane. I keep my mouth shut, but a moment later wish I'd said something, because he finishes with, "Maybe more."

He looks at me with the same blazing eyes I saw staring down the *Bliksem*, gives a wink, and heads for the door. "We'll talk more in the morning." He stops in the doorway and looks back at me.

With a grin, he sings, "The lookout in the crosstrees stood, with his spyglass in his hand. 'There's a whale, there's a whale, there's a whalefish,' he cried, and she blows at every span, brave boys, and she blows at every span."

He closes the door behind him, leaving me stunned and unsettled. I now know why none of the guys have made a pass at me. They've been forbidden. I'm off-limits, care of the first mate. And while I appreciate the fact that I haven't had to deal with sexual advances, having to turn down a horny sailor or ten is far less creepy than being claimed by the Dungeon Master. Even worse, he's just quoted an old sea shanty about whalers spotting a whale to hunt, but I got the clear impression that he is the whaler in the song, and I am the whale.

So much for "Me Tarzan, you Jane." No, I tell myself, *you Ahab, me Moby Dick, and if you hunt me, I'll kill your crew, sink the ship, and then pull you under. Dad would be proud.*

Before I can smile, my thoughts are interrupted by a loud warning klaxon and the sound of shrieking voices—the kind that say, "Someone's just been murdered."

3

After throwing on a pair of jeans, I dash up the stairs, taking them two at a time, toward the main deck. I'm pulling my sweater over my head when the ship turns hard to port. I tip to the side, slam into the stairwell wall, and fall. My head pops out of the top of the sweater, and I let out a shrill cry. I'm instantly embarrassed despite the fact that I might break my neck, but I know I look and sound like the Muppet Beaker, so there's that. But luckily the Swedish Chef is there to catch me.

Two strong arms embrace my falling body, and I jolt to a stop against a cushiony body.

"You okay?" Jenny Gillespie asks.

"I'm good," I say, standing and pushing my arms up the sleeves, trying not to look as stupid as I feel.

But Jenny is looking past me, toward the top of the stairs and the continuing shrieks of horror. She could not care less about my appearance.

I wonder if all fat people are like that—and then feel like a total asshole for thinking it. I would have fallen down ten metal steps and could have broken my neck if not for her. I decide to stop privately mocking her and other people who shop at Walmart. Okay, just Jenny. Walmartites are still fair game. It's highly doubtful anyone on this ship would shop from an evil corporate giant.

A high-pitched squeal rolls down the stairwell.

"What's going on up there?" one of the male crew members asks. I'm not sure what his name is. I think he's the cook, which does nothing to ingratiate him to me. Raw vegetables are the best thing on the menu.

I realize the question was directed at me. I'm first in line. And there are now five people behind me. "I have no idea," I say and continue my trek to the main deck.

The door has been left open, which is a no-no in the Arctic, where even during midsummer, temps can dip below freezing. I exit quickly, am struck by a cold breeze, and hug my arms around my chest and hunch down. The action saves me from a bloody fate but makes Jenny a very large target.

"Something hit me!" she shouts, clutching her chest and staggering to the side.

I race up to her, hoping she hasn't been shot. I didn't hear a gunshot and seriously doubt Greenland's whalers are using sound-suppressed handguns, never mind the accuracy it would take to shoot someone from one moving ship to another. But as ludicrous as it sounds, she *was* hit by *something*. As she sits down behind one of the Zodiacs secured to the main deck, I quickly survey our surroundings and note that the second Zodiac is missing. Strange but not a threat. I look up briefly and see a furious Captain McAfee staring down at the chaotic scene, shouting something I can't hear. When Jenny releases a string of rapid-fire *Oh my God*s, I turn back to her.

Dark red blood stains the sweater where her hands are clutched. "It hurts," she says.

"Let me look," I say.

She shakes her head. The first reaction most people have to being severely injured is the desire not to know exactly how bad it is. But I've heard enough war stories from my father to know not to screw around with injuries. If it's bad, there might only be minutes to save someone, or to say good-bye. "Let me look, now!" I shout.

My raised voice startles Jenny into compliance. She slowly moves her hands away. There's enough blood to make me gasp, but I can't see a tear in her sweater. And if it's intact, so is everything else. "You're fine," I say.

Her eyes go wide. She looks down at her chest. Gives it a pat. She looks relieved but says, "What hit me? It really hurt."

As a coppery smell tickles my nose, I begin to suspect an answer.

A wet *thwack* a moment later confirms it. A chunk of ragged, fatty meat wrapped around a thick bone lands on the deck behind me. A part of me imagines the meat on a grill, and my stomach rumbles. But Jenny stops my fantasy short.

"What is that?" she shouts, recoiling from the flesh, which has clearly been drowned in blood before it was thrown the distance between the *Bliksem* and the *Sentinel*.

I pick up the meat, drawing a squeal of disgust from Jenny.

"They're scraps," I say.

"Scraps?"

"From a kill."

"From a kill?"

Oh good Lord, Jenny! "From a whale. It's whale meat." I point to her chest. "And that's whale blood all over you."

Her pink cheeks go white, like she's some kind of color-changing octopus. Jenny's mortified face coupled with the horrified screams of the rest of the crew, who've figured out what's being hurled at them, is more than I can bear.

A snicker emerges from my lips, and I clamp my hand over it.

But Jenny has seen, and her disgust turns to righteous anger. "You think this is funny?"

Angry Jenny is much more amusing than disgusted Jenny, and I fail to contain my laughter. After five seconds, her face lightens. I've heard it said that laughter is contagious. Sitcoms use laugh tracks for that very reason, but I've never actually seen an explosive person defused by laughter. Apparently Jenny has a sense of humor buried somewhere in her girth.

Damn, how long did I last? Three minutes before I mocked her size again? I'm so evil!

We're both cackling like wounded seagulls when I glance at the wheelhouse again and find McAfee's eyes glaring down at us. His eyes lock onto mine, and I don't know if the man has telepathic powers or what, but I swear I hear him say, "There will be a reckoning."

Laughing at something like this is no doubt akin to mutiny. And I've pulled Jenny into the shitter with me. Thankfully, the captain has bigger problems to handle tonight. He'll no doubt do what he normally does—retreat to his quarters with Chase and emerge two hours later with a grand master plan I'm fairly certain will come from Chase's brain. If Chase has as much pull with the captain as I suspect, I might be able to get away with my humorous breach of protocol, but I doubt it.

I help Jenny to her feet, saying nothing about the captain. She had her back to him, so it's possible she might escape his wrath, and I don't want to worry her. Two scares in one night might be more than her heart could—*fuck! I am evil!*

"Stay here," I tell her as I work my way around the Zodiac. With whale meat being flung around like we're in the middle of some whaling-high-school food fight, it's a risky venture, but I need to see it. I need to see the Vikings hurling bloody meat. I tell myself it's for my report, but it's really just because I find it so amusing. Flinging meat in most situations would strike me as silly and wasteful, but throwing whale meat at the *Sentinel*—well, that's just pure genius.

Jenny doesn't argue, and I round the front of the Zodiac. A wall of cheering men greets me. The all-male crew of the *Bliksem* stands along the rail, dipping their hands into buckets of meat and hurling it toward the *Sentinel*. And unlike the *Sentinel's* peace-loving crew, every crew member on board the *Bliksem* throws like a man. I look to my right and see a long stretch of bloody meat sliding down the side of the ship, walls covered in whale blood. What I don't see are people. The crew has retreated from the attack, hence the cheers of the opposing crew.

Then I see the Viking, lit by the *Bliksem's* floods. He's looking right at me again. But I'm not hidden beneath a hood this time. He can see my face. My body. And I sense the eyes of a man at sea too long staring at me. I shake my head no at him.

He flips me off.

I counter his continuing barrage of rude sign language by returning a volley of my own, duplicating the cocksucker gesture his crew is so fond of. And strangely, despite being on opposing ships, separated by a hundred feet, we share a laugh.

I glance around, making sure no one has seen, and when I look back, the Viking looks worried. He stumbles a bit and then is waving his hands at me, telling me to get back. For a moment I wonder why, and then realize I'm an idiot for not seeing the same thing twice in one day.

The *Bliksem* is closing the distance.

They're going to ram us.

Tit for tat on the high seas.

Damn, someone's going to get killed if this stupidity doesn't stop. Fueled by rage, I storm past Jenny and head toward the wheelhouse door.

"What are you doing?" Jenny asks.

"McAfee is going to apologize and end this, or I'm going to throttle his ass and stage a one-man mutiny."

Jenny follows me and says, "I'm with you."

"He's likely to lock us up," I warn.

"I'd like to see him try," she says.

I climb the steps to the wheelhouse feeling more confident. If McAfee gives me trouble, I'll just have Jenny sit on—

Damn it!

4

The metal stairs clang beneath my feet as I storm up to the tall wheelhouse. The *bong, bong, bong* of my feet on the steps has alerted the bridge crew to my approach, so when I burst through the door, all eyes are on me. A gust of wind sweeps in behind me. It's a rather dramatic entrance, and I think it might help my cause.

Then I see Captain McAfee. He goes nuclear.

With a beet-red face, he shouts, "Get this trash off my bridge!"

Chase is there. He's stunned. "Captain?"

"She can't be trusted!" he shouts and then stabs a finger toward me. "How many more of you are there? What are you really doing here?"

What the hell? The level of manic craziness radiating from McAfee sends a wave of nervousness radiating out of my stomach. Still, this needs to end. Jenny gives me a little push from behind, urging me on. I recover from the captain's verbal slap and remember why I'm here.

"You need to contact the *Bliksem*, now," I say with as much authority as I can muster. "This can't continue."

"What are you talking about?" Chase asks. He's starting to get a look in his eyes, not quite as accusing as McAfee's, but suspicious.

"We throw paint at them, fine. Rotten butter? Stupid, but okay, whatever. But then we *ram* them and now they're going to ram us? How's that—"

"What?" McAfee shouts, a look of true horror entering his eyes. He dives to the port side of the wheelhouse and looks out the window at the *Bliksem*. I catch a whispered, "Oh my God." I wonder why Mr. Ram-Happy is worried about getting up close and personal, and then he shouts, "Hard to starboard! Flank speed!"

Flank speed? Seriously? Flank speed is faster than the ship's full speed. It's a fuel hog and can't be sustained for long because the engines on this refurbished ship will overheat. I've never heard the term used outside of a military context. It's a last-ditch effort reserved for emergencies like trying to evade an enemy aircraft. Granted, we're about to get T-boned by an ice-class ship, but I thought that was the game McAfee played. His level of panic now seems out of place.

Then he's got the radio in his hand. "*Bliksem, Bliksem,* this is the captain of the *Sentinel*. Stand down and we will leave you in peace."

Several of the crew in the bridge, including Chase, turn their heads toward the captain, aghast. Retreat is bad enough, but a cease-fire?

"He's probably lying," Jenny whispers.

She's right. McAfee is as untrustworthy as any genuine pirate. He'll say and do just about anything to stop the killing of whales. Anything but accept defeat. But his concern seems genuine.

When there is no reply, McAfee speaks in the radio mic again, "*Bliksem, Bliksem,* this is—"

A booming voice interrupts. At first the words are hard to make out, but I realize that the voice is speaking Greenlandic—no, not speaking, singing.

McAfee lets out an angry shout and tosses the mic to the bridge floor. He storms back toward the window, where Chase is watching the *Bliksem*'s approach.

"She's a fast ship," Chase says, matter-of-factly. "We can't out-run her, even at flank speed."

McAfee pounds his fist against the windowsill. He's like a big four-year-old who's just had his favorite toy taken away.

"You can dish it out, but you can't take it?" I can't help myself. I inherited more than my eyes from my father, and what's the point in staying silent now? I've already outed myself. Gotta get my wise-cracks in before they lock me up.

"Someone get her off of my bridge!" McAfee shouts.

When no one moves, I notice that Jenny is standing tall behind me, arms crossed, lips down-turned in a snarl. I'm not sure why Jenny is supporting me right now, but I'm glad for it.

"Where's Captain Crew Cut when you need him?" I ask. I've never used the nickname before, but have no doubt that everyone knows I'm referring to Mr. Jackson. He'd have no problem remov-ing both Jenny and me, even if we decided to put up a fight, so I'm glad he's not here, but then that's the real question. *Where is he?*

I remember the missing Zodiac and I'm struck with a realiza-tion. "You instigated this, didn't you?" I ask, stepping farther into the bridge. "Jackson's not here. A Zodiac is missing." No one on the bridge looks surprised by this information. Some of them no doubt helped launch the Zodiac.

"We did nothing to warrant this attack," Chase says, keeping a measure of calm about him.

"You mean aside from ramming them earlier?" I say.

Chase's eyes go dark for a moment, and I see an anger matched only by McAfee's.

"Ignore her," McAfee says. He turns to the crew manning their posts at radar, the wheel, weather, and charts. "Where's the nearest land?"

Land?

"We're four miles out from the mainland," someone says.

"Map shows a peninsula jutting out," someone else says. "Maybe just a mile to the east."

"Get us as close as you can," the captain says. "Where are they?"

"Closing," Chase says from his spot by the window, "but not fast. We have a minute at best."

"Too close," McAfee mutters.

"Too close for what?" I ask.

It's like I'm not in the room. No one acknowledges that I've even spoken.

That's when I notice exactly who the wheelhouse crew is tonight. Manning the wheel is Markus Jenkins, the second mate. Nick Eagon, the third mate, stands at the radar, which means the first four tiers of command are on the bridge at the same time. They normally operate in shifts. Paul Kennet, who's essentially just an able shipman, stands at the maps. He's got no real power, but his loyalty to McAfee and the *Sentinel* is unquestioned, as this is his fifth year with the organization. Aside from the missing Mr. Jackson, the entire inner circle of the *Sentinel's* crew is here. They were planning something big.

A shifting shadow by the maps reveals a sixth crew member is present. I stand on my tippy-toes and see a rainbow hemp hat that often conceals a head of dreadlocks I know well. "Peach?"

She steps out of hiding. She doesn't look angry like the others. More confused and afraid. She's holding a video camera.

Something is definitely not right here. Whatever they're up to, they recruited Peach to document the event and no doubt put a verbal spin on it.

Somewhere in the distance, I hear the high-pitched whine of a Zodiac. Its revving engine pulses as it bounces across the waves somewhere out in the darkness.

The radio crackles, and Mr. Jackson's voice fills the bridge. "Mates, you have about thirty seconds to put some distance between you and the *Bliksem!*"

Thirty seconds until what? Can he see how close the *Bliksem* is to striking us?

"She's right on top of us!" Chase shouts, his voice tinged with worry. "Brace for impact!"

I take hold of a chair that's been bolted to the floor. The ship shudders from the impact. Alarms sound.

The voice of John Nicholson, the chief engineer and one of the few people on board with whom I can have an intelligent conversation, sounds from the radio. "What the hell happened? We've got a hole in the hull down here! It's above the waterline so—"

McAfee toggles off the radio, silencing Nicholson.

What the hell?

"Get us out of here!" he yells at Jenkins.

"I doubt they're going to hit us twice," I say, but my subconscious has just put together a puzzle my conscious mind had yet to realize existed.

Thirty seconds.

Mr. Jackson said thirty seconds. But the man is precise like a Swiss clock. The *Bliksem* struck after only five seconds. No way he'd be twenty-five seconds off target. So what's coming next?

"No time!" McAfee shouts.

I see a telltale sign that tells me things are about to go to hell. I grab Jenny and tackle her to the floor. Everything moves slow. I see her face contort with hurt, maybe because I was rough, maybe because she felt betrayed by my action, or maybe because she's upset that a little person like me could take her down so easily. But her face morphs into abject fear before we hit the floor.

The *boom* is louder than anything I've ever heard. Feels like someone just shoved fondue skewers into my eardrums. Every single window shatters. Shards of glass fly out like daggers. I see them pass over my head as I'm thrown against the far wall.

My head strikes hard. I try to shake it off, but a pain-filled fog rolls into my head. As my vision fades, I see a fireball rise up past the shattered wheelhouse windows. Armageddon has come to the Arctic.

5

I come to with a deep breath that sends me into a fit of coughing. The air is no good. Tastes of smoke. When I open my eyes, that's all I can see. Thick gray smoke rolls through the wheelhouse like English fog. I pull my sweater up over my mouth and nose and say, "Hello?"

It seems a ridiculous thing to shout, like I'm some Girl Scout with a bunch of Samoas knocking on a door. So I step it up and shout, "Is anyone still here?"

The idea that I've been left alone to die of smoke inhalation fills me with vengeful anger. But then, maybe everyone is still here and just incapacitated? A deep, yet feminine, groan comes from nearby. I try to stand but fall to my side.

The ship is listing. We're going down.

I return to my hands and knees and crawl toward the groan. I find Jenny face down near the door. The air is better here. The smoke is entering from the other side of the bridge and rolling out of the door.

"Jenny," I say. "Are you hurt?"

"Head hurts," she says and then moves her limbs. "Nothing broken, though. What happened?"

"Explosion."

She looks confused for a moment, and then her eyes go wide. She remembers. "You saved me."

"We'll see about that," I say. "We're listing. Taking on water."

"We're sinking?" she asks, her voice rising with panic. She knows as well as I do that just a few minutes in the Arctic Ocean is enough to kill. If the *Sentinel* goes down, we do not want to be on it when it does. There are inflatable lifeboats and survival kits on board, but time is short and I can't leave until I know we're not leaving someone behind.

"I'll be right back," I say.

"Where are you going?" she asks. "We need to get out of here."

"I'll just be a minute." I take a deep breath and then slide into the smoke. Crawling fast, I move through the wheelhouse. At first, I'm relieved I haven't found any bodies; if there were multiple people to pull out, I'd probably die before finishing. I head for the back of the room and see an arm, limp on the floor. I crawl toward it, saying, "Hey!" But as I round the base of the map station, I see Paul Kennet's face. A shard of glass the size of a trowel is embedded deep in his neck. A river of blood seeps from his neck and flows across the listing floor, where it pools against the wall.

The smoke is thick here, so when I see the body and suck in a quick breath, smoke scratches my throat and sets me to coughing. I'm about to head for the exit when I see a second body. It's hard to identify because of the smoke, but I catch a flash of rainbow colors and know it's Peach. Dead or not, I can't leave her.

Crawling over Kennet's dead body is hard. I nearly puke twice when I feel his still-warm blood soak into my jeans at the knees. But I make it to Peach, and I'm glad to see no glass buried in her body. She's small enough that I could throw her over my shoulder, but I wouldn't make it far in the smoky gloom. So I take her by the ankle and drag her toward the door. I hear her body bumping into things as I tow her, and I cringe each time, but it's better than asphyxiating, burning alive, or drowning in freezing water, so I keep moving without looking back.

As the smoke clears and I near the door, I see that Jenny, bless her overworked heart, hasn't abandoned me. "Is there anyone else?" she asks, and looks about ready to charge into the smoke.

"Kennet," I say, "but he's dead."

Her face pales. "Dead? Are you sure? Did you check his pulse?"

I didn't, but six inches of glass in a man's throat generally qualifies him as a dead man in my book. But I don't want to tell her that, so I lie. "Yeah, let's get the hell off this ship."

Cold Arctic air relieves my lungs as we pound down the wheelhouse stairs and return to the main deck. The first thing I notice is the angle of the deck. If I sat on my ass, I'd zip right down to the ocean, which is just a few feet below the gunwales now. *We're going down fast.*

"Oh my God," Jenny says.

I expect to see her looking down at the frothy ocean, but her head is turned up a little higher. I follow her gaze and find the *Bliksem* pulling away. But she's in similar shape. A massive hole is open on her starboard bow, and a second on the aft...a portion of the ship that never touched us.

She's going down fast too, so I certainly can't seek any help there. Not that I can see her crew with all this smoke. Something deep in the *Sentinel* shakes beneath our feet. Maybe it's an explosion or air being forced out by the rushing water. I really don't give a shit. But it spurs me into action.

I thrust little Peach into Jenny's enormous hands and say, "Wait here. I'll get one of the inflatables." As I say this, Jenny's eyes flash to where the second Zodiac had been secured. Gone.

I waste no time cursing whoever took the Zodiac and our best chance of survival and instead head for the door to the lower decks. The inflatables are kept in a locker at the base of the stairs. When I open the door, I'm struck by a burst of air, pushed out by intense pressure. It's thick with the stink of oil, salt, and thirty stinky crew members. It occurs to me that this is the first time this door has been opened, which means that no one on the lower decks has yet escaped. When I hop down the stairs two at a time and land in frigid water, I see why. The interior is flooded, lit by flickering emergency lights. Three bodies float face down in the water. Everyone belowdecks was either killed by the explosion or quickly drowned.

"We're sinking faster!" I hear Jenny shout. "Hurry up!"

Opening the door released the air pressure and is allowing the ship to sink faster. Whose bright idea was it to stow the inflatables belowdecks? Ignoring the bodies and my freezing ankles, I yank open the locker and find two inflatable lifeboats.

Two. For thirty crew.

Son of a bitch! Someone needs a good swift kick in the nuts.

I yank out one of the inflatable life rafts, which looks like a huge, thick modern suitcase. Free of the locker, it falls and nearly takes my arm off. Must weigh as much as Jenny! With the big suitcase out of the locker, I notice a backpack stuffed in behind it with the word SURVIVAL handwritten across the top in black. I have no idea what's in it, but I snatch it and throw it over my shoulder. The ship suddenly lurches, and I nearly fall into the now knee-deep water, pulled down by the heavy life raft.

Jenny screams, and I run up the stairs, which are tilted so bad I'm running almost completely on the wall—not running up so much as horizontally. I have to duck to get out of the exit. And when I do, I can see why Jenny screamed. The deck is nearly at a ninety-degree angle to the water. She's knee-deep in water and standing on the ship's rail. And freezing water and sinking ship be damned, she still has Peach in her arms.

"Can you step to the side?" I shout down to her.

She looks up, sees what's in my hands, and moves to the left until she slips. She catches herself but doesn't try to move again.

"I'm going to pop this thing open. When I do, try to reach it. I'll have to slide down the deck after it."

"Just do it!" she screams.

I'm not entirely sure how do to this. I've never used a life raft, let alone an inflatable one, but a big bright yellow tag labeled PULL TO INFLATE makes it idiotproof. I give the tag a yank, and the suitcase explodes to life, pulls itself free of my grip, and falls into the water next to Jenny. At first it looks like she won't be able to reach it, but the octagonal raft just keeps on growing. The whole thing is bright yellow and has a tentlike roof with four clear plastic windows. A flashing strobe has already begun to blink at the pinnacle of the tent. She snags the raft, pulls it closer, opens the clear plastic hatch, tosses Peach inside, and looks back up at me. "C'mon!"

There's now a twenty-foot, nearly vertical drop between me and the submerged rail. I know this could hurt—a lot—but what choice do I have? I leap out of the door and press my body against the deck, hoping friction will slow me down. I cover the distance in a flash but never reach the rail. Jenny catches me below the armpits and tosses me into the life raft next to Peach. She pokes her head in after me.

"Get to the other side of the raft," she shouts. "Take Peach, too."

I'm about to argue, but then she starts climbing in and I feel the whole thing start to tip toward her. I grab Peach and drag her to the far side of the raft, which is far larger than I was expecting. I suspect Jenny might weigh more than Peach and I combined, but we've provided enough counterbalance that the raft doesn't flip.

The raft bobs up and down as we catch our breath. A moment later, a loud gurgling draws our attention out the clear plastic windows. The flashing strobe light atop our raft lights the scene like some kind of low-budget horror movie. Half of the *Sentinel* is underwater, and the rest is quickly sliding under the surface. Compressed air bursts from windows, blowing water and debris into the air.

"It's pulling us in," Jenny says, her voice a whisper.

She's right. The suction of the sinking ship is pulling us closer. A spray of water strikes my window. I jump back, and by the time I return to the window, all that's left of the *Sentinel* and who knows how many members of the crew is gone. As our raft spins in lazy circles at the center of the submerged ship's footprint, silence descends over the ocean.

6

The wail that breaks the Arctic silence is so frightening that I nearly fling myself out of the raft and into the ocean. The cold water would probably be less of a shock. It's like some kind of evil banshee has just awakened next to me. Jenny adds to the scream with one of her own. We're not going to have any trouble hailing a passing ship with these two on board.

"Paul!" It's Peach.

"Oh my God!" Jenny chimes in.

"Paul!" She must have seen the man die and is waking to the memory as though it's just happened. The light inside the raft is a diffuse yellow, and we're rolling over three-foot swells, so she's got to be completely disoriented and confused. Last she knew, she was on the bridge, being rammed by the *Bliksem*. Her screams are understandable.

"Oh my God!" Jenny, on the other hand, is just being annoying.

"No, no, no, Paul!"

"Peach," I say. Her breaths come rapid fire, as hearing her name helps her brain reconnect to reality. But I can sense she's still on the brink of madness. "Peach, it's Jane. You're safe."

"What? Where are we?"

"Life raft," I say.

"Life raft?"

"The *Sentinel* sank."

I hear a quick intake of air. Her shaking hands cover her mouth as she tries to grasp the horribleness of the situation she's awoken to. When she speaks, she sounds numb. "There was an explosion. Everything shook. My ears. Paul…He pushed me down. The glass…I saw it." There's a long expulsion of breath before she asks, "Is he…"

"He didn't make it," I say, trying to speak with a gentle voice, but I don't think there's any good way to say someone is dead.

"God," she says, and she's silent for a moment.

"Sorry I screamed," Jenny says. "You scared the shit out of me."

"How many made it off the ship?" Peach asks.

"Peach," I say, not looking forward to delivering the news, "it's just the three of us."

The silence that follows is unbearable. I prefer to get painful experiences over with fast, so I verbally vomit the answers to her unasked questions. "No one belowdecks made it. The explosion or rush of water did them in. We got the only life raft. When I came to, the bridge was full of smoke, but I checked for survivors. I found Paul first. Then you."

"She saved you," Jenny says. "Pulled you out of the smoke. Got the life raft."

"I had some help," I say, feeling embarrassed by the praise. But when Peach doesn't thank either of us, I wonder if she realizes the truth of our situation: I saved her for a much longer and more painful death of starving and freezing in the Arctic Ocean.

"You didn't see McAfee or Chase?" she finally asks.

"Nope," I say, and had planned to leave it at that, but Jenny chimes in.

"The assholes left us to go down with the ship. Took the last Zodiac."

"They haven't come looking for us?" she asks, a tinge of disbelief in her voice. She idolized Captain McAfee and supported his hard-core stance on saving whales.

"They either capsized and drowned," I say, "or made for land and didn't look back," which seems the more likely of the two options, but I keep that to myself. "We're on our own."

That sinks in like an iron anchor, and no one speaks for fifteen minutes. I sit with my arms crossed over my chest. It's chilly inside the life raft, but I think it must be made of something that retains heat because I'm not freezing. My feet are frigid from being wet, so I sit up with my back against the firm side of the raft and pull my shoes off. As I'm working off my soaked socks, a bright light blossoms from the center of the octagonal tent.

I look at the bright light and see Peach sitting back down. The light is a bright bluish LED tap light. I wouldn't have known it was there if Peach hadn't turned it on. I glance at Jenny lying down on the floor, eyes closed, head on arms. Sleeping. She's got her shoes off too, and her socks are draped over them.

"You know we don't need that, right?" I say, looking up at the light. "This far north, we're in the land, or sea, of perpetual sun."

"Knowing we have something with power kind of makes me feel better. Stupid, I know, but…" Peach shrugs and then points to the ceiling. "You can hang your socks up there."

A few vinyl lines are strung taut across the ceiling. Seems the maker of this life raft thought of everything. I drape my socks over the line and then take Jenny's massive wool socks and hang them next to mine.

"Thanks," Peach says.

"I've just hung up a pair of socks that smell like a dead fish that's been in the sun too long, and you're thanking me?"

She laughs, and I'm glad to see her smile. "For saving me."

"We're not saved yet," I say. When her smile fades some, I make a mental note never to pursue a career as a motivational speaker. *Hello, everyone, odds are most of you will never achieve your dreams, five of you will be killed in motor vehicle accidents by the end of the year, two of you will serve jail time, and at least one of you will give birth to a child who has three potential deadbeat fathers, the best of which has just five teeth.*

"It's ironic," she says, and I wonder if she's heard my mental ramblings.

"What is?" I ask.

"You saving me," she says.

"Why's that ironic?" I can't imagine an answer to this question that makes any sense. I would have pulled anyone off that ship, even Captain Crazy.

"Do you know why we were roommates?" she asks.

"Luck of the draw?"

"Chase decides who bunks with who," she says, and a theory starts to form in my mind, but she fills in the blanks before I've fully figured it out on my own. "I was spying on you. Watching you. Reading your journal. Your notes."

I frown, feeling supremely violated. I'd kept one journal tracking the actions of the *Sentinel* and a second that was personal. They're both at the bottom of the ocean now, but there were things on those pages I've never told anyone.

"Sorry," she says and at least appears honestly ashamed. Still, there's no way I'm going to offer an, "It's okay," because it's decidedly *not* okay. "They knew who you are. Who you really are. I'm pretty sure that's why they let you on the crew."

"Thought they could win me over?" I ask.

"Maybe," she says with a shrug. "I'm not really sure why they let someone like you on board."

Someone like me? I've heard Peach talking about other antiwhaling organizations like the WSPA and Greenpeace, and while she doesn't think they're being proactive enough, she respects them. She wouldn't see me as a threat.

"And who am I?" I ask. "Really?"

"They told you me you work for the US government."

I let out a guffaw that makes Jenny twitch. Peach looks at me like I'm crazy. "Relax," I say. "We've only been at sea for like an hour. I'm not going to eat you. Yet."

My humor doesn't help. Her stare has intensified. "Look, did you see the WSPA Greenland Whaling Investigation video they released a few months ago? Found all the whale meat in grocery stores? Revealed the whalers in Greenland were making a nice profit?"

"Yeah," she says. "They broke the IWC's rules. It was a solid investigation and part of the reason McAfee decided to come here."

Great, I think, *this really is all my fault*, but I continue with my dramatic reveal. "Remember the redhead with the baseball cap and sunglasses?"

"She was brilliant, yeah, but—"

"She's not a redhead," I say. "She's got short black hair and a—"

"That was *you*?" she asks loudly, but doesn't wait for confirmation. "You're WSPA?"

"Going on ten years," I say.

I can see she's confused as hell, but she shakes it off. Despite her hero abandoning us in the Arctic Ocean, she's still clinging to the idea that McAfee wouldn't lie to her. "That's your cover story."

"You read my journal," I say.

"Skimmed."

"Come across the name Michael Stone?"

She forms a half-word argument, but something clicks in her mind. "You date the director of the WSPA?"

"Dated. Past tense. He asked me to marry him. I said no. And now I'm in the Arctic Ocean, in a lifeboat."

"That sucks," she says.

"I know, right? I should have said yes."

"No, I mean that I thought you were some spook or something."

"I know," I say. "Just messing with you. Hey, now that we're being honest, since we barely have room to lie side by side, can you do me a favor and not turn our lifeboat into a shithole?"

She laughs again. It's good to hear someone laugh.

"I kept the room like that so you wouldn't see my camera."

Now it's my turn to be surprised. When my jaw drops open, she says, "Don't worry, you never did anything worth keeping. Sleeping mostly." My eyes go wide when I see her hold up a small video camera. "When something needs to be recorded for the media, they call me. Know that I can spin it if needed. An edit here, a—" She sees my shocked expression. "What?"

"You have the camera?"

"It was on my hand when I woke up," she says. "I strap it on pretty tight because McAfee has a pretty strict 'you break it, you bought it' policy. Why?"

"Were you recording when I came onto the bridge?"

"Yeah, McAfee knew you were coming. Asked me to record it."

"What?" This makes no sense. "Why did he want to record me?"

She shrugs. "All I knew is that he wanted to record something and told me to start when he saw you coming."

I can tell she doesn't have a real answer, so I file the question away for another time and ask, "Does the camera still work?"

She looks down at it and says, "Huh."

"What?"

"It's still recording." She switches the camera off.

I hold out my hand. "Mind if I take a look?"

Peach looks unsure.

Jenny suddenly sits up. "I'd like to see that, too."

Peach and I turn toward her, surprised by her sudden rising.

"What?" she asks.

"You were awake that whole time?" I ask.

"It's a defense mechanism. The guys on the *Sentinel* are all a little...gabby. Like to talk after sex. So I've learned to play dead when I don't feel like talking."

Peach lets out a *pffft* laugh that she was clearly trying to contain. "I do the same thing," she says.

I clear my throat, all business. I move my open hand closer to Peach. "The camera. Now."

7

We huddle around the camera as it powers up. We're like a bunch of tweens at a sleepover—except that we're lost in the Arctic Ocean and we'll likely die slowly. But hell, that's what some sleepovers feel like, too.

Jenny's suddenly struck by a thought. "Hey, how come we're not flipping over?"

She's right. We're all sitting on the same side of the raft and haven't capsized.

"The raft has a ballast system," Peach says. "There are four ballast bags attached to the bottom of the boat. The water in them will keep us from flipping."

"Good to know," Jenny says, happy to let it go there.

But I can't help but wonder, "How do you know so much about the raft?"

She squirms a little, but says, "I've spent some time on one before."

Jenny understands the implications of her statement before I do and gasps. "You were in the Galapagos?"

Ahh, the Galapagos, I think. The Sea Sentinel organization, of which the *Sentinel* is the flagship, has a year-round presence in the Galapagos, hounding fishermen who illegally catch sharks just for their fins—a delicacy in parts of Asia. Last year there were reports of a confrontation at sea. Witnesses said that two boats collided and sank, but no survivors were found. The identities of the ships are officially a mystery, but with one of the Sea Sentinel's Galapagos fleet missing, they were always suspected. But after an investigation revealed no missing people from the Sea Sentinel organization, they were cleared.

Until now.

The implications of this stun me. Sea Sentinel has murdered people. And Peach was part of it. She sees my growing rage.

"I didn't know they died," she says, eyes beginning to water.

"But you didn't say anything when you learned they had," I say. "Did you?"

"He told me I would go to jail," she says, and the tears break free.

"Who told you?"

"McAfee."

"He was there?" I ask. McAfee usually goes after the big PR campaigns. Whales mostly.

"Thought we were being too soft," Peach says. "Took charge for a month."

"And rammed a fishing boat."

She nods. "But it wasn't the *Bliksem*, and we weren't the *Sentinel*. Both ships just fell apart. We had a crew of ten. All of us made it into the lifeboat and spent a day at sea before Chase picked us up in a second boat."

"And they've been holding it over you since?"

She sniffs and wipes her nose. "That's why I spied on you."

"And why you were on the bridge."

Another nod. "They know…they know I won't say anything."

I start to feel bad for Peach. Despite her heart being in the right place, she fell in with people who value animals over people and who had no qualms about controlling her with fear. "Will you testify against them?"

She looks terrified by the idea.

"Look," I say. "With everything I've seen and heard, if we survive, we can both testify against them and put them in jail for what they've done. You've been used and manipulated. You're a victim, not a murderer. I guarantee you won't do time."

A weight lifts from her shoulders, and the tears return. "Thanks…but…what about the whales?"

"What?" I ask.

"Who will stand up for the whales if the *Sentinel* isn't around?"

I nearly smack her upside the head but take a deep breath and explain, "The *Sentinel*'s actions are turning public opinion *against* antiwhaling organizations. Public opinion determines what laws are put in place. And those laws might very well make the antiwhaling community the villains. Right now, the law is on our side, and yeah, whales are being killed, but far more whales will be killed when all antiwhaling organizations are shut down or have their hands tied by expanded yearly quotas. *That's* why the WSPA sent me here. If we can prove the Sea Sentinel is an extremist group and shut them down, we can get back to making *lasting* progress against the whalers."

She sits back and says nothing, absorbing what I've told her. I'm mostly impressed with the amount of chutzpah I put into my speech. Seems there's some whale-hugger in me after all.

"Umm," Jenny says. "The camera is ready."

I'd totally forgotten about the camera in my hand. I pop open the 2.5-inch view screen and hit the play button. After two seconds of black screen, there's five seconds of my room. The picture is framed by clothes. The angle of the image and the purple-and-white-striped sock helps me identify the location as a shelf in the far corner of our room that's been covered in clothes from day one. I shake my head and sigh.

"That's so *Single White Female*," Jenny says, and I'm glad we have a similar sense of humor. She'll help keep me sane over the coming days.

Peach inches closer, sees the image on screen. She offers another apology, but I'm not listening. The image has changed. It's a white linoleum floor covered with black shoe scuffs. I hear Chase's voice. Then McAfee's. The camera pans up. The bridge.

For ten minutes, we watch the inner circle of the *Sentinel* go about their business without a care in the world. McAfee's talking on the bridge phone, which is a satellite phone capable of calling other ships or someone on the other side of the planet. His face looks serious, but his conversation is private. He hangs up and turns toward Chase. "We might have a problem. The *Bliksem* is closing on our position."

"Was Jackson sp—"

"Get as many people on deck as possible. If they get close, throw everything we have at them. Get them to turn away."

"Turn away?" Chase asks.

McAfee furrows his eyebrows. "Do it, Chase. Now."

"Yes, sir," Chase says and then picks up the bridge phone and dials a three-digit extension.

"The next ten-ish minutes is when they started throwing the meat," Peach says from next to me. "You can fast forward through it."

But I don't. And when the first chunk of bloody whale meat slaps up against the bridge window and slowly slides out of view, I nearly laugh. Not so much because whale meat on a window is funny but because of the abject horror that ripples through the bridge crew when they realize what's just happened. There's screaming and wailing like some dear family member is being tortured in front of them. The terror strikes everyone, except for McAfee. He's looking out the bridge's front window.

At me, I think.

When he turns back toward the camera, I see a glimmer of a smile for a split second. Then it's gone, and he finally registers the meat on the side window. He curses loudly, almost like he knows it's what's expected of him, but his mind is elsewhere.

And that's when I arrive. The camera turns toward me as I burst onto the bridge, looking pissed and a little arrogant. *I look a little bitchy*, I think.

Jenny chuckles next to me when she sees herself step onto the bridge behind me and cross her arms. "I was doing my best Andre the Giant impression," she says, and I wonder how someone so young knows who Andre the Giant is. But I think she's from one of the southern states, so maybe she has a brother who's into wrestling. Then again, maybe she's into wrestling.

The scene plays out as I remember it. McAfee goes manic. I'm sarcastic. As we get close to the explosion, I feel Jenny and Peach both tense up next to me. We all know it's coming.

Mr. Jackson offers his thirty-second warning.

And nearly thirty seconds later, McAfee shouts, "No time!"

Then it happens—the telltale sign that sent me into action.

McAfee covers his ears and ducks. I pause the image.

"Holy shit," Jenny says.

"He *knew*," Peach adds. "That son of a bitch knew!"

"But why did he have you record it?" Jenny asks.

"Because he wanted to frame someone else for it," I say. "Someone he had collected, or fabricated, evidence against. Someone they'd been watching. Someone who wasn't who she said she was."

"You," Peach says.

I nod. "I'm his scapegoat."

Jenny has a hand over her mouth. "That's why he said those things about you when you came on the bridge."

"And I didn't deny anything," I say.

"But the tape condemns him," Jenny notes.

"Nothing that can't be edited out in post," I say and turn to Peach. "Right?"

She gives a slow nod and then surprises me by saying, "Play the rest."

She never stopped recording, so there could be some graphic images, but then I realize it might reveal what happened to the rest of the bridge crew. I hit play.

The explosion happens right away, and all three of us jump. The raft bobs in the water but doesn't come close to tipping, thanks to the ballast system. The view of the bridge becomes a pixilated mess as Peach falls to the floor. The camera lands on its side. A second later, we all jump again as Paul falls into view. His eyes are wide. Blood pulses over the large shard of glass in his neck.

We watch him die.

It's something I'll never forget—seeing the life wink out of his eyes—and something I hope to never see again. As the first tendrils of smoke wisp into the picture, voices rise up. Our view is of Paul's dead face, but the scene is easy to imagine.

"Get up!" It's McAfee. "Let's go."

"Where's Chase?" says someone.

"Over here," Chase says.

"We need to abandon ship, right now," McAfee says.

Smoke comes in heavy now.

Someone starts coughing.

"What about the others?" Chase asks.

"Dead," McAfee says, and it's hard to tell if he really believes it or if he's just saying it to get people moving. But then, with a flurry of footsteps, they're gone. After another minute, I hear myself coughing. Then a muffled conversation between Jenny and me. Nearly another minute passes. The smoke hangs thick in the air. And I crawl into view, my face contorting with disgust as I crawl over Paul's body. The video shakes and bangs and becomes fairly unwatchable as I drag Peach toward the doors. The rest of the rescue plays out this way, and I stop it once we're all safe on board the life raft and Jenny whispers, "It's pulling us in."

When I look up from the now-black screen, Peach is crying again, but this time her lip is quivering. She can barely speak. "You...you..." She gives up on speaking and throws herself at me, wrapping her arms around me and sobbing loudly into my sweater.

Now I know how my father felt. He wasn't an affectionate man, and I always went out of my way to hug him. He got all rigid and uncomfortable every time I did, and I find myself doing the same thing now. But I'm not my father. My heart's not completely made out of stone. So I force myself to give Peach a pat on her back. She covered up the murder of several fishermen, spied on me, and unknowingly helped set me up to take the fall for a murderous act of antiwhaling piracy, but she's still human.

Unlike McAfee. He's a monster. And I'm going to make damn sure he hangs for the things he's done.

8

We've been floating at the mercy of the Arctic wind and waves for nearly five hours. During the rest of the sleepless voyage, we turned our attention away from the drama of our escape and the men who left us to die. None of that will matter if we don't survive, and there's the possibility that they didn't make it either.

We've just finished taking an inventory of all the supplies included with the raft, and I'm a bit surprised. The eight-person raft has included eight sixteen-ounce bottles of water and eight-thousand-calorie food ration bars. So we won't starve.

Yet.

But there is so much more—a first aid kit, a fishing kit, sunblock, flares, smoke signals, several small packages of moist wipes, two small jackknifes, four reflective blankets, seasickness tablets, mini-binoculars, two LED flashlights, and more. They've even included a deck of playing cards to keep people from going crazy and killing each other. But they've also included a small Bible, so maybe the last person left alive can be forgiven. When I saw it, I thought of so many jokes to make—most of them inappropriate given our dire situation—but I couldn't decide between them, so I ended up staying silent. Which was a good thing, because when Jenny saw the Bible, she picked it up, put it in her pocket, and looked a little less fearful.

As a stiff breeze rattles the life raft tent, I hold out a small magnetic compass included with the raft. I turn it side to side, watching it spin. I have no idea which direction we're heading. It doesn't really matter, since there isn't much I can do about it. There are two collapsible paddles, but I don't think they'd get us far.

Peach finishes putting the supplies back in their individual pouches. When she turns back toward me, her attention moves to my side. "What's that?"

I turn around and see the backpack labeled SURVIVAL poking out from behind my back. I'd been leaning against it all night. "Found it with the life raft," I say.

"What's in it?" she asks.

"No idea," I say, pulling it out from behind me.

She sees the handwritten label. "That's Chase's handwriting."

"Open it up," Jenny says.

I unclip the top flap and unzip the zipper. I look in and smile. "Jackpot." I take out ten high-protein energy bars. Beneath them is a device I don't recognize. I pull it out. "No water, but there's this."

"It's a water filter," Jenny says, taking it from me. "Looks like it desalinates, too."

"Great," I say. "So between the water filter, the protein bars, and the fishing kit we're going to live long enough to become hairy lesbians."

Jenny and Peach both laugh, and Peach adds, "Hey, I can bat for both teams in a pinch," which sets Jenny laughing enough that the life raft canopy shakes like one of those inflatable bounce houses full of sugar-high kids.

When I reach into the pack and pull out the next item, smiles fade. It's a big black folding military knife. I disengage the blade lock and pop out the five-inch blade.

"Holy shit," Jenny says. "That's a serious knife."

"Mmm," I mumble, wondering why Chase would think to have a knife like this.

"Put it away," Peach says. "If you drop it…"

"Right," I say, pushing the blade back down. I pocket the knife and don't bother looking up to see if this bothers the other two.

There's more in the bag. I'm surprised when the next item is soft. When I pull it out, I think it's a big black, wool blanket, but there's a hood.

"A cloak?" Peach asks.

"Looks like it," I say.

"You should use it," Jenny says. I start to argue, but then notice for the first time that Jenny and Peach are both dressed for cold weather, wearing insulated, water-resistant pants and jackets. They both have hats and gloves too. In my haste to witness the hubbub on deck, I didn't bother to grab anything warmer than a sweater. If not for the tinfoil-like thermal blankets we found, I would have been much colder the last few hours. I look at Peach, and she nods in agreement.

I throw the cloak over my shoulder and pull the big hood up over my head. "I'm Ugthar, son of Grondol, beware my magic missile." Snickers fill the life raft. "Always knew Chase had to be a D&D guy."

"I think it's WOW these days," Jenny says.

"Wow, indeed," I say as I reach back into the bag, not expecting to find anything else. But I do. Its hard metallic shape is easy to identify.

Peach sees the surprise frozen on my face. "What?"

I take the gun by the handle and pull it out. Peach and Jenny lean away from the weapon. Neither say a word as I pop out the magazine, check the number of bullets, and slap it back in. "It's a forty-five-caliber Glock," I say. "Small, powerful, and accurate. Thirteen rounds."

"Uhh," Jenny says. "I'm not sure whether to be surprised by the gun or the fact that you're holding it like it's your boyfriend's unit."

I look at Jenny, then down at the gun in my hands. *Was I stroking the barrel?* I fight my embarrassment and say, "I've been to the range a few times."

"The WSPA arming people these days?" Peach asks, only half joking.

"Military brat," I say. "My father's a colonel. Took me to the range a couple times a year." I check the weapon's unique safety mechanism and tuck the weapon into my belt.

"There a reason why you're holding all the weapons?" Peach asks. She looks more afraid than confrontational.

"Aside from the fact that I know how to handle a gun and a knife? How about the fact that you were, until last night, in cahoots with the guys who were planning to pin a terrorist attack on me?"

Jenny raises both hands, "Hey, I—"

"Don't worry," I say, "I don't think either of you had anything to do with it, but it takes a little more than apologies and hugging to gain my trust. So until I trust you implicitly or there's a reason for you to have a gun, I'll hold on to the pointy things."

"Works for me," Jenny says. "With the knife and gun and cloak you kind of look like a female Van Helsing or something. It's pretty cool." She leans back, stretches with a grunt, and then adds, "Ugh, seriously?"

The comment is clearly rhetorical, but Peach asks, "What's wrong? Were you injured?"

"Nope," she says, "it's six o'clock."

I notice she's not wearing a watch. I glance at mine. Six o'clock. "How did you know the time?"

Jenny sighs. "I'm…regular."

I let out a laugh, but Peach hasn't understood. I look at her and say, "So, how does someone take a shit on this thing?"

Apparently, there's no easy way to relieve yourself on the life raft, but we work out a system that I think will work…or might result in all three of us falling into the ocean. Jenny sits on the edge of the raft with her ass hanging out over the ocean. She's leaning forward, arms outstretching and clinging to Peach and me. We're holding on tight, and leaning back, providing balance.

"Can't you go faster?" Peach asks.

With a grunt, Jenny says, "My ass is frozen, and unless you've got a bran muffin, this could take a minute. How about you guys close your eyes and I can pretend you're not here. This is embarrassing as hell."

I'm about to respond when a loud hiss bursts into the air outside the raft. For a moment, I'm terrified we're losing air, but Jenny screams and dives inside the raft.

"Something sprayed me!" she shouts.

I inch forward and lean out of the open tent door. A giant eye stares at me from the water. It's surrounded by dark gray skin. A whale.

Peach joins me. "Oh my God."

Jenny squeezes between us and sees the humpback whale watching us. "I got bideted by a whale."

The whale bobs there for a moment, inching closer. I can't help wondering what it's thinking. Its interest is palpable, like I can feel it probing my thoughts. Who's to say it can't? We don't fully understand whales. The thought of whales having some form of higher intelligence makes me cringe. If that were ever proved, there would be a lot more people like McAfee out on the oceans. Hell, I might be one of them. The encounter feels cosmic, and before I know what I'm doing, I'm reaching a hand out.

The whale dips under the water for a moment, and I think it's leaving, but then it returns. Its nose rises and touches my hand. The skin is slippery and soft, like a freshly shelled hardboiled egg. Peach and Jenny reach out and touch the whale, testing the limits of the raft's ballast system. But we stay upright and the three of us share this earthshaking moment.

The whale exhales, sending a fish-scented spray hissing into the air. With a collective shout of surprise, we fall back inside the raft. Peach is the first to recover, nearly diving back to the open hatch. "It's gone!" she says, and I think she might start crying again.

But then something strikes the bottom of the raft. It's the whale. There's no doubt. The strike feels violent, but by whale standards, it's probably just a gentle nudge. Still, Jenny starts to panic. "What's it doing?"

"It's just being curious," I say.

"Its nose was covered in barnacles," she says. "It could pop the floats, or ruin the ballasts."

Damn it. She's right.

A second bump sends the raft spinning in a lazy circle. *What the hell is it doing?*

I return to the hatch, but there's no sign of the whale. As we continue to spin around, I search the ocean until something larger catches my attention. "It turned us around," I say, excitement creeping into my voice. I look back and find Jenny and Peach looking afraid. "It turned us around."

"So?" Jenny says.

"So," I say, pointing out the hatch. "I think it wanted to show us something."

As I lean aside, they lean forward and see something amazing.
Land.

9

Peach and I hang out of the front of the raft, paddling like mad. Jenny sits behind us, holding on to our belts. If she wasn't, I'd no doubt yank myself out of the raft and into the water—that's how hard I'm paddling. We're within one hundred yards now and my arms are burning, but I ignore the pain and the knowledge that my arms will hurt worse tomorrow. And even worse the day after that. But the idea of being on land, even the frozen wasteland ahead, is intoxicating. There might be resources. Shelter. Hell, there might be people. The Arctic North of Greenland is fairly devoid of human population, but there are hunters and adventurers that come this way. At the very least, we'll be able to move in the direction we want—south—rather than be at the mercy of the wind and ocean currents.

As we get closer to land, the waves get bigger. We're fighting six-foot swells, digging up one side and falling down the other. Had I not been at sea for the past month already, I'd probably be sea-sick, but my body is accustomed to the pitch and roll of the ocean. What it's not used to is the cold. Salt water sprays in my face, over and over. The air is at least forty degrees, but the wind is fast here where the ocean temperature meets the cold air rushing down from Greenland's frozen core.

"We're not going to make it!" Peach shouts.

She's sensed the same thing I have—the waves, or maybe the tide, is fighting us. "We're going to die if we don't make it," I yell back. "Now keep paddling!"

I redouble my efforts and the burn is hard to ignore now, but I didn't fight this hard and this long to sit back and let us drift back out to sea. Peach doesn't quite see it the same way.

She stops paddling. "I can't!" She's got tears in her eyes. I'm bigger and stronger than her. Her arms are probably worse off than mine.

Before I can threaten to shoot her if she doesn't start paddling again, she's lifted up and pulled back inside. Jenny says, "Sit on her."

I feel Peach's weight on my ass, pinning me down. A moment later, Jenny lies down by my side and sets her paddle to the water. "I could have the biceps of Hulk Hogan and still not be able to pull my weight out of here."

There she goes with another wrestling comment. As we dig up and over a wave, I say, "I could go for a couple of twenty-four-inch pythons right about now."

She smiles at my quotation of how the Hulkster used to describe the girth of his biceps. "You're a wrestling fan?"

"Nah," I say. "Child of the eighties. Hogan was everywhere. You?"

"Child of Alabama," she says. "I grew up on wrestling, gravy, and butter. Can't you tell?"

I'm about to laugh when the wave crests and pitches us forward. The feeling of forward momentum is grand, but the salt water rammed up my nostrils is not. I cough and blow water from my nose as my sinuses burn. Jenny got a face-full too, and our conversation ends. We grit our teeth and tag team this son-of-a-bitch ocean like the Hart Foundation, everyone's favorite pink tights–wearing wrestling tag team.

Ten agonizing minutes later and we're just twenty feet from a beach of smooth, worn stones. But suddenly, we're not getting anywhere.

"What happened?" I shout.

"Listen," Peach says from inside the raft.

A wave picks us up and pushes us a few feet closer to shore. When we drop down, there is a sudden tug like we're caught on something, and a dull scraping sound.

"It's the ballast bags," Peach says. "They're dragging on the bottom."

"How big are they?" Jenny asks.

"They hang down two, maybe three feet," she replies.

"So we're only in three feet of water?" Jenny doesn't wait for a reply. She sits back in the raft, removes her boots, socks, and two pairs of pants. Before I can tell her she's nuts, she steps out of the raft and into the knee-deep frigid water. She lets out a shriek but takes hold of two plastic handles, leans back, and drags the raft toward the shore. Five feet from the stone-and-pebble beach, she stops. The water is only inches deep here, and our waterproof boots can handle it. Peach and I jump out and help the half-naked Jenny pull the raft all the way out of the water and over the beach.

As the ballasts lose their water, the raft becomes far lighter, and we make good time dragging the raft past the waterline and up onto a flat stone in the shadow of a fifteen-foot gray cliff.

We dive back inside. Jenny is shivering. I dry her legs with my cloak and help her back into her dry clothes. Taking them off was smart. She'd have a hard time getting warm if she had to wait for her pants to dry. Peach rubs Jenny's still-shaking legs. Jenny lies back and grunts. "This thing was a lot more comfortable out on the water."

I crouch next to them and say, "I'm going to take a look around."

Neither of them looks happy about this.

"We should stay together," Peach says.

"I'm not going far," I say. "I just want to make sure there isn't a hotel around the corner or a ship just offshore."

This seems to make sense to them, and they both nod. "I'll just be gone a few minutes. Why don't you two see about packing up all our gear so that it's mobile?"

"Mobile?" Jenny says.

"We're not staying here," I say. "If we follow the coast south we'll eventually make it to Thule."

"Thule?" Peach says. "We're just north of the Lincoln Sea. It could take weeks to walk there. Maybe longer."

"We've got food and water," I say. "We'll have to ration it, but we might be able to make it. Our other option is to sit here and wait for a rescue that might not be coming. I didn't hear anyone send a distress call before leaving the bridge, did you?"

Neither of them say a word. They know the answer.

"What about the *Bliksem*?" Jenny asks. "They might have called for help."

"Maybe," I admit, "but we don't know where that explosion went off. We don't know if any of them survived it. We can't count on that. And both ships were prepped for spending a long time at sea. No one is going to miss us for a while."

Jenny sighs. "Well, I've been meaning to lose some weight. Southwest it is."

After taking the gun, knife, and a small pair of plastic binoculars, I open the hatch and look back at them. "I'll be an hour, tops."

I step out and zip the hatch shut behind me. The cold feels like pinpricks on my legs. Next to fishnet stockings, jeans are perhaps the worst possible pants to be wearing in the cold, and I chastise myself for even bringing them. Then again, I wasn't planning on being marooned north of the Arctic Circle. I wrap the long black cloak around me, and I'm instantly thankful for whatever weird fetish drove Chase to stow it on board. The thick wool retains my body heat, and I'm quickly warmed.

It takes me five minutes to reach the cliff's end, where the rocky ground rises upward like a staircase. I climb twenty feet up, and my view of the land opens up. The barren landscape rises to a peak. Bigger than a hill but not quite a mountain. Maybe a few hundred feet tall. But it looks easily scalable.

Before heading up, I turn around and look out at the sea. The sky is deep blue and filled with wispy clouds. The ocean is a grayer blue and full of chop. In the distance, I see a huge iceberg and know we're lucky to not be stranded on it instead of land. But there isn't a ship in sight, sunken or afloat.

As I turn away from the ocean, I'm struck by a sudden feeling of rising and falling. Greenland is very seismically active, so my first thought is that I'm feeling an earthquake or erupting volcano, but there's no sound with the motion. I feel a little sick to my stomach and drop to one knee. I breathe deeply, relaxing my body. I've only got about eight ounces of water and half an energy bar in me right now, and I really need to keep it down. The feeling starts to ebb a little, and I realize I've been at sea so long I've lost my land legs. I've heard of this happening to people. They'll be in bed or sitting at a desk, and even though everything is perfectly still, they'll feel like they're rolling over the waves. It's surreal and hard on the stomach, but I push past the feeling and turn back toward the waiting climb.

My ascent turns out to be fairly easy. The stone is solid and the grade forgiving. Twenty minutes later, I reach the top and gasp. The view is amazing. I squint against the frigid wind as I look at five more wannabe mountains. A valley stretches between them, full of rocks, odd debris and…something else. I put the binoculars to my eyes and get a brief glimpse of something rectangular. But the lenses fog up fast and I lose sight of it. It looked almost like a stone foundation. Interesting, but not quite helpful enough to garner a second glance. Instead, I turn around, holding out my compass. There's ocean to the west, which is where our raft landed. More ocean to the east. And yet more ocean to the north, which is to be expected. There isn't any land north of Greenland, though there is plenty of solid ice, come winter. My view of the south is blocked by the tallest of the stone rises. "South it is," I say.

As I turn to descend back to the beach, I catch sight of something moving to the southwest. A hint of something. I follow it toward the ocean and spot an aberration in the waves. I put the binoculars to my eyes again. I scan the water quickly, hoping to find the thing again. As the lenses fog up a second time, I find it. I only see it for a moment, but the blood-red paint splattered on its hull makes the *Bliksem* easy to identify. All I can see is the bow, blackened and smoldering from fire, the last tendrils of smoke rising into the air. She apparently took a long time in sinking, but she burned as she went down. I wonder how many men were on board and how many of them drowned or burned to death. I feel a depression setting in but shrug it off with a sniff. I can't worry about the dead. The best I can do for them is survive and make sure the world learns the truth…and if Captain McAfee makes it back to civilization, make sure he spends the rest of his life in jail.

10

My trip down takes me on a slightly different path, so I'm not sure where the raft is in relation to me. I creep along the edge of the cliff and see nothing. To the left and right, still nothing. Sigh. Lost in thought, I must have veered sharply off course. I'm not too concerned; I just need to hike back to the right, where the cliff ends, and then follow the beach back.

I shouldn't have any trouble finding them.

Unless, I think, *they left.*

Maybe I misread them? Maybe they duped me? Gained my trust and abandoned me?

As my fears start to take route, logic retakes control. First, I'm a fairly good judge of character, so I'm pretty certain that neither one of them would leave me to die, especially after everything we survived together already. Second, Jenny is big, and Peach is small. They're not going anywhere fast, and they wouldn't leave (or offend) the person who not only has the compass and binoculars but also a big frickin' knife and a .45-caliber handgun.

A scream makes me jump. It came from my left. I run toward the sound.

I'm a fast runner, but the rocky terrain and my sea legs slow me down. When the second scream sounds, I'm nearly on top of it. I slow and approach the ledge. I can hear terrified whimpers now. A pair of them.

Looking over the edge, I see the bright yellow raft, but it doesn't hold my attention for long. It's the mammoth polar bear inspecting the raft that holds my eyes.

I hear Peach say, "Be quiet! It will leave if it thinks no one's in here."

But she's wrong. I can tell by the way the polar bear is swaying back and forth that it's confused but looking for a way in. A meal in the Arctic summer, with the ice sheets gone, isn't always easy for a polar bear to come by. They'll eat pretty much any meat they can find. Including people. Especially people like Jenny.

Is that mean? I wonder. *Am I still making fat jokes?* I decide I'm not. It's an honest assessment. Jenny would make an excellent meal for a hungry polar bear.

The bear tests the tent top of the raft with its paw. The raft jiggles, and Jenny lets out an ill-contained squeal. The noise makes the bear twitch back. The raft is an enigma to him, but he knows there's a meaty snack inside. Can probably smell them. And sooner or later, the world's largest meat-eating predator is going to overcome its fear of this bright yellow obstacle.

I consider my options. The knife is long and sharp, but I'd have to get down there to use it, and I'm not about to go mano a mano with a bear. The handgun is the obvious choice, but it would be loud. If there are other survivors—men from the *Bliksem* or McAfee and crew—within earshot, I'm not sure I want to announce my presence. I can't picture either group welcoming us with open arms.

That's when I notice the loose rocks around my feet. After mom died, the Colonel raised me like a boy. Even played catch. Taught me how to put pepper on a ball. Or a bottle of paint. Or a rock. I quickly pick up a stone that feels like it's a good two pounds. I heave it down at the polar bear. The rock misses by a few feet, but the sound of stone hitting stone, along with its motion, distracts the bear for a moment. I pick a smaller stone, maybe just a pound, take careful aim, and lob it over the edge. This one strikes the bear's side, bouncing off its thick hide. The bear twitches slightly, confused by the impact, but I haven't caused it any real pain.

If anything, I've made it grumpy.

It rears up on its hind legs with a roar, and I think it's about to charge the tent. If it does, I'll use the gun, but I hope to stop it before it does. I pick up another rock, smaller still, hoping a good grip will give me better accuracy and speed.

I look down at the bear, focusing on its head. Anything else is just going to piss it off. A quick stab of pain is enough to make most bears turn tail and run, especially if they don't know where it came from. Eyes locked on target, I wind up and let the stone fly, nearly throwing myself over the edge in the process. I'm so distracted by keeping myself from falling over the edge that I don't see if my aim is true. But there's a sharp roar from below, and when I regain my footing, the bear is beating a hasty retreat from the strange yellow thing that can bite from a distance.

I realize I can't get down the way I came. That would take me directly to the fleeing bear. Looking down the cliff, I can see there are plenty of handholds. So, without announcing my presence, I slide over the edge and climb down the wall. Halfway down, my arms start to shake. The adrenaline pumping through my body is wearing off, and the fatigue from my paddle frenzy is returning. I work my way down a few more feet, look down, and see a six-foot drop.

Fuck it, I think, and jump.

My knees protest when I land, but I manage to stick the landing with nothing more than a grunt.

"Was that the bear?" I hear Jenny ask. She's quickly shushed.

I walk up to the tent and know I should let them know the coast is clear, but I can't help myself. I walk up to the raft, crouch down, and shake the text. The muffled squeals nearly make me laugh, but I hold it in and grab the zipper.

As I slowly undo the zipper, I hear a mortified Jenny say, "It's undoing the zipper!" And a moment later, when the reality of her statement registers, she says, "Bears can't undo zippers."

I quickly unzip the hatch, push it open, and lean in with a smile. "Nope."

Jenny and Peach are pressed up against the far side of the raft, clinging to each other. Their horrified faces slowly morph to confusion, to relief, and finally to anger.

"You son of a bitch!" Jenny shouts, but I can see she's trying to hide a grin. "You could have told us you weren't the bear!"

"Could have?" I ask. "Yes. Should have? Maybe."

Peach hasn't moved from her position at the back of the raft. "What happened to the bear?"

"Took one look at me and headed for the hills," I joke, trying to lighten the mood.

"Seriously," she says.

"I biffed him with a couple of rocks," I say. "He took off."

This news doesn't sit well with Peach.

"What?" I ask.

"Polar bears are persistent," she says.

Everything I know about polar bears was learned from Discovery Channel specials, while Peach is a bona fide animal expert with reams of wildlife pamphlets and information tucked away in her mind. As her fear returns, all I can think is *shit, shit, shit.*

I turn around, and there it is. Two thousand pounds of white-furred fury charging toward me. Twin screams rip through the air behind me. A wind kicks up at the same time, billowing my cloak out to the side.

The high-pitched screams coupled with the sudden growth of my cloak surprise the bear. It skids to a stop and rears up. I look up at the bear, feeling its eyes on me, sizing me up.

That's when the wind fades and the screaming stops.

Suddenly, I'm just a five-foot-five woman again.

The bear drops back down and charges.

11

I move without thinking, snatching the handgun from my waist, turning it on the bear, and firing off a round from the hip. I practiced firing from the hip, years ago, when Dad and I still went to the range; always enjoyed the idea of winning an old-fashioned quick-draw shoot-out. But honestly, I always kind of sucked at it. I know now that my bad luck at the range had to do with the targets being fifty feet away. Because a giant bear five feet away is *easy* to hit.

The round strikes the bear's forehead. It pierces flesh but ricochets off the top of the bear's thick skull. The bear stumbles and slips on loose stones, stopping close enough to take a swipe at me. But the pain from the now-bleeding wound on its forehead coupled with the earsplitting report of the handgun have sent it running, hopefully for good this time.

I watch it fade from view before turning back to the raft. When I see Peach and Jenny staring at me out of the open hatch, I want to say something funny, but I'm distracted by my trembling hands. Jenny picks up the slack for me.

"Holy fucking Van Helsing!" she shouts with a big grin. She steps out of the tent and wraps her arms around me. I'm lifted off the ground in an ironic bear hug, which if not ended soon might kill me as surely as the actual bear's embrace would have.

She puts me down, and I take several deep breaths, fighting off a faintness that might be from the adrenaline rush of facing down a bear or from Jenny squeezing the air from my lungs.

Peach looks happy to be alive, but asks, "You didn't kill it, did you?"

I can't help but smile. We could have all died violently and been devoured by a polar bear, and her main concern is for the bear's welfare. *At least she's genuine*, I think. "Just gave him something to think about."

"But you did shoot him?"

"Grazed him," I say. "He'll have a cool scar to impress the females come mating season."

"How do you know it was a *him*?" Jenny asks.

"Was pretty obvious when he stood up," I say, raising an eyebrow.

"You were about to die and took the time to check out his bear junk?" She punches my shoulder, and it hurts. "You're sick, dude."

I laugh as the last of the adrenaline jitters fade. "Was kind of hard to miss."

"Hung like a horse?" Jenny says.

I shrug. "Like a bear."

Feeling some sense of normalcy returning, I tuck the gun back into my waist and ask, "How much were you able to pack up?"

"Everything," Peach says. She motions to a yellow backpack sitting next to the raft. It's stuffed full of supplies. I can tell by the color and material that it came with the raft. The SURVIVAL backpack sits next to it, just as full. "And..." she says, "check this out."

Peach picks up the raft, which is fairly light now that everything has been taken out of it. I'm not sure what she's going to do with it, but then Jenny turns her back to the raft and slips her arms through the ruined ballast bags that have been tied together like shoulder straps. It's awkward and we'll be seen coming from miles away, which is a blessing and a curse. I'd rather avoid running into McAfee and crew, but I'd also like to be rescued. Plus, this will give us shelter, comfort, and the ability to cross short distances of water if need be.

"Genius," I say. When Peach grins, I know it was her idea. I also know that I've become our small group's leader. Peach thrives on praise from her superiors. It's always bothered me. I've seen her beg for it like a dog. But it's a positive sign. Means she'll do what I tell her. And that's good, because I'm going to be pushing these two to their limits until we're rescued or dead, starting...

Now.

I pick up the two backpacks, feeling their weight in my hands, and hand the lighter one to Peach. She takes the yellow backpack and puts it over her shoulders. I throw Chase's dark gray backpack over my shoulder. "We're on a peninsula, so we're going to head south to the mainland and then follow the coast. I'm going to set the pace. I'll try not to go too fast, but we're not here because we met on a dating website, so don't expect a romantic walk along on the beach. The terrain is rough but clear. If we stay close to the water, it will be fairly even too. Good enough?"

Peach gives a furtive nod.

Jenny says, "Whatever. I just want to get out of here before Mr. Snuggles comes back."

"You named the bear that almost ate you Mr. Snuggles?" Peach says.

Jenny shrugs. "He *was* cute."

It's hard for me to not join in, but we need to get serious and I want to reach the *Bliksem* wreck sooner rather than later. If any of the crew made it to shore, I'd prefer to deal with that confrontation before I'm starving, dehydrated, and lacking the energy to flip them the bird. I wrap the cloak around me, turn my eyes south, and start walking. "Peach, bring up the rear. Keep an eye out for the bear.

Jenny falls in line behind me.

"The bear?" Peach asks. "You think it will come back?"

"No," I say, "but I'm not a bear psychologist, so who knows? Better safe than sorry. Should I aim to kill next time?"

When she doesn't answer, I know the answer is yes. She'd be offended by the act but could stop worrying about being eaten alive. What I don't mention is that we are in the land of the polar bear. Odds are good that we'll run into a few more before we find civilization.

I don't look back, but I hear two sets of feet behind me. Our expedition is under way.

An hour later, we stop at a hundred-foot-tall rise.

"Well," Jenny says, her face pink and covered in sweat, "this sucks."

I consider giving a pep talk but decide to save it for when one of us dies—assuming it's not me. I start up the hill, and Jenny groans.

"Really?" she says. "Not even a quick rest before we head up?"

I continue up but speak over my shoulder. "Somewhere behind us is a bear that would like to eat you. Every second you stand there, you're farther away from the woman with the gun."

She starts up the hill after me and says, "Bitch."

Peach follows in silence.

Despite the hill's height, the grade is forgiving and the footing is firm. I reach the top in a minute and take a seat. When Jenny reaches the top and sees me sitting, she feigns a half-serious gasp and says, "Double bitch."

Then she sees what I'm looking at. She sits on a bolder next to mine and says, "What is it?"

Rocks clatter behind us, announcing the arrival of Peach. "The *Bliksem*," she says.

Jenny squints at the smoldering hull in the distance. I hand her the small binoculars. A moment later she says, "Damn. They sank."

"And burned," Peach observes.

"Think any of them survived?" Jenny asks.

"Yup," I say with a confidence that turns both of their heads toward me.

The *Bliksem* sits about one hundred yards out and to our right. Jenny and Peach are so fixed on it that they've failed to notice the aberration to our left. I lean back so they can see the smoke drifting up toward the sky. Somewhere to the south, someone has a fire going.

"Think it's the *Bliksem*'s crew?" Jenny asks.

"We should avoid them," Peach says.

"We can't avoid them," I say. "Whoever they are, they're in our way. And if it is the *Bliksem*'s crew, we owe them our help."

"We can't trust them," Peach says.

"They might see things the other way around," I say. "Our ship sank theirs. We have a good amount of supplies. They might have injured. And they're innocent in this."

"They were killing whales," Peach says, a smidge of outrage filling her voice.

But this isn't up for debate. "And McAfee killed *people*." I point my finger toward the rising smoke. "We're going to find out who's there. If it's survivors from the *Bliksem*, we're going to help them."

"And if it's McAfee?" Jenny asks.

I strike out toward the smoke and say, "I've still got twelve bullets."

12

Fatigue begins clawing up my legs after an hour of hiking. While the flat-stone ground is great for speed and safety, it's killer on the knees. Every footstep feels like I've just kicked a wall. I weigh a buck twenty-five, but Jenny might be double that. The pain on her knees must be unbearable. Peach can't be much over one hundred pounds, but a quick glance back reveals she's just as unenthused as me.

Of course, that might be because she expects a polar bear to rush up and snatch her away.

"Are we there yet?" Jenny asks.

I cringe inwardly. I loathe when people start asking that question like it's funny. I remember an episode of *The Smurfs* where one of them, probably Brainy, annoyingly asked the question over and over. It was supposed to make kids laugh, but it just made me wish Gargamel would catch and kill the little bastards. But when I look back at Jenny's face and see her discomfort, I realize she's actually asking the question with no humorous intent.

She's right to ask, too. I thought we'd reach the source of the smoke long ago, but we haven't come across anything that looks like a campsite, occupied or abandoned. I pause and search the sky. The pillar of rising smoke is gone. I turn a full 360. Nothing. The smoke is gone.

I'm too tired to care and say, "Smoke or no smoke, this is the way we have to go. If we find the source, great. If we don't, we'll just keep moving."

Jenny sighs but doesn't complain. As bad as the pain is, none of us wants to die out here.

"But why is it gone?" Peach asks.

"Whoever it was probably moved on," I say.

"Or died," Jenny says.

I give her a look that says: *That's not helpful.*

"What?" she says defiantly. "It's true."

A third option tickles the back of my mind, but I'm feeling so lethargic I don't bother to put much thought into it. I remember days in school like this—staying up late to watch TV or go to a party and then yawning my way through a test that I could have aced otherwise. I shake my head and give my face a few brisk smacks. Getting a B in school didn't result in someone dying. Out here, we *can't* make mistakes.

So what am I missing? I treat it like a multiple choice.

Complete this sentence: The people who created the source of the smoke…

1. …are dead.

2. …have moved on.

3. …are…what? Dead or gone, what else is there?

Jenny's looking at me like I'm mad. I've been silently mouthing my thoughts and smacking myself in the face. I choose to ignore her rather than explain. With my back to the girls, I look to the south.

A small rock skitters across my path. Had the day been windy, I might have overlooked the subtle movement, but I haven't felt more than a tickle of wind for the past hour. Something knocked that rock loose. It was either the bear or answer number three:

3. …heard the gunfire, put out the fire, and set an ambush. Shit.

I fling open my cloak, draw the handgun, and point it at the stand of boulders from which the pebble emerged.

Jenny stumbles back, caught off guard by my sudden action. "What are you—"

"Come out from behind the rocks," I command in my best Colonel impersonation. "I've got a gun," I add, letting them know that I'm the one who fired it earlier. They might think I'm bluffing—I could have heard the gunshot just like they did—but all they have to do is take a peek to know I'm telling the truth. "If you don't come out right this second, I might shoot you just because you pissed me off."

A tall figure rises up from behind the rocks. No raised hands. No fear in the eyes. Just a pair of serious blue eyes staring me down. It's the Viking fond of rude hand gestures. Up close I can see his blond beard is neatly trimmed and his shoulder-length blond hair wasn't cut with an ax.

Okay, so, he's a civilized Viking. Maybe he'll quote Shakespeare as he pillages our womanhood? That's not fair. You shared a smile with the man over whale meat. He's got a sense of humor. So he'll laugh while he pillages our womanhood? Fair enough.

I track his movement around the boulders, keeping my weapon trained on his chest. He's dressed in a bright-orange winter survival suit, and I don't spot any wounds on him. His face is covered in a layer of grime, which fails to conceal the fact that the Viking is also handsome.

"Close enough," I say. He stops ten feet from me, squinting as he looks me up and down.

"It's you," he says in surprisingly perfect English, with just a hint of a Greenlander accent.

"You two know each other?" Jenny asks me.

"No," I say.

"But he recognizes you."

I try to think of a way to explain that I hand gestured oral sex at the man without looking like an idiot, decide it's not possible, and blurt it out. "He flipped me off, so I—" I simulate the gesture, pushing my cheek out with my tongue while gyrating my hand next to my mouth. "We had a laugh. It was just before we went into the wheelhouse."

"Just before they rammed us," Jenny says.

The man's face goes red with anger, and he takes a step forward. I raise the gun barrel toward his face.

He stops and says, "*You* attacked us first. With paint and that foul-smelling shit. Then *you* rammed *us*. And when we give you a taste of your own medicine, you set off two bombs. Don't talk to me about—"

"Two bombs?" I say.

"One on the bow. One aft," he says. "If we weren't triple hulled…"

He lets the sentence fade, but I get what he's saying.

"You're right," I say.

The man looks surprised by the admission. "You didn't do anything wrong," I continue. I half expect Peach to chime in here, but she stays silent, which is good because I'd like to make peace. "What was done to your ship and your crew is inexcusable. You have every right to not trust us, but—"

"Put the gun down," he says.

"Not yet," I say, feeling incredibly annoyed that the Viking interrupted my confession.

"I wasn't asking," he says.

"Look, buddy." I'm really losing my patience now. "I'm taking on a lot of weight that doesn't belong on my shoulders, so if you could just shut up and listen for a minute, I can explain everything and you can ask me to—"

He hasn't heard a word I said. I can see it in his eyes. His mind is on something else. He tilts his head to the side, looking beyond me. I hear the voice of my father echoing in my mind as he described the tactic of distraction: Killing a distracted man is easy; you just walk up behind him and put a bullet in his head. He'd finished the statement by pointing an imaginary weapon at my head and pulling the trigger. Happy memories. But an effective memory tool. Too bad I remembered too late.

The Viking's eyes are back on mine. "I wasn't asking," he says.

Shit.

I don't even need to be told where to look. I turn around without lowering the weapon, look around Jenny (whose eyes are as wide as her skin is pale), and see Peach. A wrinkly, knobby knuckled hand is wrapped around her mouth. A rusty fishing knife is held over her chest, ready to impale her.

I turn back to the Viking. *Is that a hint of a smirk I see?* "I'm starting to dislike you," I say.

"The feeling is mutual," he says, taking a step toward me. "Now, put the gun down."

He doesn't make a threat, but he doesn't need to. The knife over Peach's chest says it for him: *If I don't put the gun down, they're going to stab Peach in the heart. Checkmate. They've got me.*

But there are two problems with their plan. One, they've got a rusty fishing knife in the hands of an old coot with shaky hands, while I have a handgun in the hands of a polar bear–shooting markswoman.

And two, I'm a girl who takes after her father.

13

I cock the gun's hammer back. It's a stereotypical thing to do, popularized by Hollywood. But seeing this moment in a thousand TV shows and movies means that most people on the planet—outside of some lost Amazonian tribe—know what the action means: *I'm going to shoot your ass.*

The Viking pauses, watching my eyes. "You wouldn't," he says.

"You think I fired off a round for fun earlier?" I say. I don't actually say I shot a person—I'm not convinced I could pull off that lie—so I let him make some assumptions. Plant some doubt.

"You'd sacrifice your friend's life?" he asks.

He's searching for a chink in my armor, searching for doubt.

"Who said we're friends?" I counter.

"You're on the same crew," he says.

"Not exactly," I say. "But that's a long story I can tell you when Captain Arthritis back there drops the knife and joins you on the firing range."

The doubt I'm sowing like some frantic mind-farmer spreads to the man's eyes. But he persists. "And if he doesn't?"

"I'll shoot you both before he can work that dull blade past her sternum."

The Viking looks around me to Peach and the old man. He shakes his head slightly, seeing what I saw on my first glance. The knife is poised over the center of Peach's chest. Even if he tried to stab her, he wouldn't do more than poke through the thick fabric of her snow gear, let alone pierce bone and reach something vital. Not before I shot him, anyway.

The Viking sighs. He was, no doubt, the mastermind behind the plan to overcome an adversary with a gun. Brains over brawn. Too bad for him, I've got both. But I appreciate the fact that they chose that tactic over tossing boulders on us from above, which might have actually worked. I remind myself that these men are the victims here, not the enemy. They have every right to distrust us, and I'd like nothing more than to reverse their suppositions of us, but I can't do that until Peach is safe.

The Viking hasn't said a word yet, so I decide to give him a timetable just in case the old guy is secretly a Greenlander serial killer. "I'm going to count to five," I say. "If I don't hear the knife hit the ground before then, I'm going to shoot you in the leg." I tilt my head back without taking my eyes off the Viking. "Hear that? You have five seconds. One…"

"He doesn't speak English," the Viking says.

"Two."

Clang. The knife rattles on the ground.

The Viking shakes his head and grumbles the old man's name, "Alvin."

"Apparently he knows a countdown when he hears it," I say.

"You wouldn't have shot me," he says.

It's tempting to fire off a round, put the fear of the almighty Glock in him. But that's not what I want. I need the man to trust me, so I point the gun at the sky. The hammer clicks down without firing a round.

"You saw the safety on?" I ask, wondering how he could be so sure.

"Safety?" he says, "I've never been this close to a gun before. You…have a kind face."

Bullshit, I think. When I was a kid, I would imitate my father's best scowl—the kind he wore for new recruits—and got pretty good at it. No way this guy saw through that. Not with a gun to his face.

He must see my disbelief, because he says, "Not now. The other day."

I roll my eyes. "We were fifty feet away."

"I have good eyes," he says.

"If you two are done flirting," Jenny says, "do you think we could make nice while sitting down? I'm hungry, thirsty, and I've got cramps in both ass cheeks."

The Viking looks at the sky, considering his options. He doesn't have many. He offers his hand. "I'm Willem Olavson," he says, then motions to the old man, now standing behind him. "This is Alvin."

I shake his hand. "Jane Harper." I motion to my compatriots. "This is Jenny, and Peach. Wish the circumstances were better, Willem."

"Our camp is nearby," he says. "My father is waiting for us there."

His father, I think, suddenly remembering the old man who stumbled out of the *Bliksem*'s wheelhouse after my rotten-butter attack. His father was captain of the *Bliksem*. I try to hide my guilt but feel Willem's eyes watching me. But then, in a flash, he's not looking at me—he's looking beyond me.

I don't fully trust him yet, so I don't turn around. He's built like a true Viking and stands nearly a foot taller than me. He could overpower me and take the gun if I took my eyes off him for too long.

When Peach says, "Oh shit, not again," I turn around. One hundred feet away and closing is a charging polar bear. The red streak on its forehead confirms that this is the same bear. It's stalking us.

I step around Jenny as Peach flees to the back of the group, hiding behind Alvin, who looks just as terrified as she is. As I look away from Peach and up at Jenny, I shoot her a glance that asks, *You're not afraid?*

She understands the question and shrugs. "You're a good shot, right?"

I answer her by taking a shooter's stance, raising the gun, and looking down the sights. I line up the bear's face. I can't pierce the thick skull, and the layers of thick fur, skin, and fat would likely keep the rounds from hitting anything vital, even with a perfect body shot. So I aim for the face. A shot to an eye or its nose would put a stop to things fairly quickly. I flick off the safety as the bear closes the distance.

Before I can fire a shot, two large hands wrap around the gun, twist it, and yank it from my grasp. I expect to be shot or punched out next, but Willem says, "Save your ammunition," and hands the gun back to me.

He steps in front of me and picks up our bright yellow raft. He holds the raft up over his head, nearly doubling his height, and starts screaming.

The bear slows.

Jenny steps past me and stands next to Willem. She raises her hands and screams at the bear.

It slows again.

I see what they're doing and move to Willem's other side. I've still got the gun and know I can quick draw if need be, but Willem's plan will save ammo and is more humane. I open my cloak, flapping it open, and join the others in screaming. The bear's head cranes toward me, and it stops. Maybe it recognizes me as the person who stung it earlier. Maybe it's freaked out by the giant with a yellow head, the big red-clad woman, and the black pterodactyl flapping its wings. Whatever the case, it turns tail and runs away—again.

When it's clear the bear won't turn and make a second run, Willem says, "You shot the bear earlier, right?"

Busted. "He almost got me." I look up at Willem. "But I feel much safer now that I have a Viking with a giant…raft to protect me."

"A Viking?" he says with a grin. I've just complimented the man.

"Don't let it go to your enormous yellow head," I say, and head back toward Peach. "You okay?" I ask her.

"Like it matters," she says, surprising me with her vitriol. "I'm not your friend, remember?"

God. "I was bluffing, Peach."

"Whatever," she says, and walks away from me.

Alvin shakes his head at me disapprovingly. "Seriously?" I say, getting annoyed. "You're the one who had the knife to her chest."

Jenny puts a hand on my shoulder. "She's just freaked out. Give her some time."

She's right. Some people handle life-and-death situations with humor. Some with anger. And some with all-consuming fear. Peach has been doing well enough, but I suspect she's close to becoming unhinged. Nearly being eaten by the bear the first time would have pushed some people straight to the edge, but Peach had been held hostage, too. The bear showing up again might have finally consumed her rational mind.

I don't blame her. Most people wouldn't have come this far without cracking. But I hope Jenny is right; I hope Peach sorts things out before she makes a stupid decision and gets herself killed.

Willem steps past me. "Our camp is only a short hike from here."

"Why aren't you moving?" I ask. Making camp and sitting still doesn't make sense, unless... "You got out a distress call, didn't you?"

He nods. "I transmitted a distress call with our coordinates. I don't know if it was received, but it's something."

This is great news, but there's more to it. "But..." I say.

"That's not why we're not moving."

I look at him, waiting for the answer. "You'll probably only believe me if you see it for yourself." He motions toward a nearby mini-mountain. "I'll show you." He turns to Alvin and speaks Greenlandic, then looks to Peach and Jenny. "He'll take you to our camp. We'll join you shortly."

Jenny doesn't look pleased. "We should stay together."

"I won't be long."

"And if the bear comes back?" she asks. "You think the prune will protect us?"

I hand Jenny the Glock and point to the Internal Locking System safety feature in the back of the pistol's grip. "Just switch this, point the gun at the big white target, and squeeze the trigger until it falls down."

She takes the gun and sighs. "Please hurry," she says.

Peach says nothing, but given her permanent scowl, I'm happy she's gone mute.

Alvin moves down a stony slope. Despite being exhausted, Jenny and Peach should have no trouble keeping up with him.

Willem, on the other hand, is moving uphill fast, taking long strides with his Viking legs. I start off after him, the burn of exertion returning after just a few steps. When Peach and Jenny disappear behind a ledge, I start to feel vulnerable. I'm alone with a total stranger who has every reason to hate me. Maybe this was his new plan? Divide and conquer?

"Just so you know," I say. "I still have a very sharp knife, so don't try anything."

He looks back at me. His forehead is coated in a film of sweat, and he's breathing heavy. He's no more accustomed to this level of activity than I am. "Good," he says, between breaths. "You...can fight the bear...if he...comes back." He climbs up a five-foot ledge, turns around, and offers his hand. "We're almost there."

14

There," he says, pointing over the crest of the small mountain.

I'm winded, tired, and more than a little turned around by the time I join him and follow his pointed finger out into the distance. I stare dumbly ahead, oblivious to what he's showing me. "What am I looking at?"

He turns toward me. The expression on his face looks something like a disappointed teacher. Sorry Mr. Viking Willem, a dog didn't eat my homework but a polar bear nearly ate my face.

Asshole.

"South," he says, and I'm still clueless and even more annoyed. "You're looking south."

This is one of those moments in a movie when the camera pulls back while at the same time, zooms in. I think Spielberg did it in *Jaws,* when Chief Brody sees the shark up close for the first time. It's something they do when the main character realizes that they're even more screwed than they were before. This is my personal "we're going to need a bigger boat" moment, only I'd settle for any old boat, because that's the only way we're going to save ourselves.

We're stuck.

On an island.

"I thought this was a peninsula," I say, more to myself than to Willem.

"We did, too," he says. "That's how it appears on the maps."

"Well, someone did a shitty job making the map," I say, looking at the half-mile divide of ocean between the southern fringe of the island and the mainland. It's not a huge distance, but even from here I can see the ocean water is moving quickly through the straight. If we tried to cross in the raft—which no longer has a functioning ballast system—we'd be flipped, or dragged back out to sea…and then flipped. Frustrated, I pick up a rock and chuck it.

Willem watches the stone sail into the distance and says, "The map was probably accurate a few years ago. Maybe even last year. But the glaciers are melting fast. The island was probably connected to the mainland by ice for thousands of years."

"It's melting that fast?"

He gives me that same condescending teacher look again, like he's looking over a pair of invisible glasses.

"What?" I say, doing nothing to hide my annoyance. "Just because I'm involved in antiwhaling doesn't mean I'm a frickin' environmental encyclopedia."

He squints at me. "I bet your friends could tell me that the glaciers are melting at a rate of seven meters per day. You're American, so that's about twenty-two feet. And they could probably tell me that the melt rate of glaciers that end beneath the ocean are one hundred times faster than that."

I cross my arms. "What's your point?"

"The point is…" he says, softening his expression, "you're not like them."

This is true. But he's as much of an enigma as I am, because *he* sounds like an ecofreak.

"You weren't bothered by the whale meat," he says. "If I'm not mistaken, you actually approved of the attack. And you've got a good arm."

Shit.

"That was you with the paint," he says. It's not a question. "And that foul-smelling oil."

I sit down. The guilt is too much for my tired body. But he doesn't chew me out or pile on the guilt; he simply asks, "So, who are you?"

He crouches down in front of me, waiting for an answer.

So I tell him. Everything. The WSPA. My mission to watch the whaling techniques, to watch the actions of the *Sentinel* and her crew, and to testify on behalf of, or against, both parties if need be. I detail the events leading up to the catastrophe that brought us here, but he interrupts before I can finish that part of the story.

"So you're undercover, then?" he asks.

"Yeah."

"And the WSPA has *armed* undercover agents?" There's a bit of doubt in his voice.

"The gun isn't mine," I say. "I found it on the *Sentinel* before it sank."

He gets serious and sits down across from me. I try to avoid his eyes, but they're bright blue and hard to ignore, especially when he's leaning down, trying to get my attention. "How many?"

"How many what?"

"People," he says. "How many people were on board?"

"Thirty," I say.

He shakes his head with a sigh. "And you're the only survivors?"

I almost say yes, but then remember McAfee and crew. "We think there's another group of survivors. Captain McAfee and his lackeys. They left us for dead. But we haven't seen them. They knew about the peninsula, but they were in a Zodiac, so it's possible they made it to the mainland."

"The captain *left* you? Left three women?" The news has clearly offended his sense of chivalry. The feminist in me starts to form a rebuttal, but I decide to let it go. His concern is a welcome change from the people I normally encounter.

"The captain is a murderer," I say, my voice oozing venom. "He was responsible for the explosion."

The look on his face says that if McAfee were sitting here with us, Willem would strangle him, but he manages to ask calmly, "You're sure?"

"We have proof," I say. "He took cover before the explosion. Knew it was coming. Peach has a video of it."

"How many others were involved?" he asks.

"One for sure. Mr. Jackson, the security man." I give a couple of air quotes when I say "security." "I think he actually planted the explosives. Chase is the brains of the operation, so it was probably his plan. There might have been a few others. But most of the crew abhorred violence."

"Aside from throwing bottles."

"Right," I say, "but you saw how good they are at that, so… Did I hurt him?"

The subject change catches him off guard, and I can see he's confused by the question. "Your father. The bottle that went through the window. He looked hurt when he came out."

"The smell made him vomit," he says. "He was more embarrassed than hurt. He was laughing about it…until the *Sentinel* rammed us. And then…well, we are descended from Vikings." He smiles briefly, but it fades. "He's hurt now, though. Twisted his ankle escaping the ship. Even if this wasn't an island, we wouldn't be going anywhere fast. I can't leave him, and Alvin knows he wouldn't survive the journey. We'll either be rescued, or die here."

The conversation is turning bleak and depressing, but there are still some details I need to know. Things that, if I survive, I'll tell the world. "What about you?" I ask. "How many men on the *Bliksem*?"

"Fifteen fishermen and one stowaway," he says. "Now just three. My father, Alvin, and I were on the bridge when it happened. The explosions killed the rest."

The number of dead, over a few whales, is staggering. I try to observe a few moments of silence in their honor, but his description of the crew has me curious. "Who was the stowaway?"

"Me," he says.

"But your father—"

"Didn't want his son to fish for a living." He leans back on his arms and looks at the sky behind me. "He saved every penny he could. Pushed me in school, like a drill sergeant. And worked himself to the bone. Sent me to a boarding school in the US. From there, Harvard. I became a teacher and quickly defaulted on my loans. Things went downhill from there, and I decided to come home, live the simple life for a while. But my father hasn't noticed I'm no longer a child and turned me away. Alvin slipped me on board. My father didn't speak to me for days. And then you—the *Sentinel*—showed up. The whale meat was my idea and—" He laughs. "I saw pride in my father's eyes for the first time. All this time he's been pushing me to be someone better than him and never noticed we're not all that different."

Willem stands and brushes off his bright orange survival pants. "And now I get to watch him die."

I stand and raise my chin defiantly. "We're not done yet." His revelation about his father has stirred feelings in me that I've been avoiding for weeks. "You take after your father, and I'll take after mine. We're getting the hell off this island and back to civilization. And so is your father."

"Your father sounds like a tough guy."

"He is," I say, hearing the lie, but not correcting it. It's just a single word. *Was*. Past tense. But I'm not ready to say it yet. So I crush that morsel of pain and swallow it down for later.

"But I still disagree," he says. "We'll be lucky to survive the storm. It's going to get dark and cold."

He points behind me. I look to the north and see a dark, churning Arctic storm swirling toward us like it's the Nothing from *The NeverEnding Story*.

If that wasn't bad enough, a scream rolls up from somewhere below. It's Peach. And Jenny. And then a man. Alvin?

I find out exactly who it is a moment later when Willem lunges down the hill and shouts, "Father!"

15

As I charge down the grade after Willem, my mind races through the most likely scenarios we might find upon reaching the *Bliksem* crew's camp. The first option is that the polar bear has returned and Jenny is so freaked out she's forgotten she has a gun. The second option is that they have encountered McAfee and the two captains are trying to kill each other. Both scenarios are awful to consider but are, unfortunately, the most likely I can imagine. Whatever it is we find, I want to be ready, so I take out the knife, flick open the five-inch blade, and hope I don't trip and fall on it.

We arrive at the camp a minute later. It's a natural depression in the endless stone landscape, surrounded by several large rocks that look like they could have been placed in a semicircle by some ancient settlers. They'll help block the ocean breeze, but they won't do anything to protect us from the incoming storm. A quick scan of the area reveals no immediate danger.

No bear.

No McAfee.

Just Alvin, Peach, Jenny, and a man who I can only assume is Willem's father. They're all crouched over an object that I can't see, but it's clearly a curiosity and not a danger.

While I put my hands on my knees and catch my breath, Willem moves closer. "Father," he says in English. The captain of the *Bliksem* turns back briefly, and I see his face, thick, wrinkled tan skin, crow's-feet around his eyes, a white beard, and white, close-cut hair. Without the beard, he might look a lot like the Colonel. "What happened?" Willem asks.

His father waves him over. "Willem! Come see!"

The others make room for him in their tight semicircle. None of them has noticed me yet. They're too focused on whatever it is that made two grown women and an old man scream. I'm interested, too, but the storm rolling in keeps my attention on the north. I've spent a lot of time on the ocean. I'm pretty good at gauging storms. This one's going to be bad, and we've got about two hours before it hits us hard. Time is short.

"Jane," Willem says. "Come see this."

He sounds excited, and I wonder if he's forgotten that we're all likely to freeze, starve, or be eaten to death soon. *Like you're one to talk*, I think at myself. I've been making light of our situation since it began. Who am I to mock the way someone else handles getting crapped on by life?

As I turn around, the wind picks up behind me and flings open the cloak. I'm still holding the black-bladed knife in my hand, and the storm roils in the sky behind me. When I see the others, there are five sets of wide eyes staring at me. I look at Jenny, who's grinning. "We having another Van Helsing moment?"

"Totally," she says.

I pull the cloak down around me, pull the hood down from my head, and close the knife.

"Jane," Willem says, motioning to his father, whose bewildered look has yet to fade, "This is my father, Captain Jakob Olavson." He turns to his father and motions to me. "Father, this is Jane—"

"Muninn," Jakob says.

Willem laughs.

"What?" I ask. I don't like people laughing about me without my blessing. "Did I do something wrong?"

"Not at all," Willem says. "In fact, I think you impressed him. He called you a Raven. *Muninn.* One of Odin's ravens."

"That's a good thing?"

"It means memory, or mind, but I think the description has more to do with how you look—the cloak, the knife, your hair...your eyes."

I'm uncomfortable with the visual inspection and try to think of a way to change the subject, but Jakob picks up where his son left off. "A harbinger," he says. His English is understandable, but the accent is thick compared to Willem's. "The raven is drawn to death."

"Great," Peach says, looking down at the object they were all looking at and stepping away from it. I can't see it clearly yet, but from here it looks like just another stone.

"Father," Willem says, his single-word statement communicating something close to *Knock it off.*

But the old man's voice can't be stifled. "Odin's ravens welcomed the dead into Valhalla. Some even called him Hrafnaguð, the 'raven god.' So, you see, the birds represent great power, but their presence usually follows death."

At first I think he's talking doom and gloom about us, like we're all about to die—which might be true—but then I remember that there are thirty-something fresh corpses floating around in the Arctic Ocean, and I wonder if that's what they found. *Is it a corpse washed up on the beach? No,* I think, *we're too far from the water...*

And Jakob looks far too amused to have just seen a fresh corpse...unless maybe it's McAfee's.

"What he's not telling you," Willem says, "is that the Raven is our family's crest. For our family, the raven was a harbinger of death but not *our* deaths."

"For our enemies," Jakob says. "Our ancestors flew the raven banners before entering battle. They were buried with the warriors. They hung in our halls. And on the *Bliksem*'s bridge." The man's energy fades.

Willem puts a hand on his father's shoulder. "Show her what you found."

Jakob's brief levity is gone, but he turns around and motions to the roundish object lying on the ground. "It's here."

The others gather round again as I see the object for the first time. From where I'm standing, it looks like a stone. Granted, the color is all wrong. It's not dark gray like the other rocks. And it's very round. Most of the stones here are flat. Before I can ask, Willem picks it up in his gloved hands and turns it over.

It's a skull.

The lower jaw is missing. As are many of its teeth.

"Alas, poor Yorick," I say. "I knew him, Horatio."

Willem laughs. Everyone else looks at me like I'm possessed. I look at Peach and Jenny. "Really? Hamlet? Shakespeare? Nothing?"

"Was it a movie?" Jenny asks. She sounds serious, but I can see a glimmer of humor in her face.

I roll my eyes and look at Jakob. "Who is he?"

The old captain somehow manages to shrug using only his eyebrows.

"The rest of him is under there," Jenny says, pointing to a pile of stones. "The skull fell out when Alvin moved one of the rocks. Scared the shit out of us."

Alvin mutters something, and though I can't understand him, I think he's calling them pansies or something because he chuckles at himself, and Jakob grumbles at him.

"He's been here a long time," Willem says. "Skull structure doesn't look Inuit, either, so he's probably a Norseman." He looks at the burial mound. "This is an amazing find."

"They settled this far north?" I ask. It doesn't seem possible.

"Hunting expeditions, maybe. Whalers—"

Peach gets in a "Some things never change," but everyone ignores her.

"But settlements? No. Nothing remotely close to this. Nothing we know of, anyway. It's possible there were a lot of colonies on the western coast that we just haven't found yet. Vesterbygden is the northernmost settlement we know about, a hamlet in the west, along the Davis Straight. It's possible this man traveled with the Inuit. They traveled this far north. But he's been buried like a Norseman, so he wasn't here alone."

It's all very interesting, but I can't help wondering, "How do you know so much about them?" Before Willem can answer, I figure it out. "History teacher?"

He nods.

"No wonder you defaulted on your school loans."

He smiles at his misfortune and turns his head to the sky. The clouds are closer. Darker. He turns to his father. "Can you move?"

"Move where?" Jakob asks. "This is a barren landscape. I'd rather face my death like a man. Here with our ancestor."

I look at the burial mound as thoughts of Vikings and settlements flash through my mind. "You're wrong," I say.

Willem looks at me. "I don't think so. We need to find cover."

"Not about that," I say. "About the Vikings not settling here." I can tell he's about to shush me, so I speak fast. "When I was scouting the area earlier, I saw a structure at the center of the island."

This perks up Jakob's attention. "A structure?"

"Probably just ruins now, but it's something. And the mountains will shield us from the worst of the wind."

"Umm," Jenny says. "Don't we want to go south? Not inland, over these big effing hills?"

Fearing Willem will reveal we won't be going south anytime soon, I quickly say, "We can't head south if we're frozen solid."

She growls, but relents. "I'll get the raft."

Willem puts his hand out to Jakob. "Father?"

Jakob looks at Willem and then at me. "There is really a structure? I don't like to be lied to, Raven."

That he trusts me at all is something of a mystery to me. He knows we're from the *Sentinel* crew, but I haven't sensed any hostility from him yet, and Willem hasn't explained the situation to him. So why the kindness? "I wouldn't lie to you."

Peach huffs and starts picking up her bags. She hasn't said much and wears a permanent scowl. I'd like to explain to her that lying to people who are dangerous is not the same as lying to people who are innocent, but she'd probably just tell me that whales are innocent, so I decide to stow that delightful conversation away for another day.

Jakob takes Willem's hand and winces as he stands.

"Where are your supplies?" I ask Willem. "I can carry them while you help your father."

Willem frowns. "We're wearing all the supplies we have."

I take a protein bar from my pack, split it into three pieces and give one to Alvin, one to Willem, and one to Jakob. They quickly devour the quasi-chocolate-flavored food.

"There's more," I say, "but we need to ration it."

Jakob gives a nod and motions me forward. The group is ready to go, and it seems I'm taking the lead again.

As I step forward, Jakob says to Willem, "You see? The Raven leads our family once again. There is still hope."

The cold breeze penetrating the back of my cloak disagrees with him.

16

I can't tell if the weather is rooting for us or messing with us. We make it over the hills, struggling every step of the way, but as soon as we reach the island's core, the clouds drop trou and shit an endless stream of white.

I lead the group in a single-file line, heading for the center of the open area where I saw—where I hope I saw—some kind of shelter. If it wasn't, I'm not only going to look like a total doofus, but we'll probably die. The wind, even buffered by the tall stone hills, is brutal enough, but the storm will likely drop the temperature, too.

At first there was a good amount of complaining, mostly from Jenny, but Peach made no effort to hide her discontent, sighing loudly whenever she had to exert herself. Jakob made a noble effort to hide his discomfort, but some of the journey took them over rugged terrain, and he'd let out a grunt when Willem stumbled and Jakob suddenly had to support his full weight. But when the snow began and the wind dropped the temperature, no one made a sound. The suddenness of the shift in mood reminded me of how prey animals, once caught, lie back quietly, resigned to their fate. Is that what I'm seeing? Are we resigned to a frigid death?

Fuck that, I think. If the Colonel made it to the pearly gates and found out I died sitting on my ass, he'd block my entrance and kick me into the fiery pit himself. As nice as a fiery pit sounds right now, I'm not about to disappoint my father, at least not any more than I have already.

So I push through the storm. It's possible we've already passed the structure. Visibility is maybe ten feet, when I'm not looking down. The rocky valley floor is covered in boulders and loose sheets of shale. When I can no longer see the ground, I turn my eyes up and see nothing but white.

We're lost. Out in the open. I've killed us.

Hoping Willem will have an idea, I stop and wait for him to catch up with Jakob. Father and son look miserable, but when they see me standing still and meet my eyes, their determination is intense. Jakob stares in my eyes, reading the defeat there, but then cranes his head to the side and looks past me.

"What distresses you, Raven?" he asks. Before I can explain, he adds, "You have provided shelter as promised."

What? Do people see mirages in snow? I've never heard of such a thing, but he could be suffering from hypothermia. *Maybe he's hallucinating?*

Willem and Jakob take a few steps beyond me and stop. Jakob reaches out a hand and wipes it back and forth. It's like he's some kind of magician, because a trail of dark gray follows his hand. Then I can see it, stretching out fifteen feet in either direction. A five-foot-tall wall covered in snow. I wouldn't have known it was there until I face-planted against it.

Gripped by relief, I turn around to the others and shout, "We made it! It's here!" I run around the perimeter and find the entrance on the other side. The floor is even and free of snow near the back wall. I huddle up in the corner, and the wind disappears. The relief is instant. This might just work.

Ten minutes later, we're all piled inside the life raft, positioned in the structure's corner. It's cramped and a little ripe, but with six people inside, it's damn near warm. *We're going to make it,* I think. *And then we're going to slowly starve,* says the little red devil on my shoulder. *Maybe we'll go cannibal like that rugby team that crashed in the Andes, and then the last survivor will starve alone, or be eaten by the bear. Or maybe the bear will just tear through the tent tonight and eat us. Or—*

A staccato sound rips through the tent, sending a panicked pain through my body. I sit up and look for some sign of the bear outside the tent. I've got the gun in my hand, ready to fire. Just when I notice no one else has reacted to the noise, it repeats. I jump again, but this time I'm able to identify its source. Jenny is sleeping. And snoring. Peach is sleeping, too, as are Alvin and Jakob. Willem, on the other hand, is leaning on his elbow and looking at me—with my gun at the ready—with a smirk.

He doesn't have to say anything. I can almost hear the string of one-liners he's got on the tip of his tongue. "Shut up," I say.

Most people would still take a jab or two, but he just says, "Thanks."

"I've only prolonged the inevitable."

"It's a start," he says.

I don't want to think about our situation, and I don't want to be thanked, so I say, "So, Professor, what is this place?"

"It's Viking," he says. "The construction is similar to ruins found in the southern settlements, but the reason for it being here is a mystery." He shrugs. "I have no idea."

I sigh. "Good to know history is as interesting as I remember it from school."

He grins. "You just didn't have the right teacher." He's suddenly got that look in his eyes. You know the look—one part overconfidence, one part lost in the imaginary act of screwing. It's the same look every guy gets when it occurs to them that you're their type. It's not a universally unwanted look unless it comes from someone like Chase, who was giving me a similar stare just the other night. And if the circumstances were different, Willem's attention would be welcome. But out here, surrounded by death and cold and four sleeping, stinky companions? Hell no. I'm not some Viking wench you can seduce with a bed of hay and tankard of ale. Well, okay, that might actually work. But not now.

I'm so lost in my revolt that I don't notice him lie back and close his eyes. How long did I look at him with one Spock-like eyebrow raised? Did I offend him? Do I care?

I force these obnoxious thoughts out of my mind, lie down, and put my mind somewhere else. The problem is, I end up somewhere else I don't want to be.

My father's shouting like a drill sergeant. It doesn't faze me. It's really just a slight reaction for him. The neighbors can't hear him yet. He hasn't threatened to get a gun. He hasn't punched anything. But he's pissed. Like I knew he would be. Making my father angry has become something of an art form over the years. After years of pushing me to be something resembling the son he never had, I've learned to push back. And today, I pushed hard. I'm moving out, heading for Washington, DC, and joining Greenpeace.

His reaction is predictable. He rants about earthy-crunchy pansies, flower-wearing hippies, and tree-hugging homos. A veritable conveyor belt of foulmouthed stereotypes, that man.

I fire back, thinking my spunk and passion will impress him. It has worked in the past. Hearing a bit of himself in me always seems to make him proud, even if we're arguing about school or boys or pot. He likes that I stand up for myself, and I think many of our arguments are his way of training me for life challenges.

But this time, he wilts. He sits on the old plaid ottoman and leans his forehead down on his hands. I see his bald head turning red. I brace myself for the verbal assault. But it never comes. "Go," he says, nearly a whisper.

The whisper catches me off guard. I thought I had him cornered and out of ammunition and he's somehow pulled a knife and stabbed it into my chest. Just by whispering! My reaction to his whisper makes me angry, and I shout, "Fine!" before storming out of the house with my few possessions.

I don't see my father for a year, and then only for holidays after that. He's always distant, not quite the man who raised me. The last time I saw him was in the hospital…

Sleep spares me from the memory, but my dreams are horrible images and screaming.

I wake with a start, reaching for my gun. Willem is awake, too, and this time he shares my concern.

I assess the situation.

The tent no longer shakes. The storm subsided overnight.

The yellow fabric glows with light. The sun blazes over the hills. While the sun never sets, it does change positions in the sky, sometimes dipping and creating long shadows, but it always comes back up. Not that I'm complaining. Perpetual daylight is far better than the opposite.

I do a quick headcount. Everyone is here. Alive.

All good.

But Willem is freaked. He heard whatever woke me up and sent me scrambling for my weapon. The shrill scream from my dream repeats. The voice is high-pitched, but the scratchy vibrato mixed in sounds masculine. It's a man. And he's coming this way. Or, more likely, is being pursued by a big-ass polar bear.

Willem must have come to a similar conclusion, because he looks from my eyes to the gun in my hands to the exit and gives a nod. He braces himself, ready to spring to action.

The Colonel would've liked Willem.

I unzip the hatch and suck in a deep breath. I count to three in my head and then lunge out of the tent and raise my gun. I can't see a thing. The bright sun shining off the endless sheet of white snow blinds me, and I don't see him until he's nearly inside the Viking shelter. But when I do, I freeze.

It's Chase.

He looks wild. Insane.

He's covered in a dark red splash similar to the paint I smashed against the *Bliksem*'s hull. But the liquid covering his face and torso is a few shades darker. This is the real stuff. Chase is covered in blood. And given the amount, I think it's likely someone else is dead.

And that's when I see the bloody knife in his hand.

17

Chase's eyes flash wide when he sees me. But I'm not really sure he recognizes me, because he screams again and tries to stop. His feet slip on the fresh snow, and it sends him hard to his ass. His glasses are cracked on one side, and the other side is covered in flecks of blood, so it's possible he can't see me clearly, but the horror on his face says he's somewhere else. Not thinking. Like someone who has just witnessed a murder.

Or committed a murder.

"Chase," I say in a firm yet calm voice, "it's Jane."

I lower the gun so he can see my face behind it, but I don't divert my aim too far. It makes little difference. He scrambles away from me, breathing so heavy that spit is flying from his mouth. Or is it rabid froth? Has he gone mad?

"Chase," I shout at him, lowering the weapon completely.

"Oh my God," Jenny says as she steps out of the tent. "Is he okay?"

I ignore her. Chase is almost back to his feet, and it's clear he's going to run. And as much as I don't like him—never mind that he's covered in someone else's blood—I can't let him die.

Blood. The sight of it all over him, not knowing where it came from, keeps me from tackling him. I look to Willem and motion toward Chase with my head. He understands the request and shakes his head no. What a couple of heroes we are; afraid to save someone covered in blood. Of course we're covered in open scrapes, and getting another person's blood in a wound could be a fatal mistake. Although we'll all likely die out here anyway, so what the hell does it matter?

I take a step forward, resolved to subdue Chase, but before I get very far, a flash of red zips past me. It's Peach. Just as Chase gets his feet under him, she tackles him by the knees and brings him down like some kind of greased pig at a rodeo. Only it's not grease making him slick. It's blood.

Jenny rushes to help Peach, catches the struggling Chase by the shoulders, and pins him down with ease. He's only half her size, so there's no chance he can get up. But he continues to struggle, manic and wild. And the look in his eyes is all fear. He's not looking for a fight.

The knife says differently. Then again, he hasn't stabbed anyone yet.

Yet.

And I'm pretty sure neither Jenny nor Peach has seen the shiny silver version of the black knife I took from Chase's survival pack. I step on his wrist, pinning his hand, and the knife, to the ground.

"Hey!" Peach protests. "What the fuck!"

I apply a little pressure, and Chase's hand opens. I bend down and pluck the knife from his fingers and then hold it up for Peach to see. She hadn't seen it. I can see the shock in her eyes. But she tries to hide it. She's holding a grudge, despite the fact that I saved her life. I'm considering calling her Sour Grape from now on, but that will probably just make things worse.

The knife folds down easily. I'm about to slip it in my pants pocket with the other, think better of it, and hand it to Willem, who's standing beside me now. I crouch down and snap my fingers in Chase's face. "Chase," I say. "Snap out of it."

I'm not being gentle, I know. But anything short of shooting him is probably a mercy compared to the welcome I'd get if our roles were reversed.

His breathing slows.

Jakob and Alvin join the party, looking ready to beat Chase like a baby seal.

But he's coming around, looking at the faces around him. Then he finally looks me in the eyes.

"You're safe, now," I say. I don't really know that he wasn't safe before, but the blood seems to be a good indicator that he wasn't. That and the all-consuming fear radiating from him like heat off a parking lot in summer.

His body goes slack. Peach lets go of his legs and kneels next to him. Jenny loosens her grip but never lets go of him.

"Harper?" he finally says.

"In the flesh," I say, and then inwardly cringe. Not the best choice of words to use with a guy who has no doubt imagined me in the flesh more than once. I've also heard some Bible Belt conservatives use the term to describe themselves when their ire is raised, like the flesh itself is evil and corrupting instead of the brain, or soul, controlling it. But I don't think Chase is a Bible-thumper, so I don't think that's really an issue.

"Where am I?" he asks, looking at Willem, and then Jakob.

"We're at the center of the island," I say. "You're safe here."

"Did you just say *island*?" Peach asks, her voice suddenly frantic.

"Not now, Peach," I growl.

To her credit, Jenny takes in the information silently, looks at the sky, and then lowers her head with a sigh. Doom absorbed, accepted, and filed. Peach, on the other hand, is about to explode. She opens her mouth, and I shout at her, "Not fucking now, Peach!"

Her mouth clamps shut.

I compose myself by taking a slow breath and twisting my neck to the side, popping a few vertebrae. Feeling a little better, I motion to the three men Chase doesn't know. "This is Jakob Olavson, captain of the *Bliksem*, his son Willem, and this is Alvin. He likes knives. You two will get along."

Chase's fear vanishes and is replaced by anger. "What are you doing with them? They destroyed the *Sentinel*. Killed most of the crew."

Jakob shakes his head sadly in a way that says, "Poor, stupid boy."

"Chase," I say, realizing that he might actually be unaware of Captain McAfee's involvement in the sinking of both vessels. "These three are the only surviving members of the *Bliksem*'s crew." This news stuns him a little, but he's still tense. "They had nothing to do with the explosion."

"Then who do you thi—"

"It was McAfee," Jenny says.

Chase looks up at her, crossing his eyes as he tries to focus on her upside down. "Bullshit."

"It's true," I say.

He looks to Peach, clearly trusting her over Jenny and me, who'd no doubt be walking the plank right about now if the *Sentinel* hadn't sunk.

Peach sighs and looks at the snow-covered ground. "We have it on video. He knew about the explosion."

"Remember Mr. Jackson's countdown?" Jenny adds. "Thirty seconds. It wasn't an impact he was counting down. It was the explosion."

"But...he wouldn't. He—" His eyes lower and flick back and forth like he's scanning some invisible document. A moment later his forehead pinches tight, and he comes to some sort of conclusion. "I was afraid of this," he admits. "Not something this drastic, mind you, but he hasn't listened to my advice as much as he used to. Not since Mr. Jackson came aboard."

"Look, Chase," I say, "I'm going to give you the benefit of the doubt here and assume you knew nothing about the explosion. If you behave, you can join our little band of castaways and make us a true Gilligan seven." I get serious and lean in closer, "But if I think for a second that you had anything to do with the murders of more than thirty people, I'm going to leave you behind buck-ass naked. Understood?"

His face pales beneath the bloodstains.

"Good," I say. "Now tell me what happened."

"Huh?" He's lost in thought, probably wondering how long he'd last in the Arctic with no clothes on.

"You're covered in blood, Chase. What happened?"

He looks down at himself, and it's like he's seeing the blood for the first time. He frantically wipes it off his hands and asks, "Is it on my face? Is it on my face?"

In fact, it is on his face, but wiping it with his blood-covered gloves is just making it worse, so I lie. "No. Your face is clean." I take his glasses off his face, rub snow over them and put them back on. "Good as new, if you ignore the cracks." I stand and cross my arms. "Now. Talk."

He looks up at me, some of the fear coming back, but he manages to speak with just a hint of a warble. "After abandoning ship—"

I nearly add an "And us," but hold my tongue in a way the Colonel never could manage.

"—we made for the peninsula. But we misjudged the distance and ended up wrecking on the rocks north of here. The Zodiacs are wrecked. There were five of us when we left, Captain McAfee, me, Nick Eagon, and Markus Jenkins in one boat. Mr. Jackson rendezvoused with us shortly after." Chase's face screws up with anger. "I should have realized then, damn it!"

"Just keep going," I say. "I'm more interested in how you came to look like Charles Manson after brunch."

Jenny groans. The others look at me like I'm the one covered in blood. "Sorry. Sick sense of humor, I know." I turn to Chase. "Continue."

"By the time we reached the shore, Jenkins was gone. We don't know when we lost him. But the sea was rough and we were moving fast...I don't know—"

That Chase was getting choked up over the loss of a man scored him bonus points. It means he cares about people, too, not just whales. "We found a cave and hid inside. In the morning, Mr. Jackson and Captain McAfee went to check out where we were. I stayed with Eagon. He had a broken arm. Maybe some broken ribs. Jackson and the captain never came back, so Eagon and I spent a second night in the cave. Everything was fine when we fell asleep. But when I woke up, he was...he was screaming. I've never heard someone scream like that before. Like his voice was being forced out of him by something physical. There was a loud crunch, and I felt something. It was...warm. Wet. When I stumbled out of the cave, I saw the blood covering me clearly. Then I heard something scraping toward me. I thought it was Eagon. I called to him."

Chase pulls his knees up close and hugs them tight. I don't know many grown men who can pull their knees up tight like that, but even if they could, they probably wouldn't. It makes him look like a sad little schoolgirl. Someone to be pitied. And as he finishes his story, I do pity him.

"I heard breathing, too. Wet. Deep. I wanted to run, but I couldn't. I wanted to. I just couldn't. Like my legs were gone." He looks up at me, his eyes pleading me to believe what he's about to say. "It was his head. Someone threw Eagon's head at me." He shakes his head back and forth, as though disbelieving it himself, but keeps his gaze on me. "Harper, I don't think we're alone."

18

It's the polar bear," Jenny says to Peach. "Has to be." Jenny paces, occasionally offering a theory. But Peach just stares at the snow, clutching herself.

Willem, Jakob, and Alvin whisper to one another, their conversation private but their body language easy to read. They're on edge, disturbed by Chase's presence, and his story.

I'm crouching in a corner of the stone foundation with Chase, who is leaning back against the wall, eating half a protein bar and drinking a quarter of a water bottle. Our meager supplies are dwindling faster with each addition to our band of survivors.

Chase tips the bottle up and chugs a little too fast. I take it, tip it down, and remove it from his hands. "Slow down, Aquaman."

"Sorry," he says. "I haven't had anything to eat or drink since we arrived."

"You could have melted snow. Or ice," I point out.

He looks at all of the snow around us. "Good point. Is…there really a polar bear on the island?"

"We've run into it twice." I twist the bottle cap back on the bottle and put it in Chase's survival backpack. He sees the bag and twitches his lips. He's probably not sure if he should claim ownership. I make up his mind for him. "We know this belongs to you—*belonged* to you. It belongs to all of us now."

He grins and motions to the cloak gathered around me. "Looks better on you than me anyway."

I think he's about to hit on me again, so I steer the conversation back to the bear. Somehow talking about a man-eating bear is less offensive to me than the idea of a romantic encounter with Chase. "Do you think what you saw could have been a bear?"

He leans his head back against the cold stone behind him. "I didn't see anything. Just Eagon's head…"

There's a really big "but" implied by his tone. I say it for him. "But?"

He speaks softly. "I left out a detail. I—I wasn't sure about what I saw. Or if you would believe me."

"And now?"

"I remember it clearly, and you're being…fair."

Damn straight I am. "So what is it?"

"Eagon's head," he says. "It had been cracked open. His…brain was missing."

My crouch turns into a cross-legged sit when this news staggers me. "Missing?"

"I don't think it was a bear," Chase says. "Bears don't throw heads. And they don't eat brains. Not first, anyway." He picks up some snow and rubs it between his gloved hands, rubbing away the dried blood. "There *is* blood on my face, right? You lied to calm me down?"

I nod, still too stunned to talk.

He removes his gloves, picks up fresh snow, lets it melt some, and scrubs his face with the slush. The blood comes away, turning the snow next to him red. "You'd make a good captain," he says. "You're a natural leader. You know how to handle a gun, too. Did your father teach you?"

For a moment, I'm enraged that Chase has brought up my father. They knew who I was all along. They strung me along in order to set me up. But…Chase didn't know about the planned attack. Which means he didn't know I was going to be a scapegoat. "He did," I say.

"Teach you about leadership or guns?" he asks.

"Both," I say. "You know who I really am?"

He nods.

"Why did you think McAfee allowed me on board?"

He pushes his glasses up. "Because you had potential. You did good work for whales. You led groups of people. You handled confrontations well. And your background—your…father—meant you'd be taken seriously."Wait, you were grooming me? For a position on the *Sentinel*?" I laugh before he can answer. "How can you not know?"

"Know what?"

"I'm McAfee's scapegoat."

"Scapegoat? For what?"

I find this incredibly funny. How can Peach know, but Chase is in the dark? "For the explosion. That's why Peach was spying on me."

"She was observing you," he says. "That's a little different than—"

"She read my journals. Set up a spycam in our quarters. They weren't observing my behavior. They were gathering evidence. Framing things so that I would look like an ecoterrorist."

He looks dubious. "How do you know?"

"She told me," I say, motioning to Peach, who is staring right at us. She must have heard her name. More than once. And the tone in which it was said. Her gaze makes me uncomfortable, and in a flash, I see the truth. Peach is part of the inner circle. Even more than Chase. He's dedicated, smart, and tactical, and despite owning a gun, knives, and a creepy cloak, he's not insane. I force a smile at Peach and turn back to Chase.

He must have come to the same conclusion as me, because he looks like a man who has just been betrayed. Again. "I'm sorry," he says. "I didn't know. I swear."

I try my best to shrug it off. We're all here now, and we're all equally screwed. We can figure out who betrayed whom when we make it back to civilization. Until then, we're all on the same team. I hope.

"Jane," Willem says from the other side of the structure. He waves me over.

I give Chase a reassuring smile. "Try to rest."

Willem meets me halfway while Jakob limps to a large stone and sits down. Alvin sits in the corner, brushing snow off a rectangular stone.

"How is he?" Willem asks.

His concern surprises me, but then, nearly everything about these Viking whale hunters has defied my stereotyping. "Better," I say. "But…he doesn't think the bear killed that man."

"Neither does my father," Willem says.

"He doesn't?"

"He said a bear wouldn't throw a head, it would eat it. And he says that Chase runs slow. The bear would have caught him."

"Then what killed him?" I notice I'm saying "what" instead of "who."

He shrugs. "No idea. What I know is that we need to get off this island. My father thinks we can repair the ruined ballast by tying large rocks to the plastic still hanging from the bottom."

"But the channel is moving too fast," I complain. "We'd be swept out to sea before making it across."

"Which is why we need him"—he nods toward Chase—"to take us to where the Zodiacs landed. If we can salvage an engine, we might be able to hold it over the back while using paddles to steer."

"That's...nuts," I say.

"I'd rather die fighting for my life," he says.

I grin. "The history professor has some Viking in him after all?"

"A little," he says.

"Good for you," I say. "But we also need someone up there." I point to the tall peak at the southwestern area of the island. "If your distress call was heard, and they send someone to look, we need to be looking for them, too. We have flares and smoke signals. We shouldn't be hard to find if someone is in the area."

I take his slow nod as agreement and continue. "I originally wanted you and me on the hilltop and everyone else here, but if we can recover the engine, that changes things. Chase said they landed on the north end of the island. You, me, and Chase can try to recover an engine. It's going to weigh a lot, and you and I are the strongest."

"Don't let my father hear you say that," he says with a smile.

"Peach and Jenny will have to keep watch," I say. "Your father and Alvin can stay here, organize our supplies, and work out a ration system. The food is disappearing too fast. Sound good?"

Willem snaps off a salute. "You've done this before?"

My mind flashes back through time. Twenty years. I'm in the woods, a swamp really, with the Colonel. "With my father," I say. "He told me we were going camping. What we were really doing was surviving. Two weeks in the woods, gathering food, hunting, making our own fires and shelters. And I did most of the work." The memory, like most about my father, is bittersweet, though a little bit sweeter now that what once seemed like torture might save my life.

When I relay the plan to the others, no one looks happy. Despite their age, Alvin and Jakob aren't accustomed to letting others do the heavy lifting. Jenny and Peach fear the bear. Chase fears whatever tried to play volleyball with Eagon's brainless head. Those are all valid concerns, which I share, but we're going to have to risk our lives a little to save ourselves. And I nearly say that but decide it sounds too much like cheesy dialogue from a SyFy original movie. Instead I say, "Here are your choices: do what I say and maybe get off this island or don't do what I say and get left behind when *I* get off this island."

Whether or not they believe I'm capable of getting them, or myself, off the island, I'm not sure. But my words have the desired effect. A few minutes later Chase and Willem are waiting for me while I speak to Jenny and Peach. They've got a flare gun with two flares and two smoke signals. "You know how to use them?"

Both nod. I hand Chase's black knife to Jenny.

"Why are you giving that to her?" Peach complains.

I speak without much thought. "Because I don't trust you." It's not very diplomatic of me and only widens the divide in my group, but I have an issue with pulling punches with someone who conspired to send me to jail for life.

She looks more angry than hurt by my words, which proves I made the right choice.

"If you see the bear, or…anything else," I say to Jenny, "don't screw around. Just haul ass back here."

"Don't worry," she says. "I will. You better go, Van Slowpoke." She surprises me with a quick hug. "Be careful."

"You, too," I say. Then I add, "Both of you."

Chase and Willem are already heading north. I send Jenny and Peach southwest, wave good-bye to Alvin and Jakob, and then strike out north, toward two wrecked Zodiacs…and whatever ate Eagon's brain.

19

The flat plain to the north of the island's center ends in a steep valley between two sharp-looking peaks. It's just four feet across and rises twenty vertical feet on either side before tapering to a forty-five-degree angle. I enter first, weapon at the ready. If we encounter the polar bear here, I'll have no choice but to kill it. Or it, me.

"Jane," Chase says.

I turn around to find him frozen at the entrance. He looks frail and terrified.

I hold the handgun up for him to see. "I'm a good shot. We'll be fine," I tell him.

He points to the snow in the narrow pass. "This is the way I came."

A trail of bloodstained footprints covers the trail. I can see a spot where he must have fallen, too. His frantic escape is frozen for all to see.

"Look at me," I say. When he does, I continue. "We're going to get off this island, Chase. But the only way we can do that is with one of the Zodiac engines. We'll go as fast as we can, get back to camp, and then haul ass to the mainland. We could be out of here inside of six hours." It's a guess, really. We might have to spend another night here. But I really just need him to keep moving.

Unfortunately, it's not working.

"I can't," he says.

"Chase," Willem says in a voice that's so kind and gentle, I think he's about to tell an inspiring story from his childhood—standing up to a bully or a wild animal or whatever hardships Greenlander kids have to face. Instead, he says, "If you don't go, I'm going to throw you over my shoulder and carry you. And if the bear shows up, I'm going to drop you before running away."

Chase slowly cranes his head toward Willem. He sees the same seriousness in Willem's eyes that I do. Chase takes a slow step into the gorge. Then another. And soon we're on our way again.

Five minutes later, we're moving at a steady clip. "I misjudged you," Chase says. I think he's talking to me, so I turn around, but he's looking at Willem. "It's not often that someone can outmaneuver me. At least, not whalers."

"I'm a history professor," Willem says with a grin.

"Ahh," Chase says. "That explains it, then. The whale meat. It was…"—I can tell he's still offended by the memory, but his words don't match his expression—"…inspired."

"Thun L'Évêque, France, AD 1340," Willem says. "British attackers launched dead animals into the defending castle. The defenders reported the stench was so bad that they quickly agreed to a truce and abandoned the castle."

"Is that what you wanted?" Chase asks. "A truce?"

"And for you to abandon your attacks."

"Killing whales means that much to you?"

Chase's words are framed in antiwhaling speak, but his tone says the question is earnest, not a taunt. So I stay out of it and keep my eyes forward, waiting for a bear to rise up out of the snow or a head to come sailing my way.

"I care about my father," Willem says. "Attacking the *Bliksem* meant you were attacking my father. The paint was bad enough, but the rotten butter…I couldn't let that stand."

Chase laughs.

"What's funny about that?" Willem asks.

I realize the answer a moment after he begins to explain. "It's ironic is all. That the first real shots fired in our naval encounter were made by the one person who didn't really want to be a party to it."

Thank God Willem already knows I threw those bottles. This would be a really bad time to divide—my bullshit meter suddenly goes off the chart. Chase *is* trying to divide Willem and me. I remember Chase's last visit to my quarters. His smitten eyes *weren't* an act. This isn't about whalers versus antiwhalers. This is about Chase putting a wedge between me and Willem—the competition.

For the girl.

I'm about to turn around and give Chase a verbal kick in the nuts, but Willem beats me to the punch.

"I know," he says. "She's got a good arm."

With those words, Willem takes the wind out of Chase's sails. Not only does Willem know about my treachery, he compliments it. I glance back. Chase looks dejected. Score one for Willem. Behind Chase, Willem grins and gives me a wink. *Son of a bitch. Him, too?*

"For the record," I say, picking up the pace. "This isn't a B horror movie, so I won't be shagging anyone while the threat of death looms—"

If there is a God, I know without a doubt that he's got a sick sense of humor because as the words *death looms* come out of my mouth, I glance up and see a naked, headless, and limbless corpse impaled on a sharp rock jutting from the gorge wall. A tattoo of a breaching whale on the chest helps identify this as Eagon's body, or what remains of it.

Chase screams, but he's cut short when Willem clamps his hand over the panicked man's mouth. They struggle for a moment as

Chase tries to run, but when no bear—or anything else—appears, Chase calms, though he doesn't look up again.

"It's Eagon," I say. I'm not a forensic expert, but I'm pretty sure I can identify wounds inflicted by wide polar bear claws and big-ass polar bear teeth. So I ignore the fact that I knew this man and step closer. The stomach cavity has been ripped open. The tear is jagged, and it's dangling strings of stretched-out skin. The flesh wasn't cut. It was yanked. My stomach starts to protest. If the cold hadn't kept the body from rotting, I'd probably be retching right now. But I keep it together and look closer.

"The organs are missing," I say upon seeing the empty cavity. But that's not the most disturbing revelation. A bear could probably tear a man open, eat his soft insides, and take a few limbs for the road. What a bear could not do was slice those limbs clean off. The flesh and bone, where the one arm and both legs have been severed, are cut clean. There are no claw marks. No signs of chewing. No stretched flesh. I speak the only logical conclusion aloud. "His limbs…they were cut off."

"What?" Willem says, letting Chase go.

Both of them are drawn forward by curiosity. Willem examines the wounds while Chase takes a quick glance and stumbles away, clutching a hand over his mouth. "A bear didn't do that," he says though his hand.

"Chase," I say. "Did McAfee or Mr. Jackson have any weapons?"

"You mean like an ax or a sword? Because that's what you'd need to do that!" He's starting to crack. Tears fill his eyes.

I remind myself that he recently had a head thrown at him, and I try to stay calm. "Yes."

He shakes his head no. "Jackson had a pack. I never saw what was in it. Maybe a gun, I suppose, but not a blade."

"*You* had a blade," Willem points out to Chase.

"Not big enough to do that!" He stabs a finger toward the corpse without looking at it. "I couldn't cut through a femur with a knife!"

"Keep it down!" I hiss. "Whether this was Jackson, a bear, or something else, I don't want to be found."

"We should head back," Chase says, his hands shaking.

Willem looks unsure.

I am too. But going back means we repeat this process tomorrow, and I can hear distant waves crashing against a rocky shoreline. We're almost there. "We're going forward."

No one complains. They know it's fruitless to argue with the person holding the gun. I gave the silver knife to Willem earlier, but it's a small blade compared to whatever hacked off Eagon's limbs. But a gun beats a blade any day. So they stick with me.

We exit the chasm a minute later and arrive at a long, sloping shoreline. The flat rock slants into the ocean at a slight grade, but it's covered in large, round boulders, smoothed over time by ocean, wind, or glaciers. Maybe all three. I don't really give a shit about how the rocks were formed, only that they're blocking my view and would make a nice place for a killer to hide.

"Hold on," Willem says. He scrambles up the side of the gorge wall and then leaps to the top of a tall stone. After only a few moments, he points and says, "There. I see one of them." He climbs down and leads our charge through the stone maze.

We move fast, driven by the frantic feeling that people always experience when close to completing a goal.

"Here!" Willem shouts as we emerge from the stone maze and arrive at the ocean. The Zodiac is close to being claimed by the rising tide, but its engine is dragging on the stone shore. Willem charges into the shin-deep water, takes hold of the Zodiac, and drags it higher on the shore.

The water must be freezing, but he doesn't complain. He simply sets to work, freeing the big motor from the back of the boat, which I can now see is torn to pieces on the bottom. One of the pontoons is deflated as well. I search the interior for supplies, but it's either been emptied by Chase's group of survivors or claimed by the sea.

Chase bounces up and down, arms wrapped around his chest, nervously repeating, "Go, go, go."

Willem grunts in frustration, shaking his hand. "I can't get the bolts loose!"

Some instinctual part in our collective minds must be shouting at us to hurry up, because we're all getting panicky. *Stop*, I tell myself. *What would Dad do?*

The answer to that question is simple. Dad's philosophy was basically, *If something doesn't work, kick the shit out of it.*

I step inside the Zodiac and kick the wooden back hard. There's an encouraging crack. "Chase," I say. "Hold the engine, Willem." I motion inside the boat. When he joins me, I count to three, and we both kick the wooden back. It cracks again. Loudly. We repeat the kick three more times. On our fifth attempt, the crack sounds like a gunshot and Chase stumbles back—the engine clutched in his hands. He looks close to dropping it when Willem steps in and takes the engine from him. He hoists it over one shoulder and turns to me. "Let's go."

"That's too heavy for you alone," I say.

"That's probably true, but I'll feel better if you can shoot."

He's right. "Yeah. Sore arms are better than no arms."

Willem and Chase stare at me for a moment.

"You know you have a sick sense of humor, right?" Willem says.

He's right about that, too. And I'd like to peg that personality trait on my father, too, but the Colonel was rarely funny. Of course, Willem didn't say I was funny. Nor did he laugh.

With a sigh, I lead the way back to the gorge where Eagon's body awaits. We charge through the tight valley double time but stop cold when we reach the stone spike where Eagon's body hung.

That's right. *Hung.*

He's missing.

I've got my gun out, looking for targets. But the chasm is as empty as ever. *Did we imagine the body? Some kind of collective hallucination?* I don't bother asking, nor do I think twice about continuing back toward camp, because high in the air, arcing over the gorge, is a bright red signal flare.

20

We stumble from the gorge, following Chase's frozen, bloody footprints, and spill out into the clearing. I have a clear view of the island's interior from here, including most of the snowy peaks. I see two things simultaneously: first, the sky to the south is dark again, roiling with a storm that looks worse than the last. But in front of the storm is a sight that makes me cringe. Someone is running down one of the far hillsides. In fact it's the very small mountain where I sent Jenny and Peach to keep watch. Judging by the speed of the descending speck, I guess the runner is Peach.

My mind races for explanations. They shot off a flare. So, they saw some kind of search and rescue effort. And now Peach is running to tell us. But is that the most likely scenario? It's certainly the one I'm hoping for, but after seeing Eagon's now-missing cadaver, I suspect something dire has happened.

Willem steps up next to me. He's still holding the Zodiac engine and is out of breath from moving quickly. "Do we...still need...this?" he asks.

I know he'd love to leave the engine behind. It must weigh a ton, but something isn't right, so I disappoint him. "Hold on to it."

"But the flare," Chase says. He sounds hopeful and desperate at the same time.

Ignoring Chase, I raise a pair of small binoculars to my eyes and see a small red-suited woman more stumbling than running down the snow-covered grade. Definitely Peach. Her awkward run and the way she keeps looking over her shoulder doesn't look like someone excited about being rescued. She looks terrified.

When she trips and slides several feet, my fears are confirmed. A long red streak traces her path through the snow. I gasp and lower the binoculars. Chase snatches the binoculars from my hands and looks for himself. "Oh my God, it must have got Jenny, too!"

"We don't know that," I say, my voice sounding more panicked than I'd ever admit.

"That's not possible," Willem says. Unlike Chase and me, he sounds calm, but I think that's mostly because he hasn't looked through the binoculars. Before I can tell him so, he adds, "Whatever killed Eagon was here. It took his body. There's no way it could be in two places at once."

For a moment, his argument feels right. But Chase quickly shoots holes in it. "The polar bear could have taken the body. They're notorious scavengers. If it's meat, they'll eat it."

"And we still don't know where McAfee or Jackson are," I add. *Or if Peach can be trusted*, I think. I imagine her taking the knife from a surprised Jenny and stabbing her ample gut with the blade. How many thrusts would it take? Could Peach really kill someone? My instincts tell me Peach is innocent—of murder at least. So I make a mental note to not sound accusing when I ask about Jenny's whereabouts, and strike off toward the center of the clearing.

Chase and Willem silently follow. I know Willem is exhausted from carrying the engine, and Chase from…being Chase, but it's a straight, flat shot to the Viking ruins. I look over my shoulder, see no danger behind us, and shout, "I'm going ahead."

If either man wants to complain, they're too out of breath, voice, and opinion. I turn on the gas and sprint across the open field. I pass the Viking ruins thirty seconds later. They're about fifty feet to my right. I can't see Jakob or Alvin through the entrance, but I can't see the tent either. So I continue heading for Peach, who is running in a straight line across the plain, but not toward me or the shelter.

As I get closer, I see her eyes have kind of a blank stare. "Peach," I shout to her.

No reply.

She just keeps running.

I correct my course to intercept her and keep shouting to her. But her mind is gone. For a moment, I wonder if the bloody smear she left on the mountainside was actually her blood, but if she was bleeding that bad, I don't think she would've made it so far, so fast.

I stop in front of her, shouting her name, and try to take hold of her shoulder. But the girl is an unstoppable freight train and keeps on moving, nearly knocking me off my feet. "*Peach*, stop!" I say, my voice offering a final warning. She doesn't stop, and I don't think she's going to until she hits the ocean on the other side of the island, so I tackle her. I don't want to, but what else can I do?

We hit the frozen ground together. I shout, "Peach, it's Ja—" I catch a boot to my face before I can finish. She screams wildly and kicks, scratching at the air with her hands like something invisible is attacking her.

A large shape shifts through my periphery, and I shout in surprise, jumping back. But it's just Willem. "Fuck!" I shout. "How did you get here so fast?"

He doesn't answer. He just catches Peach's flailing arms in his hands and pushes them down to her chest. "Get on her legs," he says to me.

She's still kicking hard, and my first few attempts to grab hold of her legs fail. I shift tactics and fall on her legs, letting my weight do the work. As her screaming slows, I can hear Willem whispering to her. "It's okay. You're safe. We have you."

Part of me suddenly wishes I had a father like Willem. Kind and comforting, strong and trustworthy. Had it been the Colonel in Willem's place, he would be screaming at Peach, "Suck it up!" or "Feed on the pain, girl! It will make you stronger!"

The kicking slows and then stops.

Willem is no longer speaking.

I ease myself off, as does Willem. "She passed out," he says.

"Is she injured?" I ask.

He checks her over. "Doesn't look like it. No cuts anyway. She could have a broken bone, but I don't think so. She was moving too fast for that. Still, we should be careful moving her."

I see dark brown stains on Peach's red snow gear. "That's Jenny's blood."

"We don't know that for sure," he says. I shoot him a look that says, *cut the macho bullshit*, and he adds, "But yeah, it probably is." He looks down at himself and sees some of the blood has been transferred to his jacket as well. He mutters something in Greenlandic, looks me up and down, and says, "You're clean."

We stand over Peach, looking down at her young face. With her eyes closed, she looks peaceful, but I clearly remember the haunted look those eyes held just moments ago. They looked just like Chase's when he arrived. I have little doubt Jenny met her end atop the peak I sent them up. But I can't live without knowing for sure.

"Take her," I say to Willem, before stepping toward the crest from which Peach fled.

A strong hand takes my shoulder and spins me around. Willem looks angry. "You're not going anywhere."

I yank away from him. "Jenny is out there."

"She's dead," he says.

The words are so cold and harsh and without hope that they trigger something in me. My cool and collected facade cracks. "Fuck off!" I shout, and then take a swing. My punch connects hard with Willem's cheek, but the man does indeed have Viking blood, so he just rubs the cheek and says, "You through?"

I'm not. With a shout, I kick out with my right leg, aiming for his waist. If I connect, it will knock the wind out of him and give me time to leave. But he doesn't take the hit this time—he catches my leg and uses the momentum to pick me up and fling me.

I fall to the ground hard but quickly find my feet. Willem stands between me and my goal, arms crossed. He's stronger than me, and without a boat engine over his shoulder, he's probably faster, too. But I still have something he doesn't. I draw the handgun and aim it at his chest. "Get out of my way."

He doesn't even flinch. Instead, he takes a step toward me. "Look behind me," he says.

I glance. All I see is the small mountain.

Jenny…

"Higher," he says.

I don't want to look, but my eyes move up. The storm is there, dark and brooding. Seeing the swirling clouds somehow opens me up to feeling the frigid breeze now tearing across the plain.

"You're not going up there, and you're not going to shoot me," he says.

His confidence pisses me off, so I aim the gun higher. "We can't leave her up there." Desperation has crept into my voice again, so much so that my voice cracks. The sound of my own frailty breaks through another, more deeply buried emotional wall.

The gun lowers and then falls to the snow. I fall to my knees and Willem is there, catching me, wrapping his arms around me. I can smell Jenny's blood on him. "She's dead," I say.

I can feel him nodding.

"And you'll be dead if you go looking for her," he says.

He's right. I know he's right. But it doesn't feel right. Wouldn't the Colonel storm up the mountain, shake his fist at the storm with a booming, "Fuck you!" and find his friend, dead or alive? *But I'm not him*, I think. *And I no longer need to impress him.*

Because he's dead, too.

Before I realize it, I'm crying into Willem's shoulder. My body convulses with sobs, revealing months of suppressed mourning. I should have done this before, but there was no one to hold me then, no one to speak the words everyone needs to hear when a loved one dies.

"It will be okay," Willem says, not knowing the source of my tears is much deeper than Jenny's death.

I give a nod, lean back, and feel my tears evaporate quickly from my cheeks. The wind grows stronger by the moment. "I'll be all right," I say.

"You two were close?" he asks.

With a shake of my head, I say, "My father died. His funeral was the same day the *Sentinel* left port."

"Ahh," he says, understanding.

I skipped my father's funeral. If there's an afterlife and he's watching, I'm sure he doesn't give a shit. But I apparently do. I denied myself any closure or mourning. The man was an ass, but he was my father, too. Now that his harsh life lessons are helping keep me and others alive, I'm beginning to appreciate and miss him more than I thought possible.

A voice cuts through the wind, sharp and urgent. We turn to find Chase waving to us from the corner of the ruins. He looks urgent. When he points to the sky behind us, I remember why. The storm is coming. There is no more time for mourning.

With a sniff, I turn to Willem, motion to Peach, and say, "We can each take her under an armpit."

"You going to be all right?" he asks.

His concern is genuine and appreciated. "Fine," I say, though I'm not entirely sure that's the truth. "Just don't tell anyone I was crying like a little girl."

He says with a grin, "Done."

We pick up Peach and drag her quickly to the shelter. Alvin, Jakob, and Chase are there, waiting for us, but I don't really look at them until after we lay Peach inside the life raft's float. When I finally turn around, I'm greeted by fear-filled eyes.

Willem sees them, too, and asks, "What happened?"

Jakob stretches out his hands. He's holding the rectangular stone I saw Alvin cleaning off earlier. Close up and clean, I can see it's been etched with an array of symbols. "Alvin found this," Jakob says, handing the stone to his son. "Best if you read it yourself."

Willem takes the stone and looks it over. A moment later, I see the blood drain from his face. He sucks in a quick, shocked breath and whispers a slow "Shhhhit."

21

"What is it?" I ask.

Willem seems unable to peel his eyes away from the foot-and-a-half-long black stone. It's eight inches square on the base and slightly tapered at the top. The stone's surface looks smooth, except for the parts that have been carved with a language I don't recognize.

"It's a warning," Willem finally says.

"From who?"

He shakes his head. "I'm not sure yet. I'll need to translate the message." He spins the stone around. Text covers every side.

"You can read it?" I ask. "What language is it?"

"These are Viking runes. It's an extinct language, but my dissertation was on Norse languages. This looks like West Norse, which emerged around AD 800 and was the language of Greenland when the Vikings settled here."

"How old is it?" Chase asks. He's shivering against the storm's winds. I hadn't even noticed the worsening weather while I looked at the stone. But it's definitely getting bad.

"Best guess," Willem says. "It's been here for at least six hundred years. As long as this building, and that body we found."

"Eagon hasn't been here a thousand years," Chase says, slightly offended.

"Not Eagon," I say. "There's a Norse skeleton nearer to the ocean. Been here for a long, long time."

Chase relaxes, but something in his eyes looks disconcerted by this news. And he's right to be concerned. People have been dying on this island for a very long time. How many more bodies are waiting to be found? I think of Jenny. *At least one more.*

Alvin mumbles something and waggles a finger at the stone. Willem responds in Greenlandic. Alvin repeats himself, standing from his rock stool, and hobbles over. The man looks positively frail. He's not going to make it. No way. I turn from Alvin to Jakob. He's not quite as old as Alvin, perhaps fifteen years younger, and he's still got more muscle on him than fat. But he's injured. He's wrapped his ankle in a makeshift cast, though, so maybe there's hope. I see my father in him, and determine then and there that Jakob Olavson will survive. If any of us deserves to survive, it's the man who lost his ship and crew, and all he was trying to do was make a living.

He's strong, I think. *He can make it.* But when I look at his face, there is something different. Despair? Or is it confusion? Maybe both?

Alvin stabs an index finger at a rune carved near the bottom of one side of the miniature obelisk. "See, see," he says in thickly accented English.

"He can read it, too?" Chase asks. He's nearly shouting now to be heard over the wind. We need to take shelter, and soon.

"He can read some," Jakob says, standing up. He walks to us, his limp barely detectable. "But some runes are more recognizable than others." He pulls up his sleeve, revealing a rune tattoo. It matches the one at the bottom of the stone. "Show them," Jakob says to Willem.

With a sigh, Willem puts the stone down and rolls up his sleeve. He has the same tattoo.

"What does it mean?" I ask.

"It's our surname," Willem says. "Olavson. This warning was put here by Torstein, son of Olav." He looks me in the eyes. "Our ancestor. Perhaps the brother of a distant grandfather."

A gust of wind whips snow into my face. The sting pulls me back to the life-threatening situation at hand. That Willem's ancestor built this place and left a warning, and might very well be the body we found, is interesting. But if we don't take shelter soon, we're not going to survive long enough to appreciate this uncovered bit of history—or decipher the warning carved into the stone.

I shake the fresh snow off my cloak. "Everyone inside the tent. Leave nothing outside."

As the sun is blotted out by the storm clouds, we quickly collect our gear and load it against the back wall of the tent. We then pile inside, sitting cross-legged around Peach's unconscious body as if she's some kind of coffee table. The space is less cramped without Jenny here, but it also seems colder and less hopeful. I hadn't realized she'd become some kind of anchor for me. Now that she's gone, I feel a strange emptiness.

I watch Willem try to read the runes. He might have studied the language, but that doesn't mean he's an expert. I took three years of Latin in high school and the only things I remember are two fictional residents of Pompeii (before Vesuvius erupted) named Grumio and Metella, along with the phrase *Tuus ferox aper*, which loosely translates to "You are a ferocious boar." To make things worse, it looks like some of the runes are worn.

The small yellow tent is lit by a single LED light, and the whole thing shakes violently, beaten by the winds. The tent roof occasionally folds down on us until we all reach up and push the dome against the winds.

We sit like this for two hours, waiting for the storm to pass, or at least decrease in violence. No one sleeps. No one speaks. And the air smells strongly of Jenny's drying blood. Willem is the only one with something to do besides wonder when a cyclone will snatch up the raft and toss the lot of us out to sea.

The cold starts to seep in. We're packed in tight, but the wind is finding its way through the raft's flimsy armor. I wrap my cloak around me more tightly and fight off a shiver. When I was thirteen and living in New Hampshire, I went snowboarding at a local golf course with some new friends. I'd just met most of them and wanted to impress them, so when the cold cut through my cheap combat boots and single layer of socks, I didn't complain. Twenty minutes later, my feet throbbed with pain and I admitted defeat. I sat crouched inside a concrete tube where some construction was being done and waited for someone's mother to come pick us up. When I got home, my red feet burned. The pain was unbearable. I know now that I was close to having frostbite. And that's how I'm starting to feel now. The cold has crept past my outer layers, and it's moving through my muscles and reaching for my bones. If the sun doesn't come out soon, we're going to be in trouble. I can handle a balmy forty degrees. But this below-freezing shit, with wind thrown in, is killing me. Literally.

Chase is shivering, so I know I'm not alone. Alvin just sits still, his eyes closed, sleeping I think. Jakob has his head turned up. He watches the wind pulse through the tent in waves. But he seems unaffected by the cold so far. Willem, too. He looks nonplussed by the storm and cold, though a certain degree of fear is certainly visible in his eyes. But I think that has more to do with what he's reading than the storm around us. I watch his brow furrow deeply and wonder what he's learning. But I don't ask. I don't have the energy to speak right now.

Thirty more frigid minutes pass in slow motion. I'm thirteen again, scrunching my toes in my boots to make sure things still work. I rub my arms and legs, trying to stay in motion while sitting. I close my eyes, trying to imagine fire. I've heard that imagining heat can help you feel warmer. I don't think it actually makes you warmer. It's more a mental coping mechanism. After ten more minutes of imagining a warm, toasty fireplace, I determine the technique is useless. When I open my eyes, I'm greeted by a silver flask.

Alvin shakes the flask out to me. "Will help," he says.

"Bless your soul," I say, taking the flask and taking a swig without asking what kind of poison it contains. The minute it hits my throat, I realize I might have made a mistake. I cough and wheeze for a moment before collecting myself. The burn travels down my throat and enters my stomach before radiating out through my extremities. Like the warmth conjured by the imagination, this isn't true heat, but it certainly feels real.

Alvin smiles at my distress. I nearly call him an old bastard, but I'm feeling pretty rosy now, so I ask, "What is this?"

Jakob answers. He's smiling, too. "Alvin calls it firewater. Homemade whiskey. That's his twenty-year batch."

"Is it one hundred proof or something?" I ask. I was raised by the Colonel. I know my liquors.

"One twenty," Jakob says with a chuckle.

I can tell the act of sharing the firewater was as much a joke as an effort to help me get warm. My defiant side flares up. I raise the flask up. "To Greenlander alcoholics!" I take a long pull on the whiskey, swallow it down, and immediately start coughing. Jakob and Alvin laugh loudly as I pass the bottle to Jakob. He raises the bottle to me and takes a drink, impervious to the alcohol's burn.

Alvin takes the bottle, repeats the gesture, and takes a drink before putting the bottle away.

They haven't shared the bottle with Chase, and I can see the disappointment on his face. He's still shivering and looks envious of our laughter. But I suspect that despite welcoming Chase into our group, they haven't truly accepted him. I, on the other hand, have just scored mega brownie points with the old codgers.

"Hey," Willem says over the laughter. When no one pays attention to him, he repeats himself more loudly, "Hey!"

We stop laughing. It's hard to do. The alcohol is working wonders on my system. Death seems a distant thing now. But when I see the rune-covered block and remember Willem's mission, I sober a bit.

"Have you translated the runes?" I ask.

"Most," he says. "I don't recognize a few and a couple are illegible, but I think I can infer what was said."

"What does our forefather have to tell us?" Jakob asks.

Willem turns to his father. "That we need to get the hell off of this island."

22

Beware, all who tread on this cursed land. Only death awaits you here. Flee while you are still able."

I shiver at the words Willem has just read. He's only just begun reading his translation of the runes, and they're already ominous. He looks up, sees his audience is listening with rapt attention, and continues.

Willem looks at us and says, "Keep in mind, I'm paraphrasing," before continuing his narration. "Those now entombed on this peninsula are heroes. They bore burdens beyond imagining and sacrificed greatly. Greenland is once again a land without men. We have slain all who lived here—friends, family, the old and newborn alike. We pursued the infection north as it changed every man, woman, and child it touched into abominations...Draugar."

A gasp makes me jump. Alvin looks horrified. Jakob does, too. Something about this word—*Draugar*—frightens them more than being stranded, more than the storm, or the blood-soaked woman lying unconscious at their feet. "What's Draugar?" I ask.

To my surprise, it's Chase who answers, and he looks more excited than afraid. "The Draugar are Norse warriors raised from the dead. *Draugar* is the plural, *Draugr* is singular. They're strong but slow. Basically Viking zombies, but there are several different classes—"

Classes? Chase's role-playing speak gives away the source of his knowledge. I hold up a hand, stopping his lecture. "Stop," I say. "No offense, but I think I'd like the non-D&D version." I turn to the three men with Viking blood and raise my eyebrows.

"*Aptrgangr,*" Alvin whispers in a language I can't understand.

Jakob nods. "Again-walker."

Again-walker. Great. "So Chase is right? He's talking about zombies?"

"Not exactly," Willem says. "The Draugar are the source of modern-day zombie stories, but they're also the basis of modern vampire stories."

"Both are living dead," Chase adds.

Willem continues. "But the Draugar weren't interested in just blood or brains; they were interested in *both*. The blood kept them... fresh. The brains, I have no idea. They're described as incredibly strong and bigger when freshly infected, though I think the suspected dead were really just bloating. And obviously, they reeked of decay. They're very hard to kill. Iron weapons supposedly injure them, but separating the head from the body did the trick. Though it's believed the only true way to contain a Draugr is to entomb it. They would bury a Draugr in a stone tomb and seal it behind what they called a corpse door—basically a brick wall. They would sew the big toes together and fill the soles of the feet with pins or nails, which made walking tricky. They covered the body with hay or twigs and placed a pair of iron scissors on its chest; I have no idea why. At the time, the Norse were a mix of the old religion—Odin, Thor, Asgard—and Christianity, so there's even a few stories of holy water being used to keep them away."

"That must be why holy water works on vampires in modern fiction," Chase says.

Willem shrugs. "Probably."

"And that's what Grandpappy Olavson is telling us? That we've come across a Draugar graveyard?"

"That's just part of it," Willem says, looking back down at his notes. "He's also saying that the Draugr plague, which transferred from person to person the same way as with zombies and vampires—by a bite—spread across Greenland and that he, and his men, killed every infected person they came across, which happened to be everyone. "Wouldn't that have been recorded somewhere?" I ask. "We'd be learning about that in high school history."

Willem pats the stone lying next to him. "It *is* recorded. We just hadn't found the evidence before now. All we knew is that sometime in the early 1400s, the settlements disappeared, and no one ever knew why. Only ruins remained."

"So this story fits?" I ask.

Willem frowns. "I should probably finish reading it before we rush to believe the story or not."

Makes sense, I think. "Go ahead."

"We started as twenty men, all hunters," Willem reads. "We are now six, all showing signs of Draugr infection, which begins with mild illness and descends into madness. The strong-willed change slowly; the weak, much faster. But what is most important is that we have pursued the source of the Draugar to this frigid, desolate place and entombed it as we will now entomb ourselves. Fear the Draugr, but beware the Muninn, the source, whose resting place is appropriately marked with my family's seal, now a mark of the cursed. This message, carved in stone, is the only sentinel I can leave to stand guard. May my harsh words hasten your retreat. Torstein, Son of Olav."

"Muninn?" I ask. "Didn't you say that was one of Odin's ravens? Means 'mind,' or 'memory,' or something."

"Both," Willem says. "Perhaps they discovered the plague was being spread by the birds? I don't know."

"Or Muninn was a person," I say. "It only took a black cloak, and black hair, to make you all give me the Raven nickname."

Willem twists his lips around, pondering the ancient mystery. He looks ready to offer up another idea, but Chase beats him to the punch.

"Um," he says, sounding nervous. "Why did they pick a Raven? I mean, there are lots of black things they could have picked."

The question is directed at me. "The Raven is their family crest," I say.

Chase looks like he's just been diagnosed with terminal cancer and a few months to live.

"And...just let me get this straight," Chase says, raising a finger in the air. His hand shakes. "The Raven is the family crest of the, ahh, Olavson family. Yes? And Torstein, Son of Olav, was their ancestor? An Olavson?"

"Yes, that's right," Willem says. "Why are you—"

"So the crest carved onto the stone where this Muninn is entombed would be—"

He leaves the statement unfinished.

Willem takes the bait. "A raven."

Chase looks like the doctor has just revealed his terminal cancer is actually going to kill him in a few hours. "What is it?" I ask him.

"The cave," he says. "The cave where I hid with McAfee. And Mr. Jackson. And Eagon. It was sealed. Covered by a thick stone wall. We, uhh, we tore it down to get inside."

Willem starts rubbing his forehead. We all know how this is going to end, but we let Chase get it out.

"The largest stone in the wall," Chase says. "It was, ahh, it was marked. With a raven."

No one says a word. Four sets of eyes watch Chase.

"I think…I think it was Muninn's cave," he says. "I think the Muninn killed Eagon. We set the Raven free."

"It killed her." The soft, feminine voice makes everyone jump back and scream.

As I catch my breath, I see that Peach is awake. She's still flat on her back, but her eyes are open. The blank stare from before has dulled, but there are still traces of it hidden in her pupils.

"Killed who?" Chase asks after composing himself.

"Jenny," Peach says. "The Raven killed her. I saw it."

23

I f circumstances had been ideal, I would had have time to interview Peach, ask her to describe what she saw, how Jenny died, how she survived. Okay, ideal would actually be me on a beach, with none of these people around, sunning myself and reading a trashy novel that has nothing to do with whales, Vikings, ravens, or any other avian species. But right now, in this moment, I could have really done without the howl that rips through the tent and erases the effects of the firewater.

My body shakes with a shiver.

"What was that?" Chase says, fear creeping back into his voice.

"Wind?" Willem asks.

We all sit silently, waiting for the howl to repeat so we can identify it as wind. But the sound doesn't come. In fact, the tent has stopped shaking. Sometime in the last ten minutes while we listened to the tale of Torstein, the wind died down.

I unzip the hatch and poke my head outside. The sky is still full of gray clouds and snowflakes flutter through the sky, but the swirling black monster of a storm has moved north, out to sea. "It wasn't the wind," I say.

"It was the Raven," Peach says. She hasn't sat up. Hasn't moved. She's an Egyptian mummy lying in a sarcophagus and communicating from the afterlife. According to the long-deceased Olavson, that might actually be possible. A second shiver grips my body as a totally irrational fear tickles my mind. I look at Peach more closely. It's cold—really cold—but her forehead is slick with sweat.

"Feeling okay, Peach?" I ask.

She glances at me with a squinty-eyed glare that most women perfect in middle school.

"Never mind Peach," Chase says, sliding to the open hatch. "We're in a big yellow target." He looks through the hatch and cranes his head around, looking at the stone walls around us. "The walls are taller than the tent, so we should be okay unless it walks past the front door."

"It?" I say. "Think about what you're saying. There is no recently thawed giant raven wandering around the island killing people and playing hacky-sack with their heads. There are no zombies. No vampires. No Draugar." I set my eyes on Peach. "And we're going to find out who killed Jenny, with or without your help."

"Hey!" Chase shouts, yanking my shoulder so I'm facing him again.

I nearly punch him in the gut but manage to restrain myself.

"There might not be any of those things, but there *is* a polar bear."

Willem sidles up next to us. He speaks more gently. "And your missing captain."

Damn it. I hate being wrong. "And Mr. Jackson," I admit. "You're right. But we can't go anywhere yet. The sea will be too rough still. Even with the engine, we'll never make it across the channel."

"This girl is ill," Jakob says. He has his hand on Peach's forehead. Her eyes are closed again, and her body shivers.

What comes around goes around, I think, but I keep it to myself. Instead, I take charge. "I'm going out to look for Jenny—Jenny's body. I want to know how she died." I glance at Peach. "How she really died. Come with me or stay here, the choice is yours."

I slide from the exit and climb to my feet, careful that I don't stand taller than the wall. I don't want to expose myself until I'm certain that howl didn't come from something nearby. As I check my handgun, Chase, Willem, Jakob, and Alvin all exit the tent.

"Alvin and I will remain here," Jakob says. He points to a pile of stones that must have fallen from the upper portion of the walls long ago. "We'll fill in the doorway with those. You'll have to climb over the wall to get back in."

"Good idea," I say.

"I'm captain for a reason," Jakob says and gives me a wink.

I head for the door. Willem and Chase follow me. Neither has said so, but it's clear they're both coming. *My heroes*, I think with more than a little bit of sarcasm. It occurs to me that it's a good thing I have a filter between the things I think and the things I say or everyone would know I'm an asshole.

"We'll be back in a few hours," I say. "If we don't come back, take the raft and the engine and head for the mainland."

Jakob laughs. "If you don't come back, I will die avenging your deaths."

I laugh for a moment, too, but then realize the old Viking isn't joking. "He's serious?" I say to Willem as we strike out.

"He is," Willem says.

I like the old man even more because I can picture the Colonel saying, and meaning, the same thing, though I don't think Dad would have been levelheaded enough to let his little girl head out on her own.

A fresh half foot of snow crunches beneath my boots. My cloaks slides across the surface, and I occasionally have to shake off little ice balls that cling to it. The fresh coat of white has erased the bloody trail Peach left behind, but I remember where she came from. Where I sent her. Where I sent Jenny. I know there's no good reason to feel guilty for Jenny's death—she'd have been dead several times sooner without me—but she could have also survived.

We head up the steep, stone-covered hill in silence. It's funny how introspective people get when they think they might die. Willem is probably thinking about his father, about how it's much more likely that the old man won't make it back. Chase is probably thinking about being betrayed and picturing himself exacting his revenge dressed as a ninja or some level-seventy wizard. But neither is more pitiful than me because here I am, facing death, and I'm thinking about what they're thinking!

Willem interrupts my thoughts about his thoughts. "If we can cross the straight in the morning, I think we stand a chance of surviving. If we hug the coast, we should come across seal or walrus. So we won't starve."

"And if we can keep the tent, and keep dry, we won't freeze," Chase adds. "We might also come across a fishing ship along the way."

"Hadn't thought of that," Willem says.

And now I know just how pitiful I am. While I'm thinking about ridiculous things, these two are busy plotting our escape and survival. They haven't given up. Which makes me wonder about myself. Have I given up? Is my lack of planning a sign that I'm resigned to death?

"Raven," Willem says, but the sound of his voice is dulled by the hood over my head, never mind the fact that I'm tuned into my self-loathing and don't yet recognize the Raven nickname as belonging to me.

"Jane!" Willem hisses. Hearing my own name gets my attention. Willem and Chase have stopped a few feet behind me. Willem points to the ground at my feet. I look down and then jump away. The fresh white snow is dark red. There must have been so much blood here when the storm began that the liquid leached up through the fresh powder and stained the area red. A gust of warmer wind flows over the hill from the southern coast and carries the scent of blood and rot.

But none of it holds my attention like the fresh boot prints surrounding the bloody snow and heading off over the rise. I draw my weapon, all thoughts of Chase and Willem extinguished. I move silently, each step planned ahead and gently placed. Even crunching snow could give me away. I'm happy to see that Willem and Chase understand the need for silence as they follow, placing their feet inside my prints. We reach the crest a moment later. I lie on my stomach and poke my head over the ledge.

Three bodies occupy an outcrop of stone twenty feet below. Only one of them is dead. I can tell by the size and the remnants of a red jacket that the body is Jenny's. The other two are dressed in similar red snow gear but have their hoods up. I can't see their faces from above, but I know who they are: Captain McAfee and Mr. Jackson.

My eyes linger on Jenny's ruined body. The sight is sickening, and I fight the twisting discomfort in my gut. If I hadn't expected to find something like this, I might have lost control of my body. As it is, I'm only just hanging on. It's one thing to be killed, but then to be torn apart like this…I remember Jenny's laugh. Our shared sense of humor. I think, if we both had survived this mess, we could have been friends. My eyes grow wet, blurring my vision. *Snap out of it*, I think, blinking hard to force away the tears.

"What are we going to do?" Willem whispers to me. I'm so focused on the two men below, and what I feel about them, that his voice is like a gunshot in my ear. I flinch in surprise and manage to smack the gun against a stone. The metallic clink isn't very loud, but Jackson cocks his head to the side.

Busted.

Before I've thought about what I'm doing, I throw myself over the crest and slide down the snow-covered incline. They definitely hear me now. Both men jump away. McAfee even lets out a scream. They spin around to face me as I reach the bottom. I land on my feet just a few steps from what remains of Jenny's blood-soaked corpse. Like Eagon, she looks partially eaten, and she's missing her head.

I can't stand the sight of her, so I keep my attention where it belongs—on Jackson. "Don't fucking move!" I shout, aiming the weapon from one man to the other.

McAfee raises his hands in the air. Jackson glares at me. He's clutching a backpack in front of his chest.

Chase slides down behind me and steps up next to me.

McAfee must not have recognized me with the hood shadowing my face because his eyes go wide when he sees Chase. He drops his hands and takes a step forward. "Chase!" he says with relief.

"Captain," Chase says, sounding like the good first mate again, but when McAfee steps closer, Chase lands an impressive right hook that sends McAfee to the ground.

McAfee shakes his head, stunned. He looks up at Chase with wounded eyes. "Chase, what—"

"You killed them," Chase. "Your crew. My friends. People we were *both* responsible for. It was all you."

"Chase," Jackson says, the tone of his voice a warning, which pisses me off.

I go from thinking of ways to defuse this situation to jumping right into the mix. I pull the gun's hammer back and step toward Jackson. "Shut up, Tito," I say. When I was introduced to Mr. Jackson, I said, "Mr. Jackson, if you're nasty," and did my best Janet Jackson impersonation. His face turned bright red, and Chase asked me to apologize, which I did for the sake of my mission. But now the gloves are off and I'm free to mock his name to my heart's content. "Or is it actually Mrs. Jackson? I always wondered about you."

I can tell my jabs are having the desired effect. Jackson looks ready to explode.

For several seconds, nothing happens. We've reached a stalemate. The two men responsible for killing the crews of the *Sentinel* and the *Bliksem* are at our mercy. They deserve to die. They deserve worse. The only problem is that Chase and I aren't killers—at least not the kind that can kill defenseless men in cold blood.

Mr. Jackson realizes this around the same time I do. He throws his pack at me, and I lose sight of him for a moment. When I see him again, he's beneath me. He must have dived and rolled because he's moving fast. Too fast for me to stop. The punch to my gut knocks the wind out of me and sends me to my knees. Before I can suck in my first wheezy breath, he snatches the handgun from my hand and turns it on me, saying, "Stupid bitch."

24

Damn, damn, damn! The Colonel would not be proud if he saw me like this, on my knees at the feet of a mass murderer, gasping for breath. *Shut up*, a part of me thinks. *He'd be terrified. He was tough, and mean, but you were his girl, and he loved you.* But I also know what he'd say to me in this situation. "Go down fighting," and possibly, "Aim for his boys." And I might just do that, as soon as I catch my breath.

"Is it just you two?" Jackson asks.

I still can't speak, so I just nod. It's so much easier to lie when you don't have to mask your voice.

Chase hasn't lost his angry edge despite the power reversal. "Why did you do it?" he shouts at McAfee.

"It wasn't supposed to happen like that," McAfee says.

"So your intention wasn't to sink the *Bliksem*?" Chase says.

"What happened to the *Sentinel* was an accident," McAfee says, standing up. "I never meant to—"

"The *Bliksem*," Chase growls. "I asked you about the *Bliksem*."

McAfee is silent for a moment. The expression on his face morphs from guilt to anger. "They had it coming," he says.

Chase opens his mouth to argue, but McAfee cuts him off. "Whales have as much right to live as people do. They're intelligent, sentient creatures."

"They're…not…people!" Chase shouts.

"Oh, shut up," Jackson says and turns the pistol on Chase. And there's no doubt that he's going to shoot.

I try to lunge, but I'm still too weak.

"You're a coward," Chase says. "Both of you are cowards."

The gun's hammer starts to pull back as Jackson pulls the trigger. Chase stares him down, oddly defiant. I would have pictured him begging for his life. But here he is, moments away from taking a bullet to his head, and he's not backing down.

When McAfee starts to shout "Look out," I realize why.

A blur rises up behind Jackson, and a blade slides to a stop beneath his chin against the soft skin of his neck. Willem speaks through clenched teeth, "Drop the gun."

Jackson seems to consider his options. He could still shoot Chase. But then Willem might slice open his neck. Jackson is probably trying to determine whether, unlike me and Chase, Willem has the guts to follow through on the threat.

Jackson suddenly winces. I see a trickle of blood flow from the skin of his neck. He lowers his aim and lets the gun dangle from his finger. "Okay, okay!"

I rush in and snatch the gun away from him. "Thanks, Tito," I say, aiming the gun at him. "Now, what's in the bag?"

Jackson is reluctant to give the bag up. His fingers clutch it tightly. But there is no option here. I kick him square in the nuts. The man drops so fast that Willem has to yank his hand away to keep from slicing the man's throat open.

While Jackson writhes on the ground, I pull the backpack away from him and open it up. What I see inside makes me gasp. There are six bricks of C4, which could easily be mistaken for gray sculpting clay if not for the Ziploc bag of detonators, complete with timers, sitting on top. I place the pack on the ground and take a few steps away. C4 is very stable. You actually could sculpt with it without any fear of an explosion. Hell, you can shoot the stuff and it won't explode. But being that close to enough explosives capable of turning all of us into pink aerosol puts me on edge.

"What is it?" Chase asks as I step away.

"Evidence," I say.

Chase inspects the pack for himself. When he looks inside, his head snaps back like he's just been struck by a snake. "You did it. You really did it."

Poor guy. Some part of him was still clinging to the hope that McAfee had nothing to do with the sinking of two ships and the deaths of his friends.

While Chase focuses on the tragedies of our recent past, I return to the one lying in a bloody heap at our feet. I turn to McAfee, remove my hood, and point the gun at him. "Did you do this to Jenny?"

He looks earnestly shocked by the accusation. "What? No! We found her just a few minutes ago." He turns to me. "Do you have any food?"

I ignore the request. I might not shoot him, but I'm sure as hell not going to give him rations that could go to someone more deserving. "How have you survived the storms?"

"In caves," McAfee says. He turns to Chase. "We went back to the cave. You and Eagon weren't there."

"Eagon is dead," Chase says.

"Dead? How?"

Chase looks dazed again, like when we first found him. He motions to Jenny's body. "Same as this."

"I don't understand. What did—"

"You said 'caves,'" Willem says. "You found more than one?"

"There are caves all over the island," McAfee says. "They're natural caves, but they were all walled up. We rode out the storms in two of them. Slept in another. I think we found five in all, including the one with the raven carving."

"And the bodies inside?" Willem asks. "What about them?"

McAfee can't hide his surprise. "Have you seen them? The Vikings?"

"They're dead?" Chase asks.

"Dead? Of course they're dead," McAfee says like the question is the stupidest thing he's ever heard. "Though I don't think they've rotted much over the years. They just looked dried out."

"You'd make a horrible soldier," Jackson grumbles from the ground. He's on his hands and knees now, looking at McAfee like he's a turncoat.

I shut him up by delivering a quick kick to his gut. He rolls to the ground, holding his stomach. He lets out an angry roar and shouts, "I'm going to kill you!"

"Quiet, Latoya," I say. I probably shouldn't be antagonizing the man, but he's a dick, so, what can I do?

"Where are the caves?" Willem asks.

McAfee glances at Jackson, looking for his disapproval, but Jackson is still curled up in a ball. "All over the island. The one we rode out the last storm in is just around the corner. Maybe two hundred feet from here. I can take you there if you—"

"No," I say, and I'm surprised by the force of my voice. "We're not going anywhere near the caves."

McAfee senses we know more than he does. "Why not?" he asks.

I'm not sure I want to answer him. He's the prisoner, not me. As the man responsible for so many deaths, the only thing I want him to know is that if he survives, he'll be going to jail for the rest of his life—that is, if he's not put to death.

But I don't get the chance to tell the man, because he suddenly leaps to his feet, screams, and runs away. A white blurs explains everything.

"Polar bear!" Chase shouts, and takes off after McAfee.

As the bear rounds the corner and sets course for Willem, Jackson, and me, I level the gun and squeeze off three shots. Each round hits the bear just to the side of its head, biting through skin and muscle.

But the bear doesn't react.

Even if the shots hit nothing vital, the bear should flinch. A roar. Something. But it stays on course. "Something's not right," I say. "Run!"

I take off after Chase, with Willem hot on my heels. A moment later, a scream turns me around. I must have injured Jackson because he's struggling to get up. And he knows he's about to die. And once again, a death is my fault. I see his backpack still lying where I left it, full of explosives—which would take care of the bear and then some, but there's no way to reach them now. Jackson is on his own.

But I don't feel bad when the bear reaches him. Fifty feet away, I turn and watch. The bear smashes into him, never slowing. Its mouth wraps around his head as he screams down the bear's throat. The bear thrashes Jackson back and forth and I hear the crunch that silences the man's voice.

I start to turn away. I have no desire to watch the bear eat him. But Willem grips my arm. "Jane…" His voice is filled with dread.

The bear, which never really stopped moving, drops Jackson. But it doesn't stop for a meal. Instead, it steps over his body and charges straight toward us. I take aim and fire two more rounds. Once again, both rounds strike the bear, with no result.

Willem tugs my arm. "C'mon!" He bounds down the rocky slope, and I follow him. I know that bears can run much faster than people, but I hope that the loose shale sliding under each footstep will be enough to stumble the hulking predator enough for us to find shelter or lose it in the maze of boulders and stone spires that dot the landscape.

Chase disappears over a ridge. If we can make it there before the bear reaches us, it might not know where we've gone. So I steam ahead, not worrying about what might be in front of me, and leap over the ridge with Willem right beside me. We drop six feet, stumble, collide, and fall in a tangled mess. But the pain of falling is far less than expected.

I roll over and feel soft earth between my fingers. Sand! We've reached the south shore, and a beach. An honest-to-goodness beach. But it's not all good news. Chase and McAfee stand just a few feet away, no longer fleeing despite the threat of a killer bear tearing them to pieces. A deep, resonating roar sounds, and I glance around the two frozen men.

One hundred or so two-thousand-pound giants populate the beach. And not one of them looks happy to see us.

25

The walruses aren't aware of us until Chase charges through the pack. He moves fast, flying past the great, tan bodies before they can react to him. In thirty seconds, he clears the pack, leaps onto a low ledge, and starts climbing. He doesn't look back once. Chase might not be one of the bad guys, but he's not a great good guy either. The agitated walruses rear up, flashing their massive tusks, and find Willem, McAfee, and me standing at the fringe of their herd.

"We'll never make it," Willem says.

"We can't go back," I say. That bear will have no trouble catching and killing all three of us."

"They'll let us through," McAfee says.

The words "What are you talking about?" start to come out of my mouth, but then McAfee raises his hands and starts walking toward the herd.

"They know we're not predators. They have nothing to fear from us. They can sense it." He's closer to the herd now and the giant animals back away, shifting their bulbous bodies in great lunges. But their heads are pulled up, tusks at the ready. "We're friends," McAfee says, but he's no longer talking to Willem or me, he's speaking to the walruses. "You won't hurt me. I just want to pass by. I protect animals like you. Now you can protect me."

McAfee continues forward, and the sea of giants begins to part. The animals are agitated now, snorting and honking, but they're not attacking. Willem and I follow, but at a distance.

Twenty feet into the herd, it appears we might make it, but then everything goes to hell. The herd parts, but not for McAfee. A big bull charges out of the pack. He's no doubt the dominant bull here, and whether he senses a rival or a threat, he's ready to throw down.

McAfee stops as the giant male lifts his head high and roars. "Whoa," he says, shaking his open palms at the beast. "It's okay, we're friends."

To my surprise, the bull actually lowers its head and stares into McAfee's eyes, perhaps trying to determine whether this small man is a killer. Unfortunately for McAfee, that's exactly what he is, and the bull must sense it, because it lunges forward, pulls back its head, and slams its foot-and-a-half-long tusks into McAfee's chest. The tusks, thrust by thousands of pounds of muscle, tear through McAfee's bone, muscle, and sinew like paper. The twin spears of ivory explode out of his back, cutting off his scream. When the walrus pulls its head back, McAfee's body sticks and is lifted into the air. Blood drips from the bull's tusks and McAfee's dangling arms. The slow tug of gravity pulls the body down with a wet slurp until it falls free with a dull thud as it lands on the sandy shore.

For one still moment, all I can hear is the crashing of nearby waves. Fog rises up as the snow and ice melt in the sun. But as one hundred walrus heads turn toward Willem and me, I don't think there's any amount of fog that could hide us from them.

Our only chance is to head back and hope the bear has given up the chase. But that option is erased a moment later as the bear charges over the rise behind us and clumsily tumbles over the five-foot drop. The fall slows the bear for only a moment, though. It scrambles up and commences its insane charge.

The walruses react to the presence of the polar bear immediately. The small specimens turn and run. The larger bulls rise up, like warriors defending castle walls, spear-tusks out. They outweigh and outnumber the bear. And the bear should know this. But it shows no sign of slowing. In fact, it looks hungrier and more frantic than ever. I see the five fresh bullet wounds. The red spots are easy to find in all the white fur, but not one of the wounds is bleeding. They're just small red dots.

"Jane," Willem hisses.

I turn toward his voice. He's a few feet away and moving into the herd, which is preoccupied with the bear. I follow him quickly, and together we flee the bear along with half the herd. We move in pace with the giants, careful not to run directly in front of any tusks. A few angry roars chase us, but none of the walruses stops to take a swipe. Instinct pushes us all forward. As we approach the low outcrop of stone that Chase used to escape the beach, we have to leap over the body of a large bull, but by the time he swings around to do something about it, we're up and out of his reach.

I turn around in time to see the bear reach the noble bull walruses, still standing their ground. And what happens next…Being in the undercover documentary field, I've seen just about every nature special ever made, some for information, some shot by acquaintances. So I've seen just about every scenario of polar bear versus walrus there is—polar bear kills walrus, walrus kills polar bear, the stalemate, and polar bear kills walrus only to be killed by a rival. Most outcomes are violent and bloody, but this…this is something else.

The bear takes on the big bull, which probably outweighs the bear by a thousand pounds. It just charges straight ahead, jaws open wide. It stands about as little chance against the giant as McAfee did. The walrus slams its head down, using its tusks to kill a creature for the second time in a single minute. The bear buckles under the weight of the walrus and for a moment is pinned to the sand.

Job done, the walrus pulls its tusks out and shuffles back.

I actually let out a small shout of surprise when the bear leaps back to its feet and strikes. The walrus matches my shocked cry as the world's largest land predator wraps its long arms around the walrus. Before the walrus can react, the bear snaps its jaws onto the walrus's lower neck and bites down hard.

The walrus bellows and smashes the bear down again and again. But the bear can't be shaken.

"What the fu—"

Chase's voice makes Willem and I both jump. He's crouched down behind us, watching the scene. "Where's McAfee?" he asks.

I look for the body in the sea of fog-shrouded brown bodies and find it beneath the big bull. He's being pulverized, along with the bear.

A second large bull shuffles up next to the bear. He and the dominant male probably stab the shit out of each other when mating season rolls around, but right now, they're both part of the herd. The second male jabs the bear in the side, sliding those big tusks between the bear's ribs and piercing all sorts of vital organs. The bear is yanked away and tossed onto the sand.

And still, it comes.

This time for the second bull. The bear rounds the big bull and leaps onto its back, dragging its claws and leaving ten bloody streaks. The bull rolls and stabs at the bear again and again. More bulls join the fight. Tusks, claws, and teeth meet, and soon all of them are covered in blood.

I'm sick to my stomach. I take a deep breath and say, "I've seen enough."

Chase and Willem look equally mortified. In fact, there is a small pool of bile at Chase's feet. I didn't even hear him puke. We slide away from the scene, careful not to be spotted.

As we start up the hill, I have more questions than ever, but I keep them to myself. At this point, I don't really want answers. I just want to get the fuck off this island. "We can't stay here," I say.

Willem just charges up the hillside, his face grim. I take his fast stride as agreement. We'll pick up his father, Jakob, and Peach and make for the mainland.

Chase is a little more vocal. "Absolutely. I think I'd rather swim the distance than face that bear. But there's no way it walks away from that. No way. It got skewered, what, four times?"

"Didn't make a difference," Willem grumbles. He gives me a knowing glance that says, *You and I both know what we just saw.*

I ignore the absurdity of it all and try to focus on reality. But Chase saw the look, too.

"What are you thinking?" he asks.

Willem's only reply is a quickly sniffed breath.

"Hey," Chase complains, stopping on the side of the hill. "What is it?"

Neither Willem nor I turn around. That is, not until we hear his sharp breath. I don't know how people can hear these kinds of things, but the noise registers as a gasp of understanding.

"You don't think…" Chase says slowly. "You do. Holy shit. You think that bear was a Draugr. Is that even possible?"

Willem slows and turns around. I stop as he looks past me and faces Chase. His face is red and frightening, not so much because he's gripped in some kind of rage but because he's afraid. He points down the hill behind us and says, "You tell me."

I turn to look and wish I hadn't.

It's been ten minutes since we left the savage battle behind. The bear should be long since dead, and maybe some of the walruses with it. But there on the beach, beneath a rising curtain of fog, the battle continues. The bear, now more blood red than white, continues its one-man hack and slash attack. Behind it, several large walruses lay dead.

As much as this is the perfect time to let loose expletives that would make your mother's heart explode, the three of us remain silent. The scene is beyond description.

As my hand comes to my mouth, a flash of movement catches my attention. "What was that?" I blurt out.

"What?" Willem asks.

I point toward the dead. "I saw something else. Something smaller moving around the bodies."

"I don't see anything," Chase says.

Willem puts his hand on my shoulder. "C'mon, we shouldn't—"

A distant howl cuts through the air.

"Was that—" Chase starts.

"Wind," I say. I hope.

The sound repeats.

Not wind.

The sound came from a human being.

A man.

"My father," Willem says, and then he bolts up the rise with Chase and me on his heels.

I have no idea what we'll find when we get there. My greatest fear, the polar bear, is behind us. So whatever is making Jakob scream is something else.

Something new.

26

Chase grunts as he stumbles and falls, sliding along the smooth, slushy grade for ten feet. He comes to a stop on his back, staring at the dark blue sky. I stop and backtrack to make sure he's okay while Willem charges forward, fueled by concern for his father. We're near the bottom of the hill, and the Viking ruins are straight ahead, but no one is in sight. They're either on the other side or somewhere else.

I stand above Chase, who's blinking his eyes and staring up through his glasses. His chest heaves with each breath. "You okay?" I speak quickly, out of breath from running.

"I'm fine," he says, pushing himself up. "Go ahead."

Chase looks tired. Winded. And it's brave of him to send me ahead, but I'm not leaving him behind. I offer my hand to him.

He takes a deep breath and winces, holding his side. "I have a cramp. Just go."

I look to Willem. He's a hundred feet away now. If he finds something dangerous at the ruins, he's only going to have that knife for protection. I'm torn. Willem might need help, but leaving someone behind would be the final offense against my father. He'd probably haunt me for the rest of my life as punishment.

Motivation, I hear the Colonel say in my memory. When I had trouble in school, with my peers, or really just about anything else, my father would find a way to motivate me, usually through the threat of something worse than what I faced. *See*, he would say, *all you needed was some motivation.*

I turn my head up, widen my eyes with fear, and shout, "Polar bear!" And then I run. I don't look back. I just run. And Chase does the same. A moment later, the wiry, long-legged man passes me like he's an honest-to-goodness greyhound chasing a rabbit.

He slows as we near the ruins. As I jog closer, he turns around, chest heaving, eyes wide. He looks past me. "Where's the bear?" he shouts.

I slow as I pass him. "What bear?"

Anger fills his eyes. "You said the bear was coming."

"And you needed motivation."

He shakes his head like he can't believe what he's hearing.

"By the way," I say, "thanks for leaving me in the dust. If there had been a bear, it would have got me and not you, so well done." I only half mean it. I don't think many people put a lot of thought into their actions when they think they're about to be mauled by a bear.

But Chase lowers his head with a frown, the anger drained out of him. Before I can tell him I understand, Willem shouts, "Jane! Help!"

His voice is followed by a high-pitched wail.

"C'mon," I say to Chase, and charge around the wall. The first thing I see as I round the other side of the building is Jakob lying on the ground. At first I think he's dead, but then he moves and starts to get up. He must have fallen.

A pain-filled shout brings my attention back to the wall. Willem clings to the top of the wall, hanging a few feet above the ground. He's got a grip under Alvin's shoulders and pulls the man up. *There's something inside*, I realize.

Alvin is yanked back. His eyes go wide, and he lets out a panicked yelp. The high-pitched, angry scream repeats, and I realize the awful truth. *Peach* is inside, and they're trying to get away from *her*.

I throw myself onto the wall and heave myself up. When I see Peach on the other side of the wall, I'm stunned into silence for a moment. Her eyes are milky white. Her face—her body—is puffed up, making her look nearly twice her size. His face is twisted with rage, her bared teeth revealed by a wolflike sneer. She looks like a rabid animal, all traces of humanity erased.

"Help!" Willem shouts.

One of Alvin's pant legs is torn open. Blood seeps from the tear. Peach has a grip on both of Alvin's legs, playing tug-of-war with the old man's body. I take hold of Alvin's jacket and pull, adding my strength to Willem's. We pull Alvin up a few inches, but we're suddenly yanked back down.

Peach is incredibly strong. Even if Chase or Jakob helped, I don't think we'd win this fight.

Alvin's face is just inches from mine, so when he whispers "Draugr," I hear him loud and clear.

No way, I think. I'm not ready to go there. It's just not possible. We are not facing fucking zombie polar bears and a zombie... Peach. God, that sounds so stupid.

Then Peach goes and bites Alvin's leg. A horrible sound rises in his throat and makes my eyes tear upon hearing it. Peach comes away with a chunk of flesh and chews hungrily. She's eating him. Peach is eating Alvin!

I look at the fresh wound. It's red and bloody, but there's something else. Something small and white. And moving. *Maggots*? I think. But then they're gone, and my attention shifts to the man's pain-filled face. He shakes. His eyes are wide. "Draugr," he says again. And then he shouts it, "Draugr!"

Willem snaps his head toward me. "He's right."

"What?" I say. It's all I can manage.

"You have to shoot her," he says, and he's deadly serious.

"I can't."

"You have to!" And then he says three words that will haunt me for the rest of my life, however long or short that might be. "She's already dead!"

Wet smacking sounds draw my attention back to Peach. She's enjoying the fresh flesh in her mouth. She closes her eyes, as though gripped by ecstasy, and swallows a piece of Alvin's leg.

Something in me breaks, and my doubts wash away. Holding on to the wall with one hand, I use the other to draw my weapon. I've fired six rounds already, all at the polar bear, and none had any effect. If the bear and Peach are indeed afflicted by the same zombie-making plague, then I'm not sure this will help.

Alvin grasps my arm so tight that it hurts. "Head," he says. "In head!"

Of course. Why didn't I think of that? I mean, shooting my room-mate in the fucking head should have been the first thing that occurred to me, right?

I take aim but don't pull the trigger. I am decidedly not okay with killing someone.

Peach opens her mouth and leans in for another bite.

"Peach!" I scream.

Her head snaps up toward me. I look into her pale eyes. There's nothing there. No recognition. No remorse. No humanity.

Her eyes are dead.

She's dead.

Dead.

I pull the trigger.

The blast echoes off the hills surrounding the plain and sets my ears to ringing. Peach's head jolts from the impact, and a spray of bone and brains splashes onto the snow inside the ruins. Her grip on Alvin's legs loosens as she tips back and falls to the ground. She's motionless now. Even more dead than before.

Willem hoists Alvin up and over the wall. Alvin clenches his teeth against the pain but can't keep from shouting out when he's laid on the snow. He stares up at the sky, his breaths coming quickly. Jakob dives to his old friend's side, and they have a quick conversation I can't understand. But by the darkening look on Willem's face, I know it's not good.

Alvin grunts, clutching his stomach, which doesn't appear to be injured. I can see he's sweating now, too.

I hear the word *Draugr* a few times and put the pieces together for myself. I know enough about zombies and vampires to know that being bitten by the infected can spread the curse. In fact, the more I think about it, the more I realize how much zombies and vampires have in common. They're both living dead. They both feed on the living. Could they really just be different modern interpretations of these ancient monsters?

Jakob stands, walks to me, and opens his hand. "Gun."

I look at the weapon, still clutched in my right hand, index finger still wrapped around the trigger.

"Gun!" the old captain shouts.

His loud voice sends a jolt through my body, and I hand over the weapon without thinking about what it's going to be used for. When Jakob stalks back to Alvin, I realize what's about to happen.

But I don't do anything to stop it. I'm beyond the point of needing to be convinced. The Draugar are real. I don't know how, but they are. And the plague can be spread through a bite. But also from blood, I think. And now Alvin was missing a chunk of his leg. Judging by the way he's writhing in pain and clutching his body, he'll soon die and become a Draugr as well.

And that, it seems, is something neither he nor Jakob can stomach. Jakob stands over his friend, says a few words in Greenlandic, and pulls the trigger.

I jump with the gunshot, unable to look at the scene. But I know the old man is dead. Really dead and not coming-back dead. I didn't know him well, but I think I knew his heart. He was a good man. A good friend.

Snow crunches behind me as the smell of cordite filters past. Someone taps my shoulder. I turn and find Jakob, face grim, offering me the gun. I take it and tuck it back into my pants.

"We need to get off this island," Willem says. "Now."

I cling to the task of escape and let it distract me from the death that now surrounds us. Eagon, Jenny, Jackson, McAfee, Peach, and Alvin. Six survivors dead, all of them painfully and brutally killed. I'm beginning to think that going down with the ship might have been the better option. But there's still a chance we can get off this island. "I'll get the raft. Willem, get the engine. Chase, Jakob, grab the—"

"No time," Chase interrupts.

I wheel around on him, about to shout at him for not following orders, but the look on his face freezes me. He doesn't say a word or point or give any indication that I should look in a certain direction. He just stares into the distance.

I spin around, following his gaze, and find myself looking at a distant hilltop. A lone figure stands atop the rise, large and imposing.

"Who is that?" Willem asks. The figure is too distant to see clearly, but there's something strange about it.

I take out my small binoculars and put them to my eyes. The figure I see is beyond comprehension. It's a man, or at least it used to be. His face is sunken, and the skin is stretched like the facelift of a ninety-year-old woman. His lips are peeled back in a permanent sneer, revealing an incomplete set of teeth that look like an arrangement of black-and-white piano keys. His white eyes, which seem to be looking straight at me, send a shiver down my back. He's dressed in ragged-looking furs and a torn and weathered cape that hangs from his shoulders and snaps in the wind. A helmet rests on his head, sporting two enormous horns. In one hand he wields a large, double-bladed ax stained dark brown on the edges. *Dry blood*, I think. In the other is a shield, upon which a crest is painted. I recognize the raven image and know who I'm looking at.

The binoculars lower from my eyes, and I turn to Willem. "It's Torstein," I say.

Willem snatches the binoculars from me, looks at the ancient man for just a moment, and issues a command that we are all getting accustomed to hearing. "Run."

27

We leave everything behind. Our supplies. The raft (which is also our shelter). Food. Water. *Everything.* Our only gear is what we carry—one knife, the Glock with five remaining rounds, a protein bar in my pocket, and the clothes on our backs. In short, we're screwed, and all of us know it, but no one brings it up. Because it could be worse. That horrible...zombie Viking thing could be chasing us. But it's not. It hasn't moved from its perch high up on the distant hill. I can't see it clearly from the other side of the clearing where we've fled, but I can feel the thing watching us.

And this disturbs me greatly because it doesn't fit the zombie profile that's been ingrained in my mind by popular culture. Shouldn't it be shambling after us? Moaning and maybe calling for our brains? The fact that it's not, that it's simply observing us, means its *thinking*, which means this thing is closer to a vampire than a zombie.

Stop trying to make sense of it, I tell myself. If we base our actions on what we know about modern incarnations of zombies or vampires, we're going to make a mistake. This thing is neither zombie nor vampire. It is their predecessor, the reality that spawned two modern fictional monsters. It is Draugr, the Viking undead; a big, strong, thinking, six-hundred-year-old animated corpse.

Shit.

I slow down as we enter the gorge on the northern end of the island. This is where Chase originally fled from, where we found and then lost Eagon's body. "It's already been here," I say. "It's not going to have any problem finding us."

Willem and Chase, who have been leading the charge, pause near the mouth of the chasm. "We have a plan," Chase says.

Somehow the idea of these two working together strikes me as odd, but mortal enemies sometimes join forces to defeat a third, common enemy, so anything is possible. I raise my eyebrows, signifying that someone should fill me in.

"We're going back to the cave," Willem says. "With the raven symbol."

"The cave where Eagon was killed?" I ask, my voice oozing sarcasm and doubt. "That's a great idea. Hey, zebras, the lion is going to catch you eventually, so why don't you just go to the den and get it over with?"

"Jane," Willem says, "the cave wasn't a den; it was a prison."

"And the last thing an escaped prisoner wants to do is go back," Chase adds, pushing his glasses up. "Trust me, I know."

My sarcastic streak has a thousand insults lined up, but my rational side manages to keep my mouth under control. Mostly because they're making sense. There's no way to be sure. These things might not have any emotions at all. But if there is any emotion—or even logic—involved in the Draugr's thought process, it won't want to enter this cave, or any other cave, for a very long time. I bite my lip, trying to come up with something better, but can't. "Fine," I mutter.

We enter the gorge and leave the clearing, and the lone Draugr watchman, behind. Ten feet in, I stop. The others look back. "What now?" Willem asks.

"I just want to check something." I say, creeping back toward the entrance. Low and out of sight, I peek over a boulder just in time to see the Draugr's horned helmet disappear over the top of the hill. "It's leaving," I say.

"So?" Chase asks, eager to leave.

"So, that means it *was* watching us."

"Raven," Jakob says. "Do you know why Vikings were so successful in battle?"

His question catches me off guard. I stay silent, in part because I'm confused, but also because I don't know the answer.

"Intimidation," he says. "They attacked from the ocean and made no effort to hide the fact that they were coming. Their ships looked like dragons. They chanted and beat war drums. And they looked…" He looks motions toward the distant hill. "You saw for yourself. Many villagers fled before the Vikings attacked, allowing the Norsemen to ravage villages and monasteries at their leisure. Those who stood their ground often trembled with fright by the time the Vikings arrived, and they were easily defeated."

"You're saying that thing is trying to intimidate us?" I ask.

He nods. "Is it working?"

How Jakob is thinking so clearly is beyond me. He just shot his oldest and closest friend in the head to keep him from becoming a man-eating monster, and here he is, revealing Viking tactics. What he says makes sense, too, which I find infuriating because it means that I'm allowing myself to be manipulated. And that's something I won't allow. I squash down my fear, and say, "Not anymore." I push past the three men. "Chase, which way to the cave?"

We find the cave ten minutes later. The raven carving on the stone matches the one I saw on the Draugr's shield. This is where they buried the Raven, which is something none of us have yet seen. We descend into the hollow slowly. Willem has one of the small LED lights from the raft in his pocket. The small blue light reveals a craggy, naturally formed cave, which is essentially a large crack in the stone. The path descends at a twenty-degree angle. We follow the path for five minutes, stopping when we reach a dark brown stain on the floor. The place reeks of death and something earthy I can't identify.

"This is where Eagon died?" I ask.

"I don't want to stay here," Chase says. He doesn't answer the question, but I can see my assessment is right by the look in his eyes.

"We can't go back," Willem says. "The farther we are from the entrance, the better."

"Down," Jakob says. He heads down into the dark, fearless and determined.

We follow, happy to leave the outside world, and all that remains of Eagon, behind. But the tunnel ends fifty feet later in a small chamber the size of an RV. Willem sweeps back and forth across the space, leading with the small LED light. I stand behind him, ready to blast anything I see with the Glock, but I'd really rather not have to. Firing the weapon in an enclosed space like this would likely make all of us deaf.

As we near the back of the chamber, a reflection catches my eye. "There," I say, pointing to the light before realizing that no one can see me pointing. But Willem must have seen it, too, because he heads for the glint of light shining back at us. I crouch down next to Willem as he brushes some loose stones away, revealing a blade.

"It's a sword," he says. He quickly clears away more debris, exposing three feet of polished metal.

"An iron blade," Jakob says. He takes a careful grasp of the blade between his fingers, lifts it up, and gives it a tug. The sword slides out, pulling a hand with it.

The four of us jump back, expecting a Draugr to rise up out of the rubble. But nothing moves. The mostly skeletal hand isn't attached to a body.

Willem shines the light on the blade, revealing an ornately carved hilt. The handle is wrapped in dried, cracking leather and ends in a curved hunk of bronze that looks like a mushroom top. He picks it up, sliding the weapon out of the hand's loose grip.

"Why hasn't it rusted?" Chase asks, eyeing the sword the way he did me just a few days ago.

"Arctic air is dry," Jakob says. "Like a desert. Frozen water can't rust."

"And this island probably thawed out in the last year," Willem adds. He feels the blade edge with his thumb. "Still sharp."

Fueled by the discovery, Chase attacks the pile of rubble, lifting up stones and tossing them to the side. He stops for a moment and says, "The rest of the body is here."

Fearful that the dead man isn't quite as dead as we would like, I ready my gun. Willem raises the sword, ready to strike, and I nearly smile because he looks even more like a genuine Viking.

"Careful," Jakob warns, standing back. He's probably the smartest of all of us.

A moment later, his fears prove unfounded. Chase reveals the body dressed in the tattered remains of a tunic and various furs. A helmet sits crooked on his head. None of the telltale Draugr signs are present. He's a smallish man, perhaps five foot six, maybe a little taller with hydrated meat on his bones. There is also no hay, no scissors, no sewn toes. Nothing to indicate this was one of Torstein's infected men.

"He died sealing the Raven inside," Willem says. He lifts the helmet from the back of the man's head. The skull is crushed.

I look at the ruined wall behind the man. It doesn't take much to figure out that the man had been thrown, with great force, against the stone wall, which then crumbled and buried him. I would like to avoid whatever did this.

"Found something!" Chase says, still excited. He yanks a shield from the stones. A chunk is missing from the round, wooden shield, but it looks in good shape. I don't think it will do much against that double ax, or the rabid polar bear, but it will probably make him feel safer. And while his perceived safety might be an illusion, I still envy it. I'm not sure I'll ever feel safe again.

28

Several hours' worth of adrenaline begins to wear off as we sit on the cave floor. My muscles twitch all over my body. Willem shut his small light off to conserve the battery, so it's pitch-black. The only way I know the others are still here is because I can hear them breathing. We've all gone silent, processing the horrors of the past day in our own ways.

But the ceaseless tickle of twitching, adrenaline-deprived muscles in my arms, legs, and stomach is so intense that I can't think of anything else. On one hand, this is a blessing. I don't want to think about the things I've seen. On the other hand, it feels like something is crawling inside me. The image sticks, and I imagine small white larvae moving about my body. But I can't take credit for the horrible daydream. I've actually seen it.

In Alvin's leg wound. The small, white, maggotlike things. But did I really see them? I picture them in my body again, wriggling their small bodies beneath my skin, and I realize my subconscious has already figured it out. The little creatures didn't disappear; they entered Alvin's body. But where did they come from? The only answer I can come up with is awful.

"Willem," I say.

Someone gasps with surprise from the sound of my voice.

"What's wrong?" Chase says quickly. He sounds half-asleep.

"Just had an idea," I say. "Were you sleeping?"

"I don't know," Chase says. "I think. Maybe."

"I'm here, Jane," Willem says. His voice is so close that it's my turn to be startled. I'm beginning to hate the dark.

"Tell us," says Jakob. I can tell by the direction of his voice that he's near the cave entrance, defending us from anyone, or anything, that might decide to enter our sanctuary.

I clear my throat, looking for the right way to say this. "When you were pulling Alvin…did you see anything…unusual?"

"Everything was unusual," he says. "Can you be more specific?"

"When Peach, you know, bit him?"

"I couldn't see it from where I was," he says. I can't see him, but I can hear he doesn't like the direction this conversation is taking. "Did *you* see something?"

"So much for sleeping," Chase grumbles.

I ignore him, replaying the moment in my mind. "After she bit him, I saw the wound. There was something there. Something moving. Like insect larvae, or maggots. I don't know. They were small and white. But I only saw them for a moment before they disappeared."

"Disappeared?" Chase says. "C'mon, Jane."

"Quiet," Jakob says, his serious voice directed at Chase.

"*Disappeared* is the wrong word," I say. "I'm pretty sure they went inside him."

Silence follows for a moment, broken by Willem's voice. "So these maggots appeared when Peach bit his legs. And then they crawled into his body. He started showing signs of infection shortly after that.

"So you think…what?" Willem says. "That maggots transfer the infection?"

"I don't know," I say. "Maybe. If it's an infection, blood or other bodily fluids seem to be more likely."

"That's how it works with zombies and vampires," Chase says.

"But these aren't zombies and vampires," I say. "And this isn't a movie. Wooden stakes, crosses, and holy water won't help us."

"Shooting them in the head seemed to do the trick," Chase notes. "So the movies got something right."

"Anyway," I say with a sigh, "there is another possibility. That the maggots are some kind of parasite that hasn't been discovered before now."

Chase coughs up a mocking laugh. "You think those tiny creatures can control people? C'mon."

"Parasites take over the minds of their hosts all the time," I say. My knowledge comes from a documentary, but they don't need to know this. "There's a wasp that lays its larvae inside a caterpillar. The larvae then eat their way out of the caterpillar and attach themselves to a plant. But the caterpillar doesn't die. It survives and *defends* the larvae with its life, not because it wants to, but because one or two larvae stay behind and control the thing's mind."

"That's a caterpillar," Chase says. "The human mind is far more complex."

"Toxoplasma," I say. The word spills out from some recess of my mind. "It's a parasite that infects thousands of different warm-blooded species, including people. And when it infects people, it changes the way they think. Men become more aggressive and jealous, while women become more outgoing and receptive to the opposite sex. And both men and women had slower reaction times and became more accident prone."

"So it's a parasite that makes people have lots of sex and die young?" Chase asks. "If that's the case, I know a lot of people who might be infected."

"That's not the point," I say, growing frustrated with his devil's advocate routine. "The point is, there are parasites that can control the human mind. And there are parasites that can keep a cater-pillar that should be dead alive and animated. Maybe we're seeing something that can do both? Maybe the parasite drives the host to consume blood or brains, providing nourishment to the young living in the gut, who then mature and are passed on to the next host through a bite? I mean, they ate Eagon. And Jenny. But the rest were killed by single bites, allowing the young parasites access to a new host."

Chase speaks slowly. "That actually makes some kind of sick sense."

"It would explain why Peach and the bear were both infected," Willem says. "If the only requirement the parasite has is warm blood, then species doesn't matter. All mammalian brains can be controlled by certain chemicals, right?"

"I think so," I say. "Which is why shooting them in the head works. They still need the brain to operate the body."

"But what about that Torstein guy?" Chase asks. "He's been dead for a really long time. His brain should be as dried and shriveled as his skin."

"I don't know," I admit. "Maybe they secrete something that protects vital organs from decay, or even modify our genetic code so that the cells don't degrade? Who knows? I'm just trying to make sense of these things. I don't think we're going to get all the answers."

"She's right," Jakob says, his deep voice rumbling through the dark chamber. "We know everything we need to know: how to kill them, and what they want."

"Uhh, I missed the 'what they want' part, I guess," Chase says.

"Two things," Jakob says. "To control you or to eat you."

"Right," Chase says. "Bad and worse. Got it. So what's the plan, then?"

"Same as always," I say. "Get the hell off this island."

No one knows exactly how we'll do that, though, and silence returns to the cave. I'm sure we're all conjuring up scenarios of escape, but only one of them works. I have no doubt we'll all agree that we need to go back to the Viking ruins—where anything on the inside of the island can see us—retrieve our gear, the raft, and the engine, and then make a run for the southern coast. There is no other possible scenario for escape.

So I try to shut off my mind and get some rest. I lie on the stone floor, head leaning on my arms. It's about as comfortable as a bed of broken glass, but exhaustion soon claims my mind like a parasite and puts me to sleep.

I dream of death.

I wake to screams.

29

Sudden fear wipes the sleepiness from my mind like a manne-
quin family subjected to a nuclear blast. The problem is, when
I sit up, looking for danger, I can't see a thing. But I can hear.

There's a repetitive shuffling sound sifting through the chamber. Somebody's moving.

"What's wrong?" Willem asks from my right.

"Something touched me!" It's Chase. The high pitch of his
voice means he's horrified.

Jakob shushes us. Chase is making a lot of noise now, stumbling away from whatever threat he's imagining.

"Chase," I hiss. "Be quiet!"

Somebody grunts in reply to my voice. The sound comes from
where I imagine Chase to be, but it isn't his voice. Nor is it Willem or Jakob. The shuffling sound begins again, getting louder. The
sound comes in starts and stops.

Thud. Shhhhh.

Thud. Shhhhh.

Shambling, I think. *It's fucking shambling!*

And it's coming toward me. Speaking was a grave mistake.
Whatever monster wandered into our hideaway is as blind in the
dark as we are. It's hunting by sound, following our voices.

I clamp my mouth shut and sit still. I should probably move, but I
remain rooted in place, afraid that any sound might cause it to pounce.

I hear a tiny click to my right and recognize the sound as Willem pressing the switch on the small LED light. When he lets go, its blue light will reveal whatever is coming my way. The problem is, it will also reveal me to it. I brace myself for action and wait.

Click.

Blue light, brighter than expected, fills the chamber. We've been in the dark so long that the tiny light seems incredibly bright, and I squint as I dash to the side. A small rock snags my foot and I topple over, landing just a few feet from where I sat.

The shambling sound grows faster. Louder. It speaks as I roll over to face my death head-on like the Colonel would want.

The face gazing down at me is the last I expected.

"Jackson?" I say, staring up at the man. Blood soaks his face where he was bitten, but otherwise, he looks unscathed. Could he have survived?

My three male comrades must be wondering the same thing, because no one moves.

Then Jackson speaks, his voice wet. "I'm going to kill you."

The words slowly sink in. *I'm going to kill you.* They were the last words he spoke before the bear crushed his skull. I look more closely at his head and notice it's not quite as spherical as it used to be. It's been crushed. No way he's still alive. Not in the traditional sense, at least.

"He's one of them!" I say.

"But he's talking," Chase says. He's hiding behind the shield, crouched next to the fallen stones and the Viking body.

"'I'm going to kill you,' is the last thing he said before he died!" My words come in a frantic rush as I fumble for my gun. I don't find it tucked into my waist. A quick glance reveals I dropped it when I tried to make my escape, but it's within reaching distance. But before I can make a move, Jackson lunges.

Before Jackson reaches me, Willem leaps toward the reanimated corpse with a battle cry. He's got the sword raised up, ready to take Jackson's head off, but his shout gives the attack away. Jackson moves with surprising speed, spinning around and smashing Willem in the side with a forearm. The strike knocks Willem back. He slams into the wall and slumps to the floor.

"Willem!" I shout, which serves no purpose other than to bring Jackson's attention back to me. "Help!" I shout, reaching for the gun. I catch a glimpse of Chase on the other side of the chamber. He's free to act. Could use that shield to ram Draugr Jackson from behind. But he remains as motionless as the unconscious Willem.

I feel cold metal and fumble with the gun. I could look at the gun and pick it up quickly, but I find myself unable to take my eyes off Jackson. As a result, I'm not ready to repel his attack. He throws himself toward me, reaching out for my head. I fall on my back, pull my legs up, and plant my feet against his chest. I manage to hold him back for a moment, but he weighs more than he should, and he's using his increased strength to push himself on top of me. He opens his mouth and leans forward, straining to reach the flesh of my face just a foot away.

I wish I could say that's as bad as it gets, but he's got one more surprise for me. He hisses "I'm going to kill you" again and then sticks out his tongue. At first, I'm not sure what I'm seeing, but then a moment of clarity reveals a patch of wriggling white bodies emerging from the tip of his tongue. I can see each one clearly. They have two black specks for eyes. The mouths are small, but as they open and close, I see tiny little needlelike teeth. Their segmented white bodies writhe back and forth, pushing out of his flesh. And in a moment, they're going to fall on my face. Maybe crawl into my mouth, or my nose, ears, and eyes. A bite might not even be necessary!

I look into his dead, white eyes, hoping to see a trace of humanity left. No such luck. I thought his eyes had been whitened by some form of undead cataracts, but up close I can see that his eyes have become clear membranes. The whiteness comes from the writhing mass of parasites *filling* his eyeballs. Jackson no longer sees with his own eyes. Instead, a mass of tiny black eyes stare out *through* Jackson's eyeballs and somehow transfer the visual data to his body.

One of the parasitic killers frees itself from Jackson's tongue. It dangles above my mouth, held up by viscous slime, wriggling, chomping its tiny jaws.

I want to scream for help again, but can't. The parasite could fall right into my mouth.

The parasite is just inches from my face when Jackson is yanked back. The tendril of slime stretches and snaps, dropping the parasite as I flinch away.

Jackson roars in frustration, but his voice is replaced by a sudden slippery crunching sound. The Draugr falls to the ground at my feet. Jakob lands on its back, hacking away at the spine with Alvin's rusty fishing knife.

Knowing I'm safe, I jump to my feet, frantically searching my body. I find the mucus-covered parasite wriggling down my sleeve, headed toward the cuff of my sweater. I flick the small creature to the cave floor and then crush it beneath my boot.

Jakob stands, out of breath, and wipes his blood-covered hands on his pant legs.

"Will kill you," Jackson croaks out.

"He's not dead!" Chase shouts from his hiding spot.

"Severed the spine," Jakob says. "Alive, but cannot move."

I notice several white maggot-things crawling out of the knife wound in the back of Jackson's neck, but they're not going anywhere fast. "Keep away from him."

"What happened?" Willem sits up, rubbing his head and looking at Jackson's still body.

"You tried to play Viking," I say. "Didn't work out so well."

He blinks hard. "Tell me about it."

"Next time don't scream as you attack." I reach out my hand and help him to his feet.

"Thanks for the tip," he says.

"Kill you," Jackson says, his voice fading.

Chase finally finds his courage and comes out of hiding. He crouches next to Jackson. "What do you want?"

"What are you doing?" I ask.

"Trying to communicate," he says and then repeats, "What do you want?" like he's talking to a really old lady, one loud syllable at a time.

"Kill…you."

"That's not an answer," I say. "It's just repeating the last thing he said. Can probably trigger whatever part of the brain that is. Makes the reanimated corpse that much more believable. If Jackson had said, 'Help me, please,' before he died, this might have worked out differently."

Jackson says, "Kill," one more time before Willem drives the sword through the paralyzed Draugr's skull and brain, silencing him for good. But a new voice, more mangled than Jackson's, picks up where he left off, only this time the message is much more peaceful. "It's okay, we're friends."

McAfee's last words.

30

McAfee's body defies logic. The two large holes in his chest are the least of his problems. His face is flattened and smeared with blood. The rest of his body looks compressed. I remember the large bull pounding his body into the sand. It must have broken all his ribs and crushed the rest of him. His arms look rubbery—probably filled with broken bones. His legs appear solid, but one is twisted to the side at an odd angle.

Now this *looks like a zombie*, I think, but the familiar image does little to comfort me.

"It's okay," McAfee says. He speaks out the side of his mouth, unable to open his jaw fully. It's crooked and looks to be broken on one side. "We're friends."

As though to prove the truth of his statement, McAfee raises his arms toward me and charges forward. He's faster than anticipated and nearly reaches me, but I manage to roll away.

McAfee is fast and probably strong, but he's not agile. As I roll to the side, he turns to watch me though his bleached eyes and doesn't see the approaching wall. He smashes into the wall and falls to the floor.

"Run!" I shout.

Chase leads our exodus from the chamber and into the tunnel. As we run for the surface, the light in the tunnel shifts from the light blue of the LED light Willem carries to a bright yellow. A glowing circle reveals the exit ahead of us, beaming with the promises of freedom and daylight.

The sun, I think with relief.

I'm doing it again; attributing what I know about modern vampires to the Draugar, which we've already seen operating in the daylight—perpetual daylight. As my legs start to ache from the uphill run, I start to think. The Draugar obviously know where we are. But only Jackson and McAfee came into the cave.

Why?

The answer comes quick. Willem and Chase were right about the cave. The others couldn't or wouldn't enter. But Jackson and McAfee were new Draugar. They'd have no memory of the caves. No fear. No apprehension. But they were injured. Weaponless. Clumsy.

The light ahead blooms bright. The fresh air of day rolls past us. It feels warm, maybe fifty degrees, but it carries a scent that makes me shiver. The smell is earthy, and I quickly realize why Jackson and McAfee entered the cave alone.

They were never meant to kill us, I think. *They were sent to flush us out!*

"Chase, wait!" I shout too late. He runs out of the cave and is bathed in bright yellow sunlight. It looks so welcome, so peaceful. And quiet. Nothing happens.

"What's wrong?" Willem asks me.

Chase stands outside the cave, looking back and forth, seeing nothing. My fear fades as we enter the sun. "Nothing, I just thought—"

Chase turns to greet us. His head snaps up. His eyes go wide. A scream unlike anything I've ever heard rises in his throat. I look up and find a silhouette of something big, framed by the sun. Something swoops past my head. Chase flinches down and raises the shield. The instinctual defensive posture saves his life as a double-sided ax strikes the wood. The shield explodes into fragments, and Chase is sent sailing. But he wasn't cut in half, which I'm pretty sure was the attacker's intent.

As the ax is pulled back up, Willem, Jakob, and I waste no time fleeing the cave and following Chase as he slides down the hillside.

"Chase!" Willem shouts as he bounds closer to the now-still figure.

As much as I still don't like or trust Chase, I sigh with relief when he picks up his head and curses. Willem yanks the skinny man to his feet and is rewarded with a shout of pain. Chase clenches the arm that held the now-destroyed shield.

"Is it broken?" I ask.

"I don't think so," Chase says, giving his arm a cursory wiggle. He winces but appears to have no trouble moving it.

"Hurry," Jakob says, stopping next to the group. "Torstein comes."

Four sets of eyes look up the rocky slope as Torstein jumps down from his perch above the cave entrance. The dead man is massive, at least a foot taller than Willem, but he lacks the bulk he might have once had. His body looks dried and withered. Of course, he seems to have no trouble wielding that giant ax. It, along with the horned helmet and tattered cape, make him look like something straight out of Chase's role-playing games. In fact, as I look at our group, me with the hooded cloak, Willem with the sword—we're all starting to look like characters out of a fantasy novel.

Torstein takes a step toward us, and it's clear he's not going to be sprinting anytime soon. His joints are stiff, and I swear I can hear them grind as he takes another step. He won't be able to catch us in an outright race, which is good, but he's also not going to get tired, need to sleep, or get hungry.

Well, maybe hungry—he did eat Eagon and Jenny, after all— but I don't think he needs to eat. Not like the living do, anyway.

We turn and run, not really sure where we're headed, except that it's away from the ax-wielding Draugr. The decline takes us to a beach with gray sand and a stand of stone obelisks, rising out of the sand like tree trunks. I approach one of the natural structures and run a hand over it. The stone is smooth, polished by eroding tides. I can't see the water, but I can hear it, somewhere beyond the tall stones.

With Torstein descending the hillside behind us at a slow but steady pace, I step into the labyrinth of stone.

"We can't go in there," Chase says. "We don't know where it goes."

"I'm pretty sure it leads to the ocean," I say, motioning to my ears.

"I know that," he says, "but—"

"There isn't time to debate, Chase," I say and point to the lumbering Draugr following us. "As long as he can see us, he can follow us. And we're eventually going to get tired. So unless you want to live in a B horror movie where the casually strolling psycho killer can catch victims running full speed, I suggest we use these stones for cover and then follow the coast one way or the other before cutting back to the center, grabbing our gear, and getting off this hellhole of an island."

"There's still a fifty-fifty chance he'll follow us."

"Chase," I say, my patience gone. "Shut up." I enter the field of stones.

"Follow the Raven," Jakob says, giving Chase a shove. It's the first time I've seen the old captain lose his patience. He's lost his best friend and his ship. He's been walking and running on an injured ankle without much complaint. In fact, I forgot all about his ankle until now. I glance back and see just the slightest limp in his gait.

Chase obeys, perhaps not wanting to be left behind, or maybe just eager to please whatever captain is giving him orders.

Willem stands outside the field for a moment, holding his sword. He looks like he's going to do something stupid and noble like waiting for Torstein so the two distant relatives can duke it out and settle things the Viking way. Instead, Willem just shakes his head and follows us.

Just fifty feet in, we lose sight of the island behind us. After another fifty, we reach the edge of the ocean. The rocks shrink in size, looking more like stalactites fallen from a cave ceiling, worn thin at the base where the water constantly eats them away. The view of the ocean and the blue sky full of white, soft clouds belies the horror of this place. The stark beauty is just a mask. Something sinister lives in the frozen north. Something old. Something evil.

I frown at the view, taunted by it. This might actually be a nice place to die, to be buried, but not like this. Not eaten alive or turned into an ever-living abomination. Something rises from the ocean in the distance. A plume of steam reveals a whale.

Fucking whales, I think. *I wouldn't be here if it weren't for you*. If I make it out of this alive, I determine to become a whaler and hunt the giants into extinction. I'm going to eat whale steaks, light my fucking house with whale oil, and open a fast-food chain in Japan that sells nothing but deep-fried whale nuggets.

"What's that?" Chase asks, pointing at the ocean.

I'm completely annoyed that the whale-loving idiot doesn't recognize them, and I don't bother to follow his pointed finger to its
target. "They're whales." *Asshole.*

I'm near screaming as the frustration of everything we've
encountered and survived starts to weigh on me. All because of a
pretty view.

"Not them," Chase says. He takes my head in his hands, and
I nearly shove my hand down his throat and rip out his heart. But
he shifts my gaze just enough so that I see what he's talking about.

A swirl of water, like a whale's "footprint," reveals something
rising. It's not a whale. Too close. Too shallow. It could be a walrus, which wouldn't be good, but we could lose it in the maze, no
problem.

When the thing rises from the ocean dripping gouts of water
and trailing a mass of seaweed, I'm not sure what I'm looking at.
But then the details resolve and I stare into the empty gaze of a
bald-headed, tunic-clad, Viking Draugr. This one's skin is loose,
probably from soaking in the ocean, but it's a sickly green color
and hangs in flaccid sheets that reveal he used to be a man of some
bulk. The loose skin covers shriveled muscles, taut sinews, and old
bones. In fact, its left arm is exposed, and I can see gleaming white
bones and shifting ligaments. The thing is like a living puppet. But
it's loose, unlike Torstein, and it can move much faster. It charges
through the water, slowed by the surf.

This is a trap, I think, but I never get to reveal my thoughts. Our
group flees back into the maze, confused, separated, and inside of
a few seconds—

—lost.

31

Somewhere, Chase screams. I think he must have been caught and killed, but then he shouts a warning, "There are more of them!"

Before I can heed his warning, I'm struck from the side and slammed into one of the stone spires. I right myself in time to see a short Draugr picking itself up, just a few feet away. The thing is dressed in brown, tattered leather and has long braided hair, partially peeled away from its skull. A double-braided beard wiggles at its chin as the hungry mouth snaps open and closed, filling the air with the *click, click, click* of chomping teeth.

My head spins from the impact, and I struggle to get up. The Draugr, who feels no pain, has no trouble hopping back to its fur-wrapped feet. It charges again, white-spotted tongue extended, ready to inject my body with its parasitic youth.

I force myself up, but the world spins around me as my head throbs in pain. I fall back to one knee, unable to move my legs. With the short Draugr just five feet away, I whip out my Glock and fire two shots toward the thing's head. Either the rounds have no effect or I've missed.

The gun is knocked from my hand as the Draugr lunges.

I clench my eyes shut.

I hear the impact but never feel it.

My eyes pop open, and I see Willem atop the Draugr's back. He must have tackled it at the last moment. He raises the Viking sword above his head and brings it down hard, splitting the short Draugr's head like a melon. There's a grating slurp as he withdraws the blade and prepares to strike again. But the monster doesn't move.

Clinging to the stone tower, I pull myself up and tuck my handgun back into the waist of my pants. We're surrounded by the tall stones. I think I see movement in the maze. Flashes of people. Of Draugar. But it could just be my spinning vision. I jump when Willem appears at my side and puts an arm around my back, supporting some of my weight.

"Can you move?" he whispers, looking into the maze with eagerness in his eyes. He doesn't want to run, I realize. He wants to find his father.

I nod and say, "I'm fine. Go."

He lets go of my back, but despite my best efforts, my legs start to buckle. I claw at the stone, dragging my nails across the polished surface, trying to stay upright. My fall doesn't stop until Willem catches me.

He pulls me up close, squeezing me tight enough to hurt my ribs. He looks back into the stone labyrinth with sad eyes.

"Leave me," I say. "He's your father."

"My father would never leave you," he says. "Neither will I."

He's right, I think. I can't picture the old man ever leaving a damsel in distress, even if there was a chance Willem would die. These Greenlanders have honor in them, or perhaps sexism. Either way, Willem isn't about to leave my side or endanger my life.

"Chase! Jakob!" I shout as loud as I can. "Get to the ruins! We'll meet you there!"

I hear a distant, indistinct reply from Chase but nothing from Jakob. A flash of green weaving through the stones catches my attention. My shouting attracted some attention. "The green one's coming."

We turn and hobble away, moving as quickly as we can, which isn't very fast. I do my best to help, but every time I push off with my feet, I head in the wrong direction, betrayed by my distorted equilibrium. If not for the stones, the big Draugr would have probably caught us by now.

Willem changes tactics and throws me over his shoulder. While this arrangement is very uncomfortable for me, we make much better time and soon get clear of the stone spires. The beach widens, but it's now covered in large, round boulders.

This looks familiar, I think, though it's hard to tell while being jostled up and down. I try to determine where we are, but my train of thought derails when the floppy-skinned Draugr emerges from the stone forest and locks his white eyes on mine. As he charges at us, I see that he carries a large, two-handed mallet shrouded with seaweed. I can't imagine Willem fending this thing off with just the sword. I have the gun still, but can't trust my aim. Not with my vision swimming.

"He's coming!" I shout, head turned down toward the sand.

Willem tries to pick up the pace, but the surge only lasts a moment. I can feel him weakening under my weight. *We're not going to outrun that thing*, I think. Then I see something that gives me an idea.

"Willem, stop!"

He slows and says, "What?" sounding incredulous.

"Look," I say, pushing off him. He puts me down. I'm still woozy, but the world isn't spinning anymore. I stagger a few feet back and point out the trail of footprints in the sand. "This is the way we came. To get the Zodiac engine."

"So?"

"So the other engine might still be there," I say. "A one hundred–horsepower blade could come in handy. At the very least, we might be able to hide in the boulders."

He looks into the field of boulders, his eyes following the path of our footprints, then back up to the approaching Draugr.

Every second of indecision allows the monster to get closer. As adrenaline begins to clear my mind, I remember that I've taken charge on more than one occasion thus far. I'm the fucking Raven, after all. I take Willem by the shirt and drag him toward the boulders and the possibility of a modern-day weapon.

We follow our footprints through the maze. If the parasites operating the Draugr's body have as much intelligence as they seem to, it will have no trouble following our path, too.

The crashing of waves signifies our arrival at the shore. The destroyed Zodiac has been washed ashore, its engine removed by Willem and I, and one of its two pontoons flattened. But the second mauled Zodiac is nowhere to be seen.

"It's gone!" Willem says, sounding defeated.

I climb up a boulder and scan the area. I quickly spot the Zodiac and feel a glimmer of hope. It's short-lived. The Zodiac shifts, and I realize it's not resting on the beach; it's floating in a bed of seaweed, forty feet from shore. Out of reach.

Before I can curse our bad luck, a flash of green catches my eye. The Draugr is here! And Willem hasn't seen it yet.

Fear flashes in my eyes, alerting Willem to the danger, but the hammer is already arcing toward his head. Without thought, I replicate Willem's earlier dive-tackle rescue. I manage to knock the hammer off course—it smashes a six-inch deep divot into the sand instead of Willem's head—but I don't land atop the giant and smash his brains. I bounce off the large, strong body. I reach out and grasp hold of something soft and pliable, hoping to bring the thing down with me and give Willem a chance to finish it off.

I feel a brief tug as the fabric goes taut, but I keep falling. A loud tearing sound fills the air. I fall in a heap on the sand, covered by a blanket of soft, slimy—oh God. A triangle of hair covers the center of the sheet, and to the side…a nipple. I've peeled the skin right off it!

I kick out from under the blanket of skin, more disgusted than afraid, and wish I'd stayed hidden beneath it. The Draugr turns to face me, its insides revealed. There are ancient strands of muscle covered in some kind of oozing film. I see organs, shrunken but still there and pulsing with the motion of thousands of white larvae-like parasites. I've heard that in the future we will have colonies of nanite robots living in our bodies, destroying viruses, curing cancer, and modifying our genetic code. This looks like a natural version of that symbiosis, except the nanobots are controlling body and mind and have an insatiable drive to propagate the species.

Scrambling backward, my hand hits something rubbery and pliable. My mind still on the hideous skin, I shriek and yank my hand away. But there's nothing to fear this time. It's the Zodiac's inflated pontoon. I push myself over it, glad to have something between me and the Draugr, even if it is an insignificant obstacle.

There's a flurry of excited movement inside the Draugr's exposed interior, and the ancient man lifts the massive hammer, clutched in both hands, over his head. I nearly vomit when the thing's flaccid bingo arms undulate like two limp jellyfish. Movement above brings my gaze back to the hammer. The weapon has a long reach, and at this range, it'll have no trouble striking my legs.

The hammer descends, then swings wildly off course. My mind registers what happened just a moment later. Willem's sword has cut through the Draugr's upper arm, severing it. The hammer swings right, missing my leg. But the severed arm, no longer controlled, loses its grip on the hammer and flings toward me. I cover my head just in time as the limb strikes me hard and bounces away.

I flinch away from the severed limb, looking for parasites that aren't there.

The Draugr spins around, swinging the hammer in a wide arc that could knock a man's head clean off. Willem ducks the blow and swings out with his sword. To my surprise, the Draugr actually goes on the defensive, taking a step back, right onto the Zodiac's pontoon.

The weight of the Draugr compresses the pontoon, but the strong material bounces back and rolls beneath the dead man's foot. He falls back hard, slamming onto the sand. Had he been a living man, there would have been a shout of surprise followed by an *oof* as the wind left his lungs. But the only sign that the Draugr is caught off guard is that it drops the giant hammer.

I dive to the side to avoid the falling behemoth but can't avoid being sprayed by sand kicked up by his fall.

"Shoot it!" Willem shouts. He looks winded. Maybe injured.

And he's right. The thing is at my mercy. But I've only got three rounds left. Better to save them when there's another option. As the thing struggles to sit up with just one arm and barely any stomach muscles to speak of, I pick up the hammer. The thing weighs a ton, and for a moment, I think I won't be able to swing it.

The Draugr sits up but can't figure out how to stand with the Zodiac pontoon beneath its legs.

How could something smart enough to set a trap get confused by a pontoon? I wonder. But I don't spend any time wondering about it. This thing's eternal lifespan is about to be cut short. I hoist the hammer up onto my shoulder. The weight of it nearly pulls me over backward, but I spread my feet apart, regain my balance, and swing the hammer like a little kid at a "test your strength" carnival game.

The hammer finds its mark atop the Draugr's skull, and although there's no ringing bell, there is a sickening, wet crunch. When I pull the hammer away and drop it onto the beach, I see the damage I've done. The Draugr's head has been compressed down, into its body, like a turtle retreating into its shell. The top of its skull is cracked open. Gouts of white, writhing worms wriggle out. I step away from the mess, a sinister grin on my face, and say, "Give the girl a prize."

But when I look to Willem, I see my celebration is premature. Despite the Draugr's demise, Willem looks terrified as he looks over my head at a distant peak. I don't see anything there when I look, so I ask, "What is it? What did you see?"

"I—I don't know," he says. "I saw something up there. Something big. Watching us. It looked—" He shakes his head like he can't believe what he's about to say. His eyes look disturbed as he speaks again. "It looked like a raven. I think...I think I just saw Muninn."

32

I think…we've gone…far enough," I say, trying to catch my breath. After our encounter with the hammer-wielding, loose-skinned Draugr and Willem's sighting of "the Raven," about which Torstein carved the warning, we flee. I've never run so far, so fast in my life. I feel like a kid again, running up the creaky basement stairs, certain that something would jump out and attack me at any moment. The difference is that now, my fear of monsters is justified.

Willem slows but doesn't stop. "We should keep moving."

"This is an island," I say. "If we keep moving, we're going to end up where we began."

This stops him in his tracks. He rubs his forehead, and I can tell he feels stupid. "Sorry," he says. "I just—"

"Don't worry about it," I say, resting my hands on my knees. My cloak feels like it weighs a thousand pounds. I take it off and place it on the sand.

"Wow," Willem says, looking at me.

For crying out loud, I think. My sweater is form fitting, I know, but we're running for our lives and he can't help commenting on the view. "Willem," I say, ready to deliver a verbal beat down, but when I see his eyes, I notice he's not looking at my chest; he's looking at my back.

"What is it?" I ask, my voice changing tone in an instant as I picture a swarm of those maggot things crawling over my back, burrowing through my flesh.

"You're steaming," he says.

I glance over my shoulder and see a swirling curtain of steam rising. *Warm sweat, meet cold air, and its friend dehydration.* I find some snow in the shadow of a rock and shovel a handful into my mouth. It's slushy but drinkable. I didn't realize how thirsty I was until this moment. I scoop up another handful and drink it down. "You should have some," I tell Willem. "Keep hydrated or—"

Sudden pain pulses behind my eyes. I stagger back, placing my hands on my head. Willem dashes to my side, holding me, and says, "What's wrong? Did they get you?"

Despite the pain and circumstances, I let out a laugh and say, "Brain freeze."

"Brain freeze?" Apparently, he's never heard the American term describing the sudden, sharp headache that can occur with eating frozen food.

"From the snow," I explain.

"Ohh," he says. "Push your tongue against the roof of your mouth."

I do, and the pain subsides. When it does, I notice he's still holding me. I glance down at his arms and then up into his eyes. "Thanks."

There's a moment there. A connection. The kind teenagers first experience at summer camp or behind bleachers or someplace else equally nonromantic. It's that thing that makes you cramp up inside and sucks your breath away. It's kind of a painful experience, actually, but in our minds, or maybe our hearts, we know it means something. It's typically less intense when experienced as an adult, but this hits me hard. Maybe it's exhaustion or adrenaline or fear, but this is intense. And uncomfortable.

I push against his arms, and whatever spell that bound him in that pose breaks. He steps back, looking sheepish.

But my stomach doesn't recover from the moment. Twisting pain grips my cold gut. Drinking the ice water has awoken my appetite.

While Willem helps himself to a snowy drink, I take out the protein bar stashed in my pocket, tear off the wrapper, and break it in half. I give one half to Willem and scarf down the rest. Tastes like cocoa powder–sprinkled cardboard, but I can feel the vitamin-fortified snack delivering an energy boost to my system already.

"Shouldn't we save some?" Willem asks.

I reply through a mouthful of food. "Rationing works when you're waiting for rescue. Not so much when you're being chased. If we crash before getting off this island, they'll catch us. We need to stay strong."

"And smart," Willem adds. "We fell into their trap like a bunch of stupid animals."

"Speaking of stupid," I say, "I know they're not really zombies, so we shouldn't expect them to be totally brain dead, and they're not really vampires, so they're not playing chess in some castle, either. But these things have been in the ground for hundreds of years. How do they still have brains sharp enough to lay traps?"

"Or use weapons," Willem says.

"Right."

"I'm not sure," he says. "But maybe it has something to do with that slime inside the body. Did you see it? Inside the last one when, you know—"

The memory of the peeled sheet of skin falling on top of me returns and sours my stomach for a moment. "I remember."

"It looked like the organs, the important ones anyway, had been coated in the stuff. Maybe it protects them. Keeps them from aging normally. If they do the same thing to the brain, maybe they're still functioning at a higher level."

"You don't think they're still aware? Still human in there some-where? Can you imagine that kind of hell? Being a prisoner in your own mind forever? Having your memory and knowledge hijacked but your will trapped? It must be hell."

Willem pauses, chewing the last bite of his bar. My imagination has soured what little flavor it had. He forces it down with a grimace. "We need to get back to the ruins. If my father and Chase survived…"

I realize that I've made him even more worried. We won't be able to leave this island if we don't find Jakob, and if he's already one of them… "He'll make it," I say with as much conviction as I can muster. We both know I'm talking about his father.

Willem shakes his head. "He was injured."

"He's tougher than both of us," I say. "Now shut up about it, and let's figure out where we are."

After another drink of slush, the cold starts to sting my back. The air is warm today, but the breeze rolling in off the ocean is frigid and saps the warmth from my body. I sling my cloak back on and hide my head beneath the hood. *Mental note: Grow hair out for next Arctic trip. Scratch that—fuck the Arctic. Go to the Bahamas.*

I take a long look at our surroundings. Something about it looks familiar. "This isn't far from where I landed with Jenny and Peach." Mentioning the pair makes me cringe with survivor's guilt. They made it off that damn boat. Why couldn't that have been enough? Why did we have to land on this freak-show island and not the mainland?

Pushing my regrets aside, I point to an area where the stone hillside slopes right down to the beach instead of ending in a drop-off. "I think that's where I first left the beach." I check the area and find depressions in the loose stone that could have been made by boots. "This is the place."

I point up to the hill rising high above us. "I first saw the ruins from up there. Felt so far away then. The backside of this hill is steep, though. Would make for a hard walk, but it's doable." I point down the beach. "That way is south, where we met."

"We know the way to the ruins from there," he says. "We could make good time."

He's right, but there's one thing he hasn't remembered yet. "But…this stretch of beach is where we first encountered the polar bear. Then again, with you. Not much farther beyond that is where the bear killed—or whatever—Jackson and McAfee."

"And the walruses," he adds.

"Right," I say. "So I think it's safe to assume that living or undead, the bear patrols this coastline."

"Or it's just running laps," he points out.

"Or maybe the walruses took care of it in the end." I know it's hopeful thinking, which I'm loath to do. I prefer realism. But things are so unreal, I think a little hope will do us some good. Willem seems to disagree.

"I doubt it," he says. "Not planning on seeing the bear again could be dangerous."

"Okay, Captain Greenland," I say. "What do you plan to do about the Draugr polar bear that is stronger and faster than you, not to mention the fact that it has lots of sharp teeth and claws, and the only way to kill it is by destroying its brain, which, by the way, is protected by a thick skull that already deflected a perfect forty-five-caliber shot?" I catch my breath, hands on hips, and wait for an answer I know he doesn't have.

"We could blow it up," he says.

The ridiculousness of his statement makes me laugh. "Blow it up? How are we going to do that, McGyver? You have some household chemicals I don't know about? Maybe a bottle of hairspray and a microwave? That seems to work well in the mov—"

Shit. He's right. "C4," I say, barely a whisper.

He's nodding, and thank God, not mocking me.

"Jackson had a lot?" he asks.

"A ton," I say, eyes widening with the realization that there is a weapon on this island that can not only blow up a zombie polar bear but Draugar and whatever the hell the Raven is too.

"You know how to use it?" he asks.

"I have a general grasp of explosives," I say. "And it didn't look too hard to figure out. Blast caps. Timers. And a shit-ton of C4."

"Shit-ton?" he says, grinning.

"What?"

"Your…unique sense of humor is coming back," he says. I must look like I'm about to go on the defensive because he adds, "You were kind of a drag for a little while." I'm about to lay into him when he grins. "It's not so much unique as morbid. Borderline inappropriate."

I can't help but smile, despite being stranded on a giant piece of frozen crap. "Yeah, well, it seems to be rubbing off on you."

"So it would seem," he says, but his smile fades as he sets his mind back to the task. "So, what's the plan? Follow the coast, grab the C4, and head for the ruins?"

"Sounds about right to me."

"And if we come across the polar bear—"

"We blow it the fuck up."

"You know," he says, as we start down the beach, "Out of all of the military tactics developed throughout history, 'blow it the fuck up' never fails."

"That's why it was my father's favorite," I say.

"Were you two close?"

The question stings. "Once upon a time, maybe. When I was still trying to please him. He was mostly an asshole."

"An asshole you talk about a lot."

"I do?" I ask, but the question isn't for Willem. It's for me. I decide to be honest with myself and realize that the Colonel has been on my mind a lot. Much more than usual, which is none. "I guess, even though I haven't seen him much, I miss him. Knowing I won't see him again. Knowing we'll never get a chance to..."

"Heal old wounds," he says.

"I was trying to think of something that sounded less wussy, but yeah."

"Sounds like the kind of guy that would understand."

"*Not care* is more likely."

"I never met the man, and I know that's not true," he says. "Any father who spends two weeks in the woods alone with *you* must care."

I laugh and let out a sad sob at the same time. I forgot I'd told Willem about that. He's got a point, but I think the real lesson here is that Willem still has a chance to save his father and not live with this kind of regret. Before I can say as much, a high-pitched sound catches my attention. It fades in and out, as crashing waves and brisk wind occasionally wash it out.

"What is that?"

He listens, and the sound repeats. It's high-pitched but not like a scream. There's no emotion in it, but there is a warble. "Sounds like a monotone crow call."

"Or a raven," he says.

"Right." That this sound could be the emotionless call of the mysterious raven makes me uncomfortable. I think I'd rather it sound crazed than robotic.

"But it sounds far away."

"Doesn't mean it won't get closer. We should go," I say, and then break into a jog. Willem falls in line behind me, and our jog becomes a run, but not like before when desperation and fear fueled us. This time we're fueled by hope. We can finally fight back, maybe survive, and maybe raise a little hell of our own.

33

A five-foot drop catches me off guard. I manage to land on my feet but then stumble and fall unceremoniously on my face. But it's not the drop that stumbles me; it's the ground upon which I land. It's soft. I lift my head up and spit sandy grit from my mouth. A beach. I don't remember there being a beach between where I met Willem and the spot where Jackson was killed.

Willem jumps down next to me and helps me up. As he brushes the sand off my back, I see the mainland across the channel and realize what we've done.

"What's that they say about the best laid plans of mice and men?" I ask.

"Go often askew," he replies, and I think he's actually quoting whatever poem that line comes from. He proves this theory correct when he continues. "And leave us nothing but grief and pain."

"You can stop there, Mr. Sunshine," I say before pointing out the beach. "We overshot our target. This is the beach where—"

"The walruses," he says, sounding stunned. "They're gone."

He's right. There isn't a single living thing left on the beach. There isn't a single corpse either, for that matter. The beach is empty. Curiosity pulls us farther out on to the sand. Tall waves crest and crash to our right. The foamy water hisses as it slides up the sand and slips away, tinged pink.

Dark brown patches of sand stretch into the distance. Blood covers the beach. On the plus side, the beach is empty, and launching our raft from here shouldn't be much trouble. On the downside, it's an awful reminder that the horrors we witnessed on this beach are real. A line of pink water traces the shoreline where the rising tide leaches the blood away, pulling it into the ocean.

A loud hiss snaps my attention out to the channel. A plume of steam. Whales. Taunting me again. Steam rises again, but this time it's followed by a tall black dorsal fin. *Orcas*. No doubt drawn by the thousands of gallons of walrus blood seeping into the ocean. Seeing them in the water between here and the mainland feels like a dark harbinger. But despite being nicknamed killer whales, they've never killed and eaten a human in the wild. Sure, they freak out and chomp down on a Sea World trainer every now and again, but lock me up in a cell for no good reason and I'm liable to do the same. Instead of fearing the creatures, I feel fearful *for* them.

"Run," I say to them. "Get out of here."

"They're safe in the water," Willem says, watching as the pod moves through the channel, hunting.

I'm not sure I agree, but I don't argue the point. Our safety needs to be first and foremost on our minds. Any lapse in focus could—

Speak of the devil.

A distant, bouncing ball of white appears on the beach. "Willem!" I shout before giving his sleeve an urgent yank and throwing myself back up the five-foot wall.

He shouts some kind of Greenlandic curse behind me, and then he's got his hand on my ass, shoving me up faster. I turn around as he climbs up and yank him to the top.

Paying attention to my surroundings this time, I backtrack and quickly find the spot where Jackson met his fate for the first time.

But I don't spot the backpack. *It has to be here*, I think, as I begin searching behind the strewn boulders and loose fallen stones.

"Here!" Willem shouts, holding up the backpack victoriously.

I kneel beside him and yank the pack open. Everything's here. I take a blast cap and timer out of the Ziploc bag.

"What are you doing?" Willem asks. It's clear he wants to run.

"We're going to have to stop running eventually," I say. "No time like the present, right?"

He doesn't agree, but he doesn't run either. While I try to figure out the explosives, he keeps an eye out behind us.

The blast caps and timers look to be made for each other, and they snap together easily. I look for any other missing pieces, find none, and slide the pointy end of the blast cap into the C4. It feels too easy, but McAfee probably had these custom made. His crew is often lacking in the IQ department, and he had equipment special ordered so that monkeys could figure it out. Seems his theory applied to weapons-grade explosives, too.

I look up and see Willem inching back toward the beach. "What are you doing?"

"I don't see the bear," he says. "I think it might have—"

The bear rises up over the five-foot wall, standing on its hind legs and trying to find purchase with its forelimb claws. If it gets up now, we're dead. But I can't run. Not right away. The thing's horrible condition freezes my gaze for a moment. Its face is ruined, peeled away from one side where a tusk must have penetrated and pulled the skin free. Half of its teeth are exposed, along with a portion of cheekbone and forehead. The wounds I gave the bear are invisible now, masked by an array of large puncture wounds covering the rest of its body. It should be dead a hundred times over, but here it is, rising up to devour us.

My sense returns with a surge of adrenaline. "Willem!" He turns and runs toward me. Without a word between us, we charge up the hillside. Once we crest this hill, it's a straight and clear slope down to the ruins. If we can take care of the bear, we should be able to grab our gear, return to the beach, and head for the mainland inside of an hour.

"Did you figure it out?" Willem asks, looking at the backpack in my hand.

I show him my other hand and the brick of C4 it holds. "I think."

"You think?"

"You want to give a try?" I say. My thighs begin to burn from the uphill run.

He looks at the brick and shakes his head. As his head turns to the side, his eyes widen. "Here it comes!"

The bear is below us and bounding over the rock-strewn hillside like a monster truck over Matchbox cars. I see one of its legs bend at a sick angle, no doubt broken during its battle with the walrus herd. The wound is severe, but it seems to only slow the bear a little— enough for us to reach the top.

The downslope of the hill is mostly clear. We'll be able to run quickly. The bear will run quicker. I pause at the top.

"What are you doing?" Willem shouts, frantic.

"Count," I say. I'm out of breath. "Count how many seconds… until it reaches the top."

He nods and nearly throws me over the edge.

My knees protest the pell-mell run. Each impact jars my body.

"Twenty-one seconds!" Willem shouts.

The bear is just twenty-one seconds behind us. It will decrease that distance as it comes down the hill. With shaky hands from fright, not to mention sprinting downhill, I set the timer.

Nineteen seconds.

I drop the brick of C4, and for the first time wonder just how big of a bang I'm going to get out of that brick. Something in me says it's going to be big. "We need to find cover!" I shout.

Fifteen seconds.

"There!" Willem shouts, pointing to what looks like a drop-off. But it's not close, and I can't move any faster.

Ten seconds.

We're not going to make it, I think. I glance back and see the bear. It looks closer than I expected. I don't see the brick of C4 anywhere. Did the bear already pass it?

Five seconds.

Pain lances up my arm, snapping my attention forward. Willem yanks me to the side and over the edge of a rise. We drop several feet and strike hard stone. Willem takes the brunt of the impact as I fall on top of him.

Two seconds.

"Cover your ears," I shout.

I block my ears at the moment of detonation.

The sound hits me first, pulsing through my body and sucking the air from my lungs. Then a deep, resonating rumble rolls through the earth beneath me. The shockwave will no doubt reach the other side of the island and send ripples out into the Arctic Ocean.

With the main force of the explosion past, I stand to my feet and help Willem up.

"Did we get it?" he asks.

Stones trickle down from above and fall into our hiding place. The bear's head slides into view, staring down at us with dead, white eyes.

And then it falls.

We both jump back, startled, but relieved to find the bear is missing most of its body. I feel like I should say something, some kind of cool movie hero quote. But before I get a chance to come up with something witty, a grinding sound catches my attention. My first thought is that we started an avalanche, which seems likely now that I'm thinking about it. *Who sets off C4 on the side of a stone-strewn hill while standing at the bottom of it?* We're lucky we didn't bury ourselves.

The grinding continues as I search for its source. I find it closer than expected when a loose stone falls free and lands at my feet, revealing a black gap. What first looked like the remnants of some ancient rockslide now looks like a rock wall. Built by human hands.

Something on the fallen rock catches my attention. I pick up and inspect the surface. There's a rune. I show it to Willem.

"The dog hunter," he says, reading the rune.

"They hunted dogs?"

"No," he says. "A hunter who used dogs. To track. To kill. This is a corpse door."

The stones shift and collapse, opening a hole big enough to drive a truck through.

From what I understand, the corpse door is the last line of defense against a Draugr, and we've just opened it. As a deep growl echoes from somewhere behind the door, we back away and then run, neither one of us wanting to think about what we might have just set free.

34

We make it to the base of the hill before hearing anything behind us, but when a howl rolls down the hill,
I nearly fall on my face. The chorus of five ragged
canine voices is one of the most horrible sounds I've ever heard. It's
so awful, I can't help it; I turn back and look.

I wish I hadn't.

There's a human Draugr standing in front of the cave. He's
short, but wide, and powerful looking. His face is peeled back like
Torstein's, and a skull cap rests on his head, covering an explosion
of gray hair. He's dressed in fluffy, tan furs, which seem to be dis-
integrating in the breeze, spewing clouds of fur into the air like
milkweed in the fall. There's no hammer or sword or ax or any other
manmade weapon to speak of. Instead, he holds five taut leashes.

The undead dogs strain against their bonds, eyes locked on the
only moving prey in sight—Willem and me. They're hard to see
because their tan fur matches the skins the human Draugr wears.
But I can see their permanently bared teeth quite clearly. Each dog
looks to be about fifty pounds, and while they're withered from the
dry Arctic air, they're no doubt stronger than they were in life. Like
the furs of the human Draugr, the dogs' fluffy tan fur billows and
spins around them, caught up by the wind.

"Elkhounds," Willem says. "They've been popular hunting dogs
of Norsemen for seven thousand years."

"Then let's get going while we've still got a head start," I say. "We can hold them off inside the ruins."

"No." Willem looks to the ruins. "If my father made it there, I don't want to lead the Draugr straight to him."

"I hate to break it to you," I say, "but we just rang the world's loudest dinner bell. Every Draugr on the island is probably headed this way."

Our moment of indecision is interrupted by a deep laugh, like a dry Jabba the Hut from *Star Wars*. The dog-master raises the gloved hand holding the leashes. His fingers open. The leashes fall to the ground. There is a moment of confusion as the dogs continue to strain against the leashes, but there's nothing holding them back. Are they free, or did the master step forward? A single angry-sounding grunt, barked from the dog-master's mouth, clears their minds and sends the pack sprinting toward us.

I turn and run for the ruins. Not only do I disagree with Willem on this point, but there is nowhere else to go. Willem seems to have come to the same conclusion, because he's right next to me, running for all he's worth.

Or is he?

He's in good shape and has longer legs. He should be leaving me in the dust.

"Don't wait for me!" I shout.

"I'm not going to leave you!"

Son of a— "If you get there first, you can be ready to help me over the top." I glance back. The cloak whips out behind me as I run, making it hard to see, and no doubt slowing me down. My instincts say to cut it loose and run faster, but I'll freeze without it. The cloak drops for a moment and gives me a clear view. The five dogs reach the flat plain. One of them trips and spills into a heap. It rolls to its feet but now runs on just three legs.

The canine bones have become brittle.

My logic must make sense to Willem because he pulls ahead of me. I know I suggested it, but being left behind like this is a horrible feeling. What's that people say about surviving a bear attack? You just need to be faster than the other guy. That probably applies to undead hunting dogs, too. And I'm the slow one.

I can hear the clack of ancient claws on the stone ground behind me, growing louder by the moment.

Willem reaches the tall walls of the Viking ruins. He could throw himself over the top and save himself. But he stops, links his fingers, and leans down. I've done enough outdoor group activities to know a ten-finger boost when I see one. I focus on his hands. If I can leap and get a foot into his big hands, he'll be able to use my momentum and launch me over the wall. And he shouldn't have any trouble pulling his tall self over behind me.

But before I reach him, my cloak snaps tight around my neck. The sudden stop pulls me back off my feet like I've just been clothes-lined by Jimmy "Superfly" Snuka. Struggling to catch my breath, I reach up and try to free myself from the cloak. Cold air be damned. But it's being pulled too hard. I look up and see two of the undead dogs, now missing half their hair, yanking on the cloak with their jaws. Two more dogs are approaching. The fifth, limping mutt is still some distance off. And behind him, the dog-master strides confidently toward us.

I'm caught, but the dogs don't seem any more intelligent than usual, as they mistake my clothing for a part of my body worth attacking. Of course, maybe they've been trained to keep prey alive so that their master can make the killing blow. Whatever the case, I need to be gone. Now.

I draw the Glock. Three rounds left. Five dogs. I can't shoot them all, but I can take care of the two dragging me across the ground. I take aim upside down and squeeze off a round. The shot finds its mark on the dog's forehead. Unlike the polar bear, the dog's skull can't stand up to a .45 round. The bullet shatters the old bone and pulverizes whatever brain is gel-protected inside. The dog twitches and falls. Its companion simply pulls harder as the other two approach.

I hear Willem shout the way people do when facing an angry dog. I don't think it helps with living dogs any more than it does with living-dead dogs. "Their bones are weak," I shout to him, taking aim at the second dog holding my cloak.

I pull the trigger and flinch at the sound of the gunshot. My ears ring and throb with pain. But the second dog is dead. Again. And I'm free. I launch to my feet as the other dogs arrive. One heads for Willem, the other for me. I take aim, but the dog weaves back and forth. This is my last shot. I need to make it count.

My back presses against the stone wall. I look down the sight like my father taught me. Both eyes open. Deep breath. Let it out. Squeeze the trigger gently and—

Something tight wraps around my chest, under my arms. It's like an anaconda has me. I'm yanked off my feet. "Willem!" I shout as he kicks one of the dogs hard in the head. There's a loud crack, and the dog falls. Willem finishes the job by taking the thing's head off with his sword. He turns to me, eyes wide, as I'm pulled up and over the wall.

"Jane!" I hear him shout, but I can't see anything but the blue sky above as I fall inside the ruins.

I land on something soft and hear a very human-sounding *oof* beneath me. The anaconda lets go and I roll away, bring my gun up, and point it in Jakob's face. "Jakob!" I shout in surprise, lowering the weapon. Chase is on the ground behind him. He must have been holding Jakob up when we all fell inside.

Willem shouts in pain outside the ruins. His voice is followed by the metallic ting of metal striking bone. Then his hands clasp the top of the wall and he hoists himself up and over.

There's no greeting when he lands. No hug for his father. Willem sits up, unlaces his boot like it's on fire, and yanks it off. The boot lands next to me, and I see a puncture in its top, just the right size for a canine tooth.

Willem's sock comes off next. It, too, has a hole. He grips his bare foot and pulls it up. We crouch next to him, all looking for the same thing.

Blood.

But other than a pink divot, there is no wound. Willem sighs with relief.

Jakob falls to his knees next to Willem and presses his son's head against his chest. "Thank God."

"I'm fine, father," Willem says, clearly not accustomed to his father's affection. When Jakob doesn't let go, Willem says something in Greenlandic. I have no idea what the words are, but they seem to placate the old man. He lets go, and the conversation, now private thanks to the language barrier, continues quickly and ends with an embrace between father and son. And though I have no idea what either man has said, I'm moved to tears when I see both rugged-looking Viking men cry.

Chase shatters the moment with a whispered, "Everyone shut up! Here it comes!"

Willem quickly turns his sock inside out before putting it back on his foot and then shakes out the boot. Nothing but lint. No parasites. He puts the boot back on, ties the laces, and waits in silence with the rest of us.

The first thing we hear is sniffing. The one remaining dog searches for us. Then there are footfalls, big and heavy. The dog-hunter arrives. I can see his shadow moving past the cracks in the wall. When his gloved hand grasps the top of the wall, I tense and prepare to fight.

Again.

35

The shuffling and sniffing outside the wall continues for about thirty seconds. Then the dog-master pulls his hand away, and we can hear the pair retreat. When the footsteps fade into the distance, everyone relaxes. But I'd like to know I'm not being outfoxed yet again, so I move to poke my head over the wall for a look-see.

"Don't," Chase says. "They seem to forget about you if they don't see you for a while. If it sees you, it will come back."

"You're sure?" I ask. "They seem smarter than that."

"Being smart and having a good memory are two different things," he says.

I'm not sure I agree with his assessment, but I don't want to risk being wrong. The cold stone of the floor in the ruins makes an uncomfortable seat, but I plop down like it's a plush faux-leather recliner and sigh. The sun is warm on my face. The air is fresh with evaporating water. For a moment, one of the thousand knots screwed into my back loosens.

That's when I open my eyes and see the life raft. It's torn to shreds. I snap up. "What happened?" Our only way off this island has been destroyed.

"Not sure," Chase says. "We found it this way."

"How could they know?" I ask, raising my voice. "It's fucking yellow plastic! They're undead *Vikings*. How could they know it was a way off the island?"

"Maybe the bright color drew them to it?" Willem says.

"Or the smell of it," Chase adds. "We did spend several nights inside. It must smell like us."

I'm not sure how the Draugar could smell anything over their own stink, but it could make sense. There was just one problem. "Did you fix the wall?"

"What?" Chase says.

"The wall." I point to the portion of the structure that once had a doorway, but was blocked up by Jakob and Alvin. "If they got inside, who fixed the wall?"

"The wall," Jakob says, his voice grave, "was not ruined."

"So there is a Draugr that can get inside and out again without a door." I shake my head in exasperation. Chase takes it for chastisement.

"Hey," he says. "It's not our fault we—"

"We should have seen it," Jakob says. "It's the kind of mistake that costs lives. You are a first mate. You know such things to be true."

"The Devil's in the details," Chase mutters.

"Indeed." Jakob holds up a backpack. The familiar word SUR-VIVAL is scrawled across the back. "They did, however, leave us our food and water."

Willem and I help ourselves to some fresh water, but we leave the few remaining snack bars for another time.

After twisting the cap back on a water bottle, I return it to the backpack and ask, "So how did you escape?"

"We ran, mostly," Chase says.

"Our friend is being modest," Jakob says.

Two things leap out at me. Jakob has just referred to Chase, the first mate of the ship that sank the *Bliksem*, as a friend. Second, since when is Chase modest?

"Saved my life," Jakob says. "Twice."

Chase makes a lazy attempt at hiding his proud grin. "I found him on the sand."

"I twisted my ankle again," Jakob explains.

"Anyway," Chase says. Telling the tale of his heroics is probably a new experience for him. "Right after I help him up, one of them—a Draugr—finds us."

"The blacksmith," Jakob grumbles. "Still wore his tools around his waist." He leans forward, reaches behind him, and pulls out an iron-headed mallet. It's nowhere near as big as the one Floppy-Skin used, but the head looks dense and heavy. It could do some serious damage and is easier to hold.

"So, Jakob starts waving his arms and shouting. I see he's distracting the thing—"

At these words, Jakob frowns, but I keep quiet.

"The blacksmith goes after him. And he stands his ground. I've never seen anything like it. The thing loses track of me. I run up behind it, grab the hammer, and just start whacking the shit out of it. I can hear its bones breaking. But it doesn't stop. I give it a good hit in the leg, but there's nothing solid there, or at least too much muscle covering the bone."

Chase is really excited. He rubs his hands together quickly. I can picture him acting this way while in the heat of role-playing battle.

"You guys were probably popular in school, right?" he asks, looking from me to Willem.

I started at a new school every two to three years of my life, so I was the perpetual new kid and rarely popular, but I doubt I was ever unpopular in the way Chase must have been, so I stay quiet.

"Of course you were. So, when someone is walking, you can kick his leg, just as he picks it up off the ground. It shifts the foot behind the leg and wham, instant trip. I had the technique used on me on more than a few occasions but had never really tried it. But the concept is simple. So when the Draugr closed in and picked up its foot, I kicked that son of a bitch as hard as I could." Chase laughs. "Fell flat on his face, right at Jakob's feet."

"He helped carry my weight all the way here," Jakob says.

"You didn't kill it?" I ask. "When it was on the ground?"

Chase's proud smile fades some. "I wasn't really thinking too well at that point."

"The boy did well," Jakob says.

Willem claps Chase on the shoulder and nods in acknowledgment of a job well done. "Thank you."

"So what are we up against, then?" I ask. I doubt we're going to have long to figure things out, so the more time we spend preparing, and not telling stories, the better off we'll be. That doesn't mean I don't think we're going to die, just that I'd like to give the fight an old-fashioned Alamo try.

"Torstein," Jakob says with disdain.

"The blacksmith," Chase says. He looks at me and adds, "Sorry."

"The dog-master," I say. "And his last limpy dog."

"What about the big guy with seaweed and the hammer?" Chase asks.

"Dead," I say.

Chase looks impressed but then says, "Why didn't you keep the hammer?"

I'm about to tell him to sit on Torstein's horn and rotate, but he sees my flash of anger, holds up his hands, and says, "Just messing with you. Geez, Jane."

My anger hasn't completely faded when I say, "Oh yeah, I blew the polar bear into shish kabob–size chunks, too."

Chase looks startled, like he is just finding this out, but he's really just remembering. "We heard that!"

"And felt it," Jakob says.

"You found Jackson's pack?" Chase asks.

I pull out the backpack and open it up, revealing five bricks of C4 and the bag of timers and blast caps.

"Holy shit," Chase says. "Five bricks and four Draugar. We might actually stand a chance."

"Five," Willem says.

Chase turns to him. "What?"

"Five Draugar."

"You saw another?" Jakob asks.

Willem's mouth twitches. He doesn't want to say it. So I do.

I drop the bomb fast and bluntly. "Muninn."

Jakob's eyes go wide. "You saw the Raven?"

Willem nods. "For just a moment. It watched us from a hilltop."

"We haven't seen it since," I say. Sensing a rapid decline in morale, I add, "Look, Raven or not, it can be killed. It can be destroyed. These Draugar aren't supernatural. They're a highly evolved parasite that can be squashed under our boots. The Raven is probably just one of the original Draugar they chased to this island."

"Draugar don't run away," Jakob says.

I roll my eyes. "Fine. That's not the point. The point is, this thing is not supernatural. It's not Odin's pet. It's alive, or used to be, and if Torstein and his merry band of hunters had C4, we wouldn't be having this conversation because the Raven would have been blown to bits six hundred years ago."

Jakob smiles when I finish my rant. He nudges Willem. "We have our own Raven."

Ugh.

"You have my blessing to marry this one," the old man adds with a chuckle.

Double ugh.

The joke is meant as a jab at me, I know, but when Willem doesn't exactly decline his father's blessing, my cheeks get hot.

Chase doesn't like the new direction of the conversation, either. "What do we have for weapons? Aside from the C4?" He pulls out a knife and puts it down.

For some reason, the appearance of a new knife strikes me as odd. "Where did you get that?"

"Back pocket," Chase says and then shrugs. "I like knives."

I sometimes wonder if Chase is a few screws loose from being a serial killer, but then, having a serial killer on the team might not be a bad thing. I draw the Glock and put it down. "One round left."

Jakob places his hammer down.

Willem adds the sword.

"Not much," Chase says.

"Oh!" says Jakob. He leans back and drags the now-useless Zodiac engine into the weapons cache.

Willem smiles at his father, and then me, who suggested the very same thing not too long ago. "Peas in a pod."

"So aside from one bullet, and the C4, this fight will be up close and personal, which works in their favor. So let's plan on finishing this with the C4 from a distance. If they can set a trap, so can we," Chase says.

I'm about to protest Chase taking charge but then remember that this is his thing. He's good at strategizing. It's the implementation of that strategy where he lacks ability. But he did save Jakob, so maybe he's changing…finding his spine. It would be nice to have

JEREMY BISHOP   217

him not bolt at the first sign of danger for a change. "So what's the plan?"

"We get them here and make a run for the gorge. When they follow us inside, we bring down the walls with the C4 and bury them."

The boldness and simplicity of the plan surprises me. It requires some close-up contact with the Draugar, fending them off at the walls, but it's as good a plan as any. "That could work," I say.

Chase looks surprised. "Really?"

"Assuming there aren't too many more Draugar on the loose," Willem says. "Even if we don't get them all, we should get a few."

"And have C4 to spare," I say. "But we need to do this soon, before they come up with something better."

"So the last question is," Chase says. "How do we want to get their attention?"

As though in response to his question, a shrill, high-pitched shriek blares. The sound echoes in the valley. It's so close that I flail and dive to the side. When the sound repeats, I recognize it for what it is.

A telephone.

36

The pulsing ring of the phone is a double-edged sword. On one side, it means we can contact the outside world and arrange rescue. On the other, I fear the sound will attract the Draugar before we're prepared for them. But these thoughts are fleeting as I pinpoint the source of the noise—Jackson's backpack.

I pick up the pack, rip it open, and overturn it, shaking its contents out. The bag of detonators falls out, followed by five bricks of C4 explosive. And then, a sight that seems more surprising than the Draugar, a phone about four times the size of the average cell phone, sporting a thick black antenna on top.

"A satellite phone!" Chase cheers.

I accept the call, feeling surreal as I put the receiver up to my ear and say, "Hello?" like I've just answered a call in my kitchen.

The man on the other end speaks in Greenlandic.

I interrupt him with, "English. Speak English, please!"

"Apologies," says the man in heavily accented English. "This is the Greenland Coast Guard cutter *Odin*, responding to a distress call from a…Michael Jackson."

I nearly laugh but contain it. *No wonder Jackson hated my Jackson family taunting. His first name was actually Michael.*

"We have reached the coordinates provided," the man says over the phone, "but see no vessel in distress. We also called before, but received no answer."

I remember the strange monotone sound Willem and I had heard earlier and attributed to Muninn. *It was the phone!* If only we'd recognized the sound for what it was, we might be stepping aboard a ship right now instead of reenacting a World War One trench warfare scene.

The *Odin* crewman continues, "May I please speak to the man who called in so that I might verify this number?"

"Yes," I say. "I mean, no. You have the right number, but Mr. Jackson is…indisposed. He can't come to the phone."

"To whom am I speaking?"

"Jane Harper. I was a crew member aboard the *Sentinel*."

The man is silent on the other end.

"The call we received was for a ship called *Bliksem*."

What the hell? Had Jackson placed the call before the *Bliksem* sank? *Of course he did.* Making the call for the *Bliksem* would make Jackson and McAfee look like the good guys. They called it in before the explosion went off, beating the *Bliksem* crew to the punch.

I hear paper shuffling, and then the man's voice grows suspicious. "What did you say your name was?"

"Look," I say, "both ships sank. The *Bliksem* and the *Sentinel*. The surviving crew are stuck on an island."

"There are no islands on our charts, *Miss Harper*." The man goes cold, saying my name like it's bile in his mouth. Whatever Jackson told them in his first call must have framed me by name as the eco-terrorist responsible. They no doubt claimed to have subdued me as well.

The phone is yanked out of my hand. Jakob puts it to his ear. "This is Jakob Olavson, captain of the *Bliksem*. To whom am *I* speaking?"

He listens for a moment, beard twitching as he grinds his teeth. "Yes," he says. "Hull identification number?" He sounds incredulous but then rattles off a twelve-digit code starting with three letters. He listens for a moment, face turning red, and then says, "Jane Harper did no such thing. No."

And I have proof, I think, remembering the video. I throw open the destroyed life raft and quickly locate the now-ruined video camera. I eject the memory card and hold it up victoriously. "I have proof!"

Jakob pulls the phone away from his ear. "They want to know where we are."

Chase offers his hand. Jakob hands him the phone. Chase puts the phone to his ear and switches to his official-sounding first-mate voice. "*Odin*, this is Greg Chase, first mate of the *Sentinel*. Please confirm you are at last known location of the *Bliksem*." He listens. "Okay, about a mile north of your position is an island—" I hear the squawk of a voice interrupt him. "I know it's not on the charts. You'll see it as a peninsula. It was connected to the mainland by an ice bridge that has melted. Right. No, listen…"

Chase takes the phone away from his ear and pushes a button. For a moment, I think he's hung up on the man and tightness grips my chest.

"Can you hear me?" Chase asks.

"Yes," the man replies, now on speakerphone.

Chase hits a few more buttons on the phone and the reads off a series of coordinates to the man.

"Okay," the *Odin* crewman says. "Okay, we have you. We're underway."

"Copy that," Chase says. "What is your estimated time of arrival?"

"Uh, one hour. The sea is getting rough."

"Hold on," Chase says to the man. He turns to Willem and me. "Is the south shore clear now?"

"Yeah," I say. "Last time we saw it, there weren't any walruses. The polar bear is dead."

"Did she say polar bear?" the crewman says. I have forgotten the speakerphone is on.

"There was a polar bear on the island," Chase says. "It's not a problem now. The south shore between the island and the mainland is the safest place to land a small boat. It's a sandy beach with no rocks. The rest of the island is much more dangerous."

"South shore," the crewman says. "Copy that. How many survivors should we prepare for?"

Chase looks at the group. He doesn't need to count, he just doesn't want to give the number. "Four," he finally says.

"*Four?*" The man sounds stunned.

"There were more than sixty lost," Chase says. "Most at sea. Some on the island."

The crewman clears his throat, regaining his composure. "I see…"

"The men you send to pick us up," I say, "make sure they're armed."

"*Armed?*"

My voice coupled with the request for an armed pickup has the man on edge again.

"We…have hidden from the polar bear," I say. "But it's still here. And dangerous." It's a lie, but the truth might make them think the whole thing is a prank.

"Thanks for the warning," the man says. "Is there anything else?"

"Just hurry," Chase says.

"Copy that. We're on our way."

"See you in an hour." Chase hangs up the phone. His eyes glow with excitement as he looks at the three of us. "Our plan stays the same."

"Shouldn't we just run for the coast?" Willem asks.

"We'd get there too soon and would be defenseless with our backs to the ocean," Chase says. His voice is followed by the sound of metal being dragged over stone.

They're coming.

"We stick to the plan," Chase says. "Get them all here. Make a run for the gorge. Blow it and bury them. And then we'll follow the west coast down to the south beach."

I've been down the west coast of the island several times now and feel confident we can make decent time, especially without having to worry about the polar bear. "Let's do it," I say, picking up my gun.

As the others reach for their weapons, a shadow cuts across the floor of the ruins. A shadow…from above.

37

The four of us dive away from the middle of the ruins like a grenade has fallen there. Of course, that isn't far from the truth. The last remaining Draugr dog lands but is far from graceful. With one of its legs already ruined, it takes all the weight from its upper body on its single forelimb. With a crack, the leg breaks and the dog falls forward. But the thing isn't fazed by the injury. With its ass in the air, the Draugr dog runs with its back legs, pushing its body around in circles, biting at everything around it.

The thing comes around toward me, and I jump over its head. If the dog could leap, or even turn quickly, it might have gotten a bite, but it's stuck in a counterclockwise spin. I could probably shoot it, but it's moving fast and wouldn't be an easy target. I'm about to suggest someone with a blunt object put the thing out of its misery when Willem steps forward and swings a well-timed strike. The sword blade separates head from torso.

Momentum and perhaps the dog's nervous system keep the body running and spinning for two more laps. As it spins, white blood oozes from the body and head. Then the body falls limp next to the head and I get a good look at the blood.

It's not blood.

It's a pool of white, larvaelike parasites. And they're on the move, squirming toward the four of us, slowly but surely.

"They're outsmarting us again!" I shout. "They *wanted* us to kill the dog!"

My assessment is greeted by three frowns.

"Get anything flammable you can find and throw it on top of them!" Chase shouts. He digs into his survival pack and pulls out a flare. Understanding the plan, we toss useless supplies, wrappers, space blankets, and anything else that might burn atop the spreading army of parasites. The dried-out dog will burn best, but the rest should help the flames spread.

Chase takes the plastic cap off the flare and then strikes the ignition surface against its rough end. The flare works a lot like an oversized match, and like a match, doesn't take on the first try. Chase quickly strikes the flare against the sandpaper-like cap again and it catches. Red flame blooms from the end. Instead of throwing the flare down, Chase eases forward, squishing a few parasites, and places the flare on a patch of fluffy fur still attached to the dog's side.

The hair bursts into flame so bright it makes me squint. The fire quickly spreads out to the rest of the carcass and then to the human detritus we've spread around it.

The heat and smell of burning hair and melting plastic pushes us to the walls, which might have also been the purpose of the Draugr version of Monty Python's cow catapult. As though to prove me right, the wall shakes from an impact. A stone falls and nearly strikes my head.

A gloved hand reaches over and nearly catches my hood, but I duck down beneath it. I recognize the hand as the dog-master's.

"Raven!" Jakob shouts, and I think *where*? But when I turn to the man, I see he's speaking to me. Talk about an unfortunate nickname. He holds up the blacksmith hammer. "Take it!"

He tosses the hammer to me, and I catch it by the handle. The hammer's head is a little smaller than a modern sledgehammer, and the handle is about the size of the average nail hammer. That means it's heavy as hell, but I can hold it in one hand, which I do. I put my whole body into the swing and crush the dog-master's hand. The bone-crunching impact must register with some small part of the Draugr's mind as a bad thing, because he quickly withdraws his hand.

Or he's changing strategies now that they're all around us. Through swirling smoke I see a thin shadow moving beyond the wall to my left where Chase crouches. He's quickly packing up the C4, detonators, and sat-phone. *Good thinking.* Willem stands to my right. Beyond his wall is the clinking of metal tools. The black-smith. And behind the wall opposite me, where Jakob repeatedly yanks the Zodiac's start cord, I see two large horns. They seem to be rising up in the air, but I realize they're just getting closer.

Torstein is coming. And he'll be tall enough to look over the top.

A shift of light to my left tears my eyes away from the approach-ing Viking. The shadow flickering between the gaps in the wall by Chase is moving.

Up.

Whatever this is, it must be the Draugr that entered the ruins earlier and destroyed the life raft.

"Chase!" I shout as the thing rises up above him. The Draugr leaps to the top of the wall and nearly loses its balance on a loose stone. But it rights itself and looks down at Chase. Despite being severely disfigured by time and dehydration, I can still tell that this was once a boy. Maybe a young teenager. He's dressed in furs, like the others, but has a thick black belt around his waist and a single tool hanging from it. A hammer. *The blacksmith's apprentice,* I realize.

The apprentice steps to the side, where the stone wall is stronger. His body tenses as his eyes watch Chase's feeble attempt to scramble away. He looks like a cat about to pounce.

I draw my arm back and throw the blacksmith's hammer with all the strength I can muster. I feel the *tink, tink, tink* of muscles pulling in my arm. But my throw is good, though slightly off target. I had hoped to strike the undead teen in the head, but the weight of the hammer pulls it down prematurely and strikes the boy in the center of his chest. The impact knocks him back. His feet slip out, and when he falls, his legs catch the wall and spin him ass over tea kettle. I can't see the entire fall, but I imagine it's the kind of unceremonious and embarrassing spill that, if videotaped, would end up on YouTube and *Tosh.0*. What sucks is that when the boy falls, the hammer, which I see is actually embedded in his chest, goes with him.

Two rumbles fill the ruins at once. The first is the Zodiac engine as it roars to life. The spinning propeller is a wonderful thing to see. The second rumble is the top half of the wall behind Jakob crumbling down.

Jakob hobbles away from the falling wall, but a few of the stones catch his foot. His injured foot. He shouts in pain but manages to stay on his feet. Willem catches his father and helps him stay up.

The wall behind them crumbles under a fresh blow from Torstein's giant, double-bladed ax. He's exposed from the waist up. This close up I can see his braided blond beard and hair. His eyes are large and white, twitching with movement. The parasites are watching us. The Viking giant still retains a lot of his muscle, which makes him stronger than the others.

Is that why the wall is crumbling beneath his blows and not the others? I wonder. *Or do they want our attention on him?*

Before I can voice my concern, Willem snatches the boat engine from his father, hoists the spinning propeller up in front of him, twists the throttle, and charges Torstein. The big Draugr swings his ax at Willem, but the blow is blocked by the wall, which crumbles some more.

Willem climbs up the spilled stones and shoves the propeller at Torstein's chest. The blades bite flesh with a wet grinding sound. Bits and pieces of partially decayed skin and bone spray out like Fourth of July fireworks.

But Torstein is undaunted by the attack. He raises the ax over his head. If he brings it down, he might well split Willem in half.

Willem shoves hard, burying the propeller blade deep into Torstein's chest. *Is he trying to reach Torstein's spine?* I think. If he is, the attempt fails when the blade catches on something it can't chew through. And when the blade stops spinning, the engine starts spinning. The sudden twist of the engine throws Willem to the floor just as Torstein brings the blade down. Luck saves Willem twice in the span of a few seconds.

As the engine spins, its weight and momentum throws Torstein off balance, and the giant stumbles back for a moment, taking the engine with him.

We'd do a lot better if we didn't keep handing them our weapons!
"We need to get out of here!" I shout.

"We're still surrounded," Chase replies.

"Which way is north?" I ask. I'm so turned around I can't tell.

I scan the walls. Torstein battles to remove the engine on one end. A moving shadow to my left reveals the boy is recovering. The wall to my right shakes from repeated strikes where the blacksmith attempts to break through. And the wall behind me—

Chase points to the wall, eyes wide with fright. "That way," he says. "North is that way."

The dog-master pulls himself nearly to the top of the wall behind me. Torstein *was* distracting us.

"Willem!" I shout. "The sword!"

Willem pulls the sword out from his belt and moves to strike the dog-master.

"No!" I shout. "There's a better way!" I reach out for the sword. Willem looks doubtful for a moment but then hands the weapon over. I move to the fire at the center of the ruins. The flames have dulled, though the stench has not. An occasional pop and sizzle marks the death of another parasite. But I'm not interested in any of that.

I shove the tip of the blade into the still-burning dog's eye socket. I lift the head up, take aim, and fling the thing. It sails through the air like Greek fire from a catapult and strikes the dog-master's shoulder. It's a glancing blow, but it's enough. The copious amount of furs the dog-master wears burst into flames. The heat forces us all back a few steps, but then the undead bonfire falls back off the wall and the heat is hidden behind the stones.

Given the intensity of the flames, I'm sure the dog-master is done for. The path north is clear.

"Time to go," I say.

"Willem," Jakob says, limping toward his son. "Leave me here."

"What?" Willem looks horrified. "Never."

"I can barely walk," Jakob says. "You won't make it with me."

For a moment, Willem looks like he might actually be considering it. I sense there's some kind of macho Viking "Let me die in battle" bullshit happening here and put a stop to it before it can go any further.

"The hell is wrong with you two?" I say. "Willem, pick your fucking father up and carry him." I turn to Chase. "Think you can set the explosives?"

"No problem," he says.

"Just wait to set the timer," I say.

Chase salutes.

"I'll cover our rear," I say.

Willem looks about ready to argue, but I cut him off. "You have your father. Chase has the explosives." I brandish the sword and gun. "And I've got the weapons. Now help me push."

I turn to the north-facing wall and push against it. It shifts a little, but not enough. Chase throws himself against the wall. Then Willem. Even Jakob, standing on one leg, puts his weight into it. The wall tilts away from us and then spills over, covering the smoldering dog-master with a thousand pounds of stone.

The other walls are weakened by the sudden crumbling and begin to fall inward. Before being crushed, Chase leads the charge out over the dog-master's corpse. Willem throws his father over his shoulder and follows. I leave the ruins just as the walls collapse, and three sets of white eyes turn toward me. Seeing the three of them, out in the open like this, is terrifying. But perhaps even more frightening is the fact that the Raven is nowhere to be seen.

A problem for another time, I think, and then leap off the crumbled wall and hit the ground running.

38

Halfway to the gorge, I glance over my shoulder and see brown teeth stretching out toward me. The apprentice is quick! But there's something different about him, something that keeps me from panicking at his proximity. He's smaller than the others, but that's not it. Nor is it the fact that he's not brandishing a weapon of some sort.

Then I see it. It's his mouth. His stretched-back skin and open maw give me a view of his mouth that only a dentist could love. And what I see is a normal-looking tongue. Well, as normal as it could after being preserved by clear slime for six hundred years. Unlike the others, the apprentice's tongue has no white dots. The parasites controlling him aren't trying to infect me.

They're trying to eat me.

And while that *should* disturb me, being eaten alive would be a far better fate than becoming a Draugr. Not only would I be under the control of parasites and potentially attack and kill people, but I'd also have to spend the rest of my eternal life with this rank-ass Viking zombie horde.

The apprentice's teeth clack together as he takes a bite and finds only empty space. I take a wild swing with the sword and have the same crappy luck as the Draugr. Running and fighting at the same time is hard, and for fifty feet we repeat the dance of missed bites and sword swings.

As my shoulder starts to burn from the previous day's furious rowing and today's repetitive swinging, and I start to feel rather stupid, I change things up. Instead of swinging after he bites, I let him take three bites in a row. Each is closer then the last, but I want him in close, and I want to find his rhythm. By the fifth bite, I've got the timing down; he takes a chomp every three steps.

On his sixth attempt, I swing with the sword and make contact. The impact shudders up my arm, and I nearly lose my grip on the sword. When I can't pull the blade back, I realize it's snagged on something. I look back and see it wedged in the apprentice's face. With a twist, I yank the blade free and get a good look at the damage. I've severed his lower jaw, and tongue, clean off. If my strike had been harder, I might have taken off his head. On the plus side, he won't be eating anyone soon.

But that doesn't mean he can't still take me down and hold me until pappy blacksmith arrives. The big Draugr's jangling tool belt is loud as he charges toward me, just twenty feet back. Torstein brings up the rear. He's moving fast but not nearly fast enough. That sounds wrong, but I want these three together in the gorge.

Of course, I don't want them this close to me either, or I get buried along with them. I need to do something to slow them down.

I still have just one round left in the gun, but I'm holding the gun in my left hand and I'm running. So odds are I'll miss. I could probably hack the legs off the apprentice, but then he wouldn't get buried. Inspiration comes from Chase's story of how he tripped the blacksmith.

With the apprentice still hot on my heels, and making the occasional lunge forward like he's still got a lower jaw, I veer to the side and slow myself just enough so that he pulls up beside me. He bites at open air again—I swear he's the dumbest of the Draugar, which might actually be because he was a boy rather than an experienced hunter when they took his mind. When he realizes I'm next to him instead of in front of him, he begins to close the gap.

When I strike, I'm sure there are a thousand little parasite minds in his body all thinking, "What the fuck just happened!" I take the sword and poke it between his legs. When he takes his next step, both legs strike the flat side of the hard metal, and the undead kid launches forward. One more clumsy fall for the zombie YouTube sensation. *If only I had Peach's camera.*

The trouble is, when the apprentice's legs lock onto the sword, it's yanked from my hands and sent spinning back toward the blacksmith. No time to go back for it. But the same motion that took my sword also frees the hammer embedded in the apprentice's chest. I stop for the briefest of moments, snag the hammer, and start my sprint again.

To my delight, the blacksmith stumbles over his apprentice and slows. I can picture the scene, had the man still been living. He'd curse the boy loudly, maybe even strike him, and no doubt work him hard for weeks. But now he just stumbles and moves forward without so much as a stern look. My imagining reminds me that these were once people. And maybe their consciousnesses are still alive in there somewhere. These men once fought hard to wipe this plague from the face of the Earth. They sacrificed so much, killing friends and family and chasing the Raven to this godforsaken place, only to become the thing they hated most.

I'll do my best to kill you all, I think. Then I'm at the gorge. Willem is far ahead. He disappears around a bend. Chase is nowhere in sight.

A quick look back reveals the blacksmith closing in. The apprentice is right behind him. Torstein has closed the gap a bit, but he's still not part of the group.

Another quick sprint brings me to a bend where I'll lose sight of the Draugar. The blacksmith and apprentice enter the gorge, undeterred. But Torstein stops at the entrance. I can feel him looking at me, his perpetual grin mocking me like he's got everything all figured out.

"C'mon!" I yell at him, feeling a little like Arnold Schwarzenegger in *Predator*. "Come get me!"

But the giant won't budge, and his friends close the distance. I round the corner, see Chase in the distance, and start counting how long it takes me to bridge the gap.

Twenty-seven seconds as I reach his side. Willem and Jakob wait for us farther down the path. Jakob stands on one foot. Willem stretches his back.

"Twenty-seven seconds!" I say quickly, out of breath.

"What?" Chase says.

"The timers! Set them for twenty-seven—"

"Oh!" he says. "Good thinking."

"Start them when they come around the corn—"

Here they come. They're screwing up the timing. "Go!" I shout.

"I'm trying! Go ahead!" Chase is working the small timer quickly. This is the first time he's looked at it, and it takes him a few seconds to figure out. When it looks like he's got it, I take his advice and run for it. It feels strange leaving Chase behind. I'm used to it being the other way around.

"All set!" he shouts from behind me, but the C4 is going to explode about ten seconds too late. Maybe some shrapnel will get them.

Up ahead, Willem and Jakob take cover behind a five-foot-thick outcrop of stone. It should protect us from the blast, assuming we don't collapse the entire gorge.

As I slide to a stop next to Willem, Chase is still fifty feet back, and he's not running very fast. Then I see why. He's setting a second timer. Holy shit. And a third!

"Chase," I say, my voice full of concern.

The Draugar pass the first explosive. Ten seconds remain on the timer.

Chase lobs one brick of C4 and then the other.

Then he runs like the roadrunner on speed. He's nearly reached our hiding spot when the first explosion tears through the gorge.

And then through Chase's body.

hase's scream lasts just a fraction of a second before he's past us and either dead or unconscious. That I actually heard him over the explosion is a testament to the power of his lungs. I don't know if he survived the blast, but I do know that he won't survive the next two. A cloud of gray dust billows past, fouling the air and concealing Chase's body. I cover my mouth with my arm and search for Chase. He lays in a heap, just ten feet away, but fully exposed.

Without looking to see if the first explosion did its job, I lunge for Chase's limp body.

"Jane!" Willem shouts. "Don't!"

But I can't just leave Chase there, not when he finally switched his wiring over from flight to fight. I grab the first part of his body I reach—his left foot—and drag him toward shelter. Halfway there, Willem takes his other leg, and together we heave him behind the outcrop just as the chasm turns to hell.

The first explosion was bad enough. It felt like a punch to the gut, made my ears ring and choked the air with dust. The second, and then third, are much closer. The sound, contained and ampli-fied within the gorge, drops me to my knees. The impact, even hidden behind the thick wall of stone, is like a sledgehammer to the back of my head, knocking me flat on my back. And the air, hot, fast, and full of tiny stone particles, does nothing to replenish the oxygen sucked from my lungs. All this happens in a single second.

For several more seconds after the explosion, I lay unconscious. I have no idea how long. All I know is that I'm shaken awake.

Chase leans over me. His glasses are missing. Blood streaks down his face. But he's alive. I smile up at him, happy to see him alive. And the little prick goes and lays a kiss on me.

I push him away, and he says, "Sorry, I'm just glad to see you alive."

I push myself up, and the world spins around me. I wave my hand in front of my face in a feeble attempt to clear the dust away. When that doesn't work, I lift the inside of my cloak up and breathe through the fabric. "Are you okay?" I ask. "We thought you were dead."

"So did I," Chase says. He rubs the blood from his forehead. "I think I caught a rock to the head. Maybe a few on my body, too, but it will hurt worse tomorrow than it does today."

As my head clears, I hear a groan beside me.

My vision only spins a little as I turn toward the sound. Willem sits up, rubbing his ears, which appear to be bleeding some. Jakob lies motionless next to him. Willem shakes his father's leg. "Father. Father!"

Jakob stirs. He blinks his eyes wide a few times. And then he begins to laugh. It's the kind of, "Holy shit, we just blew something up" laugh familiar to teenage boys, and apparently Vikings. What's amazing is that it's catchy. Dazed, injured, and beaten, the four of us laugh like drunken sailors.

As my humor fades, I push myself up and peek around the stone barrier that saved our lives. The destruction is profound. The gorge no longer exists. Both sides have collapsed, bridging two of the steep hills with a thirty-foot-tall stack of boulders.

The others fall silent as they step out of hiding, view our handi-work, and perhaps contemplate just how close we came to blowing ourselves to bits.

Chase points to the ground at our feet. The blacksmith's head lays there, hairless and smoldering. Its jaws lay open, like it's laughing, and its wide white eyes stare at the sky. Seeing the once-horrible monster without its body, frozen in such a humorous pose, bring my giggles back. I try to keep it in, but when Willem cracks too, we all begin laughing again. Maybe it's the absurdity of everything we've seen. Maybe we're just all happy to be alive. I'm not really sure why we're laughing. It just feels right.

That is, until two horns appear at the top of the thirty-foot pile of freshly toppled stone. The horns rise up, revealing first helmet, then head, and then towering body. Torstein survived the blast. In fact, he looks like he avoided it all together, and I doubt the sound, shockwave, or air-sucking power had any effect on his body.

"Give me a brick of C4!" I shout.

Chase spins around, looking for the backpack. For a moment I fear it's been buried, but then he spots it beneath some rubble, rips it open, and begins assembling a bomb.

As he works, Willem, Jakob, and I stare up at Torstein. He doesn't move; he just stares right back at us, holding that ax over his shoulder like it's just another day at the Viking office.

"Okay," Chase says. "Okay! You set the timer."

He hands the brick of C4 to me. As I try to gauge how long it will take the C4 to cover the distance between me and Torstein, I see movement and glance up.

Torstein cocks his head to the side like he's listening to some-thing. Then, without a second glance back at us, he turns and bounds down the far side of the rock pile, out of view. And out of range. *Does he understand what I was trying to do? Or is there another reason he's leaving? Another plan at work?*

Then it hits me.

The Raven.

The boat.

They've been trapped on this island for six hundred years. The caves aren't the only thing they're eager to leave behind. If they can reach the boat before us, they might make it to the mainland. And then...I don't want to even think about what kind of plague would be unleashed. Greenland would quickly become hell on Earth. The nation-cleansing act of Torstein and his band of zombie killers would have to be repeated but on a much grander scale. While Torstein might have had to kill a few thousand Greenlanders, there were now sixty thousand. And when winter arrives and the Arctic ice links Greenland to Canada, Alaska, and Siberia, the plague would spread worldwide. Yet another reason to go to the Bahamas. Islands, and Australia, would be the only safe places on Earth. I suppose Antarctica would be safe too, but my new policy regarding polar environments rules that out.

"They're going to beat us to the boat," I say.

"How could they know about boats?" Chase says.

"The Vikings were a seafaring culture," Willem says. "They knew everything about boats."

I shake my head, frustration mounting. "So let's call the *Odin* and have them pick us up on this side of the island, rocks be damned. I'll swim out to them if I have to."

Chase takes the sat-phone from Jackson's backpack and frowns. He pushes a few buttons on the phone and then hands it to me. The front face is cracked, and while the power light is on, there's no response when I push any of the buttons. It's the south shore or nothing.

"We need to hurry," Jakob says.

Willem bends down to Jakob. "Father…"

"Sorry, son," the old captain says as he leans over his son's shoulder and is hoisted into the air.

Willem grunts from the effort. "C'mon," he says, leading the way. "I can't carry this old sack of shit all day."

Jakob grins until Willem takes off toward the northern coast.

We follow the familiar coastline around the island as quick as we can. I take the lead, ready with handgun and hammer, though both weapons seem feeble compared to Torstein's giant ax. At least Chase is ready with the C4. Two bricks remain, and both are good to go once the timers are set.

When the terrain is level, Willem and Chase both support Jakob's weight. When the path is rough, Willem takes his father's burden on his own shoulders. Halfway there, the effort starts to take its toll on Willem. His face is red, his hair is soaked with sweat, and his breathing sounds wheezy.

After reaching the top of a short climb along the island's west coast, Willem puts his father down. I recognize the place. We're close to the first Viking body. Head between his legs, Willem apologizes and says, "Two minutes. Just need to catch my breath."

Not one of us understands how hard it must be to carry his father's bulk. I doubt Chase or I could carry the man one hundred yards without collapsing. Even though Willem is quick and strong, I doubt even he could make it if not fueled by concern for his father's well-being.

Unfortunately, Willem chose the wrong time to take a break.

Torstein's body blocks out the sun as he pulls himself up over a tall spire of stone and lands in front of us. But he doesn't attack. The giant Viking just stands his ground, holding his ax like it's a gate.

"You want a shrubbery or something?" I say to him.

"Python," Chase says with a snicker.

Are we all so brazen now that our first reaction to a living dead monster is to quote movies at it?

"Chase," I say, holding out my hand to him.

He knows exactly what I want and reaches into the backpack for some C4. When he places the brick in my hand, my fingers lose their strength. Not because the C4 is heavy but because I'm terrified. There's something behind Torstein. Something black. And it sucks away my bravery like the apprentice wanted to suck away my blood.

The C4 falls from my hand and tumbles away. I don't even turn to look for it. I can't. The thing sliding out from behind Torstein has my undivided attention.

The Raven is here.

40

A gust of frigid wind carried in by the ocean sweeps past. The black form comes to life, twisting and shifting in the breeze with a dry scratching sound. *Feathers*, I think. *It actually has black feathers.*

This can't really be an oversized bird, I tell myself. Wouldn't it just fly off the island? Of course, it looks like it could be about the size of an ostrich, sans the long legs and long neck.

Then, in a snap of motion, the thing turns its head toward me. Dead black eyes stare at me. A long, sharp beak points directly at my face. It twists its head slowly to one side.

Why is it just looking at me? I think and then wonder if it's because I'm holding the weapons. The truth, however, is far worse than that.

"Jane?" it says.

I stagger back. Not only can this thing talk, but it also knows my fucking name? With that one word, the Raven makes me powerless. I doubt I'll even defend myself if it decides to attack.

But it doesn't.

It slowly moves around Torstein until it's standing directly in front of him, just ten feet away from me. "Jane, you don't need to be afraid."

The hell I don't.

When it speaks this time, I notice that the beak isn't opening and closing. In fact, I can see the whole thing more clearly now. The beak and eyes aren't real. It's a mask. And the feathers aren't part of its body; it's a cloak, like mine, but covered in thousands of actual raven feathers.

"Who are you?" Willem asks. He still looks exhausted, but he's caught his breath. While my repulsion has made me fearful, his now fuels a growing rage.

The beaked head snaps toward Willem. The thing looks him up and down but doesn't speak. It turns back to me and says, "Jane—"

"Stop saying my name," I grumble. Willem's anger helps me turn the tables on my fear.

"Perhaps I should call you Raven?" it asks. "That's what they called me, too, before…" Two arms rise up, like wings, but I can see black-gloved hands on either side. They're just sleeves, I tell myself. "…I became this."

The voice sound familiar somehow, but off just enough that I can't peg where I know it from. Is it really possible that I've met whomever this is before?

Looks like I'm about to find out. The Raven's hands reach around to the mask. After untying two black cords, the mask comes loose and slides away. The face that's revealed shocks me and everyone else.

"What the fuck?" Chase says. "Jenny?"

The voice clicks. It's Jenny's, but it's off. Same voice box, different—

Oh my God.

I saw Jenny's body. But not her head.

I nearly throw up, but anger keeps it down. "It's not Jenny."

"She's right there," Chase yells, thrusting a rigid hand toward the Raven.

"It's not her," I say, sounding ill. "It just has her head."

The Raven smiles Jenny's familiar grin. "Jenny is here, Raven. Her mind. Her memory. It's how I know about you." She turns to Chase. "And you, Chase." She turns to Willem and Jakob. "And you as well. It's how I speak your language. And how I know about the world outside this prison."

She nearly spits the word *prison*. I was right; she wants off this island in a bad way. But is she really a she?

"Who are you?" I ask. "Really?"

"I am many parts," she says. "Before being driven to this place, before taking this face, I was a woman. You would call me a Norse woman. They called me a witch."

"I can't imagine why," I say. I'm not sure the thing can understand sarcasm, but then it smiles. It not only understands, but it also doesn't mind the jab. It's beyond the kind of emotional taunting that would upset most people, like a hard mental nipple twist.

"My parents called me Áshildr," she says.

Upon hearing the name, Torstein looks down at the Raven. It's the first sign that the big Viking is even listening.

Willem reacts to the name, too. "Áshildr! The last record of Greenland before they were wiped out came from a ship that reported the capture of a witch."

The Raven actually looks a little surprised. "You know of me?"

"When I studied the disappearances of the Greenlanders, I came across the account of your capture. You were to be burned at the stake. But that's not why I remember your name."

Raven-Jenny looks distraught for a brief moment and then cuts off Willem's explanation, her voice carrying just a trace of emotion for the first time. "I was sixteen but had the heart of a much younger girl. One day while out exploring, I came across a vessel.

Like an urn, perhaps the size of an oil drum. When I touched it, it opened. I remember waking up, lying on the wet grass, staring at the blue sky above. The vessel stood open and empty. Despite being alone, I heard a voice. It spoke to me kindly. And it made me a bargain. In exchange for eternal life, I would hide their Queen inside my body. I did not know at the time that my body already belonged to them, but for the Queen to take root, the host has to be willing. My consciousness merged with the Queen's, and we began the glorious work of giving birth to her children—"

"You mean those maggots?" Chase says.

"That is how they appear to you," Jenny-Raven says. "But they are so much more. Together, they can communicate and think on a level beyond that of humans. The more there are, the smarter they become. It's like an effing hive mind."

That last sentence sounds so much like Jenny it turns my stomach. It seems that while the Raven now speaks English, it speaks *Jenny's* brand of English.

"Where are you from?" I ask.

Jenny smiles. "All of your questions will be answered, Raven." She takes a step toward me. "Had the body of Áshildr not been imprisoned in this place, she could have lived forever. But her— my—consciousness still resides as part of the whole, her body has been ruined, despite our best efforts to repair it."

The Raven sounds confused. There's a little Queen maggot in there, some Áshildr, and even some Jenny now, not to mention a collective consciousness from thousands of parasitic creatures. And what are they? Some plague wiped out and hidden on Greenland by humanity long before the Vikings? Are they alien? I suppose it doesn't really matter where they're from. They can be stopped, and now we know how: the Queen. Torstein must have figured this out, too. Otherwise, why chase the Raven all the way up here? The question is, why did he bury her instead of destroying her?

The Raven takes hold of her feathered cloak and draws it open like a flasher. The body beneath staggers me. The core of the thing is a nearly petrified, naked sixteen-year-old girl. Much of her skin is missing and torn. Just beneath her skin is an army of parasites squirming around, coating surfaces with protective mucus. Her arms and legs, however, belong to a Caucasian man. I see a familiar tattoo on one of the legs. *She has Eagon's limbs!* The whole thing looks like it's bound together by the parasite secretions.

"This body cannot be sustained. So now the Queen makes her offer again." She reaches out to me. "You have shown yourself to be strong, resourceful, and intelligent. Eternal life in exchange for your servitude. Your mind will remain. Your body, yours to control. Your intellect, expanded."

"My thirst for blood and brains, unquenchable," I say.

Jenny makes a humor-filled expression I've seen several times before, and her voice takes over again. "It's an acquired taste. You'll get used to it. Vampirism is hip. So are zombies. Win-win. Do you accept?"

Hell fucking no, I think, but I can't say that. I'm pretty sure that if I do, Torstein will descend on us like a grizzly bear that just woke up during a prostate exam.

"You'll let them live?" I ask.

"We will all escape together," Jenny says.

"But not him?" I say, pointing to Torstein. "He stays here?"

Emotion takes hold of the monster again. "He can rot here for the next six hundred years."

Torstein looks down at the Raven again. *What's he thinking? Can he think?*

I step toward the Raven, reaching out with my empty left hand.

"Jane," Willem warns.

"It's the only way," I say.

"Jane, don't," Chase says.

Jakob joins the chorus of worried male voices. "Raven…"

The Queen parasite-controlled Draugrstein's monster reaches out for me with Eagon's hand. "Raven," she says. "It will be your name for all eternity." Her hand snaps out like a striking snake and wraps around my wrist, squeezing until I scream in pain.

41

Raven-Jenny yanks me toward her, arms open to embrace me. I'm about to fall into her arms, which I think would be a very bad life choice. I lean back and fight, but the pain in my left wrist is intense. I think I can actually feel broken bones grinding. Before I black out from the pain, I give in to the pull and launch forward. But the move is intentional. The Raven kept her nasty surprise hidden beneath her cloak. So did I.

The hammer swings high over my head. I put all my weight and momentum into the strike. The dense metal hammer head shatters the Raven's wrist. The grip on my wrist disappears as—I'm not entirely sure what to call her: Jenny, Raven, Áshildr, Muninn— screams in pain.

She can feel pain, I realize. *She's really not like the other Draugar.*

I move to press the attack, but my upper hand is short-lived.

"Jane!" Willem shouts. "Look out!"

When I hear the loud whoosh behind me, I know it's already too late. There's no avoiding what's coming. Torstein is too close and too good with that ax. Ironically, it's Muninn who saves me, shouting, "Don't kill her!"

Rather than lopping my head off, Torstein twists the ax and strikes me with the large flat of the blade. It's not a killing blow, but the impact sends me rolling down a short hill. I come to a stop at a pile of stones.

"Jane!" Willem shouts. He's out of sight. On the other side of this stone ridge.

"I'm okay!" I call back.

But I'm not really, because Torstein is blocking the way, and Muninn is coming down the slope toward me.

"I thought I had to be willing?" I ask. I struggle to stand, using my one good hand to push myself up. When I breathe, my back throbs with pain where Torstein's ax blade struck slightly off center. I might have a few broken ribs, but that's a lot better than a broken spine.

"For a permanent bonding, yes," Muninn says. "But you will last until I find a willing host. You don't think it will be hard for me to find someone interested in eternal life, do you?"

Great, I think, *not only does she understand sarcasm, she uses it, too*. I think about her question. Death terrifies people. But vampires are so en vogue right now that there are probably a bevy of teen girls, or boys, for that matter—the Queen might not have a gender preference—that would jump at the chance to be a bloodsucking member of the living dead.

I get my feet under me and stand. I let her see that I've still got the hammer and she slows. She might be stronger than me, and I can't let her get too close, but this is a fight I could potentially win.

Muninn stops. "Father," she says.

Father? What the hell? And then Torstein turns toward her.

Torstein is Áshildr's father?

The ramifications of this strike me hard. Torstein didn't just imprison the plague-carrier in this place; he entombed his own daughter. That must be why he didn't just kill her. Despite the fact that she wiped out the entire Norse population of Greenland, Torstein couldn't bring himself to slay his own daughter. I try to picture myself in his enormous boots, looking down at my sixteen-year-old daughter, who, unlike the rest of the plague victims, looks healthy and perhaps innocent. He would have loved her. Would have sacrificed for her. The way Jakob would for Willem. The way the Colonel would have for me. Good fathers can't imagine doing harm or allowing harm to come to their own children. But he couldn't let her leave either, so he trapped her here, and as punishment for his failures, he buried himself alongside her.

It's a tragic tale but ultimately a mistake. Torstein *should* have killed her. That would have been true mercy. Because whether he knew it or not, she was no longer his daughter. She was—she *is*—something else. Something less than, or perhaps more than, human.

She looks up into her father's white, parasite-filled eyes, and says, "Kill the others."

I suspect the command could have been given without speaking. It's how Muninn moved the Draugar like chess pieces, watching from a distance and outmaneuvering us. So her speaking the words aloud, in *English*, means they were for our benefit. To frighten us. *Bitch*.

Torstein turns away from us. I can't see Jakob, Willem, or Chase, but I know he's locked on to them. His body tenses, ready to strike. But before he can launch himself forward, a large rock strikes his face. There's a crack of breaking bone, but Torstein shows no reaction.

Chase suddenly appears at the top of the rise, another large stone raised above his head.

They're not going down without a fight, I think, feeling a bit of pride for the man Chase has become.

And then he goes and lets out a battle cry. *Stupid, stupid, stupid!* Torstein whips his head toward Chase and swings out with his ax.

The first strike is so fast and powerful that I don't think Chase is even aware that his hands have been lopped off at the wrist until the big rock drops on his head. Before shock even has a chance to set in, the ax returns and separates head from body. Chase's dead body falls to the ground and rolls down the stone decline toward me. It stops halfway, snagged on a rough patch of stone. A river of blood flows down the stone, oozing from his wrists and neck. My lips tremble as I stare down at Chase's body.

"I can make him stop," Muninn whispers.

I jump back with a scream. She's right next to me.

"Accept the Queen and the others can live."

I can't watch the others die, and I'm close to accepting the offer when Willem rushes up over the ridge. He's fueled by rage and tackles Torstein by the waist. It's a solid hit that any football player would be proud off, but it doesn't even stagger Torstein. The giant strikes Willem hard on the back with his boxing glove–size fist. Willem shouts in pain and drops to his knees.

But he's not done. A glint of silver reveals the knife in his hand. He swings high and stabs the knife into Torstein's gut. He follows the stab with a punch from his other hand, which disappears inside the giant's belly. He pulls his hand out again, shakes off the few parasites clinging to him, and strikes again with the knife, this time burying it in Torstein's chest.

It's a mortal blow. But Torstein is no longer mortal. Before Willem can withdraw the blade, Torstein takes Willem's wrist and yanks him off his feet. There's a wet pop that gets a horrible scream out of Willem before he passes out. I can see by the angle of his arm that his shoulder has been yanked from its socket.

Torstein raises the ax. The swing will cut Willem in half at the waist.

"No!" I shout. "Stop! I'll do it!"

Torstein pauses. I don't think he understands me, but my upstretched hand and pleading voice probably communicate my supplication. He looks to Muninn. She says nothing to him, but the giant doesn't swing.

Muninn steps closer to me, opening her raven feather cloak and revealing her hideous body. The parasites writhe madly, as though excited by anticipation. Will they be joining the Queen inside me? I see something large moving beneath the dry skin of Áshildr's chest.

"Drop your weapon," Muninn says.

I toss the hammer to the side. It strikes a stone, which rolls off the pile and reveals the skull we found when we first met Jakob and Alvin. That non-Draugr body is buried behind me. I lean back against the stones, instinct pushing me away from Muninn. Once again, the gun could solve this situation, but it's tucked into the left side of my pants and I don't think I can reach it with my right hand. Besides, that wouldn't kill the Queen, and it wouldn't stop Torstein. I've only got one option left available: Surrender and save my friends. I promised Willem that Jakob would make it off this island alive, and I keep my promises.

"No!" Jakob hobbles to the top of the rise. But he's not speaking to me or Muninn. He's talking to Torstein.

Jakob yells something in a language I don't understand, but it must be Old Norse. I hear "Torstein" and "Olav." The rest is gibberish. But the old Norseman's tone and body language say he's trying to give the Draugr an old-fashioned familial talking to.

Torstein's head twitches to the side.

Is he listening?

Muninn certainly is. She's not even looking at me. Instead, she's staring intensely at Torstein.

Be careful, Jakob…

"*Tillit!*" Jakob shouts, pointing at Willem. He shouts something else and pulls up his sleeve, revealing the raven tattoo that both he and Willem have. "*Tillit!*"

Look, I think.

And to my surprise, and Muninn's, the giant turns his head. First to Jakob's arm, then Willem's, and then to his own. The very same raven tattoo, though faded from time, has been branded into Torstein's skin. The raven. The family crest.

And then something occurs to me. The Raven—Muninn—was never meant to instill fear. It was a term of endearment, the way Jakob uses it with me. The Olavsons were, and are, proud of their heritage, of their family crest. Dressed in a cloak of raven feathers, the sixteen-year-old Áshildr might have looked stunning. A grand gift from a father in love with his daughter.

I shake my head at the tragedy of it all.

Muninn actually hisses at Torstein. Her Jenny-eyebrows furrow deeply. And Torstein finally reacts. He tosses Willem down the hill. His body bounces over Chase's corpse and slides the rest of the way to the bottom. Jakob charges his undead ancestor, but a backhand smack from Torstein sends him sprawling down the hill after his son.

He steps down the hill, ax on his shoulder. He rounds the unconscious forms of Jakob and Willem and stands behind Muninn. Her eyes are back on me now.

She's all malice and hatred. Even if I gave myself willingly, I don't think she would let Willem or Jakob live. In fact, the Queen—whatever it is—will probably get a kick out of torturing my psyche for all eternity. It's the kind of fate twisted, fundamentalist nut jobs dream up to scare people into believing in God. But this—*this* could actually happen.

I push away, sliding over the top of the burial mound. I fall back with a yelp and pull several of the stones with me. I scramble to my feet and see the Glock has fallen out of my pants. I scoop it up with my right hand and level it at Muninn's head.

She grins.

I hate being right. Shooting her in the head won't change anything, but it will make me feel better. At least until the Queen burrows her way inside my body.

Muninn takes a step toward me. More stones fall, drawing her eyes down. She gasps. I didn't think the thing was capable of being surprised, certainly not by a skeleton, but she looks horrified. It's the same face Jenny made when facing the polar bear. "*Mor,*" she says in a tone bordering on affection.

Torstein turns his head toward the body. The ax lowers to the ground.

What's happening?

I stand on my toes to see the corpse better. A skeletal arm dangles form the side. The jawless skull rests at the top. But the rest of the body is wrapped in a ragged red cloth that looks like it's held together by grime. But the most striking thing about the cloth is the raven symbol at its center. The Olavson family crest.

42

I'm not sure what's happening, but it seems profound. Both Muninn and Torstein seem to have forgotten me. Will they see me if I move? Can I escape? Is there time to try waking Jakob or Willem?

Before I have time to consider these things, Muninn whips her head back to me. Her eyes twitch. The thing is crazed and looks less like Jenny than ever. Then I see why. Her face is alive with movement. The parasites in her body are surging toward the surface. If she gets too close, I might find myself covered in the things. She opens her feathered cloak, opening the sides like two great wings. Her body roils with tiny bodies. The center of her chest pulses. Then a hole appears. A parasite head the size of a baseball slides out.

The Queen.

Like the others, she's got two black spots for eyes, each the size of a pencil eraser. Her mouth opens wide, revealing nail-like teeth. Clear mucus oozes from her jaws as they snap open and closed, ready to chew their way into my body. I'm not sure, but I think the mucus that covers everything, including the Queen's body, will keep me from bleeding out or dying from the injuries she'll deliver by burrowing through my insides.

"*Kona.*" The deep voice startles me.

Was that Torstein?

Muninn cranes her head around toward her father's undead body. She seems as surprised as I am to hear him speak.

"*Kona*," he says again, and then turns and looks at Muninn, or is he seeing Áshildr now? "*Datter.*"

His head lowers, white eyes on the ax in his hands. He shakes his head as though gripped by shame.

A shudder runs up Muninn's back, ruffling the feather cloak with a hiss. "*Far?*" Muninn says, but the voice isn't Jenny's. It's that of a sixteen-year-old girl, afraid and confused.

"*Forlate, Datter,*" Torstein says. His voice is scratchy and dry but carries an ancient heartache that nearly brings a sob from my mouth.

A second shudder runs up Muninn's back, and her seething anger returns. She hisses at Torstein, no doubt trying to regain control of his mind. But something in the man's posture has changed. He looks tired but resolved. Muninn gasps when the ax rises up above her. As the mighty weapon drops down like the blade of a guillotine, Muninn shrieks. I hear the girl, and Jenny, and a thousand little inhuman squeals.

The blade passes through Muninn's body and clangs when it strikes stone. Feathers part as the cloak splits down the middle. One half of Muninn's body falls atop the skeleton. Then the other. Small white parasites flee into the stones, but I don't think they'll survive long without a host.

Then I see her.

The Queen.

Her segmented, wormlike body is about a foot and a half long, like a white kielbasa with rubber bands squeezing it every inch or so. It wriggles into the stones.

"Oh no you don't," I say. I tuck the handgun into my waist and reach into the stones with my good hand. I feel her squishy, slick body and squeeze. The Queen twists and writhes like a worm about to be hooked. I grip the thing just below its head and tighten my grip.

This creature is clearly a form of sentient life. Whether from Earth or someplace beyond, I don't know. It would be the greatest scientific discovery of all time. Its ability to keep people alive might cure a thousand different ailments and save millions of lives.

Or it might kill every last person on the planet.

With a quick squeeze, I burst the fucking thing's head and throw it to the ground.

With Muninn and the Queen both dead, I remember Torstein. The big Viking stands motionless, staring down at what remains of his daughter's body and the skeleton beneath. The mighty ax rests at his feet. His fighting days are over.

I skirt around him and kneel beside Willem. He's alive, but his shoulder is still dislocated. I gently adjust the arm, pulling it out straight to line up the joint, and then I shove with all my strength.

Willem hollers in pain as he comes to. It sounds like the pain is sharp, but with the joint back in place, it seems to fade fast. He spins around, looking for danger. His last memory was of dangling in Torstein's grip. He sees the Viking standing next to us and pushes away.

"It's okay," I say. "It's over." I move to the side and let him see Muninn's body.

Willem looks from the two halves of the body to the ax. "Did he?"

"Some part of him remembers," I say. "Family is important to you Olavsons."

Understanding flashes on his face. "Áshildr the witch. Her last name was recorded as daughter of Torstein." He looks at the skeleton.

"Also an Olavson," I say. "The body is wrapped in red fabric. The raven crest is at the center. I think he recognized the body. So did Áshildr." Torstein's words come back to me. "Kona."

"What?" Willem looks surprised by the word.

"Kona," I repeat. "He said it when he saw the body. He called Áshildr datter. And before he…you know. He said, 'Forlate, Datter.' Do you know what it means?"

"Wife," he says. "She was his wife."

"You said the skeleton was a man," I say.

"I'm a history professor, not a CSI," he says, rubbing his shoulder.

"Torstein's sentinel told of six men in his party. We met them all. Why didn't he mention his wife?"

"Honestly?" he says. "Because she was a woman. Just the way things were back then." He looks up at the Viking. "Seems pretty clear that his feelings for her were powerful, though. And 'Forlate, Datter.' Forlate means 'forgive.' Datter is—"

"Daughter," I say, understanding. "He was asking her for forgiveness. Not for what he was about to do but for what he didn't do six hundred years ago."

"Willem," Jakob groans as he sits up. He seems totally disinterested in how things have resolved when he says, "How much time?"

Willem's eyes go wide. "I don't know."

I think they're talking about the boat and say, "I think they'll wait."

Willem stands but winces when he does. He pulls Jakob up onto his one good foot. The attempt to put Jakob over his shoulder is pitiful. His wounds are too severe.

"My wrist is broken," I say, holding up my left hand. "But I can take him on my right side if you can get him on the left."

Willem and Jakob both agree to the arrangement, and then we're moving. We're almost jogging when I say, "We need to slow down. I can't—"

"Here!" Willem shouts, then directs us to a large boulder. We set Jakob down behind the stone. Willem looks back to Torstein. We're at least a hundred yards away, but the man still looks huge. He stands like a statue, his horns rising high into the air, his braided hair and beard caught up by the wind. He's a legend in the flesh—zombie, vampire, Viking.

And then, he's nothing.

A fireball rips him to pieces and rises up into the air.

Willem grabs me and yanks me behind the stone as the boom and shockwave hits us. The impact is powerful but nothing compared to what we experienced in the gorge.

"What just happened?" I ask, searching my mind for some memory of an explosive being planted. Then I remember it. Willem. "You had C4 in your hand," I say. "When you punched him?"

Willem nods slow and sure, and when he does, I see a little bit of Torstein, son of Olav, in him. As much as I should fear the name, I realize that despite nearly killing all of us, Torstein is a hero. He cleansed Greenland of the plague and probably saved the rest of the world from exposure. His only mistake was loving his family. And in the end, it was that same love that gave him the strength to set things right, once and for all. I see that same strength in Willem and think the Olavson family line is worth preserving. With that in mind, I kiss Willem on the lips.

Jakob clears his throat. "Listen," he says. "Our ride approaches."

The high-pitched buzz and rhythmic *whump* of a boat engine tearing over ocean waves reaches my ears and brings a smile to my face. *It's time to get the hell off this island.*

43

I get that feeling again, like I'm a kid fleeing the basement. But it doesn't make sense. We're home free, making good time along the coast, and our ride is no doubt waiting for us at the south beach. I no longer hear the sound of the engine, so they've definitely stopped.

So what has my subconscious all riled up?

The Raven is dead, as is the Queen.

Torstein is dust in the wind, literally.

All of his original six-man party is accounted for: the blacksmith, the apprentice, the dog-master, bingo arms, the short fry, and Torstein himself. All five dogs are dead, too.

We pass the familiar spot where we found Jenny's body.

Jenny's now-missing body.

But it wasn't here when we came back for the C4, I realize. How I missed that then is beyond me. But it could have easily been the polar bear or the Raven or Torstein who took the body. Eagon's body disappeared, too. Maybe Draugar have a waste not, want not personality?

The beach is just ahead. I can hear the waves breaking. When we reach the five-foot drop to the beach, Willem goes down first. His shoulder feels better now, and he's able to help Jakob down. I sit on my ass and push myself over the edge, landing on my feet.

I should be running over the sand, looking for our ride, getting aid for Jakob. But I take my post under his shoulder, and the three of us start for the water. We're just fifteen feet from where the outcrop of island stone ends and we'll get a clear view of the beach and our salvation.

But before we get there, my thoughts turn toward that feeling again. It's probably paranoia, but I can't stop it.

Peach, I think. I don't remember seeing Peach's body. "What happened to Peach?" I ask.

"We threw her over the wall," Jakob says with a wince as his bad foot hits the sand. We're having trouble keeping him lifted up on the loose ground. "She was outside the ruins before you two returned. Why?"

"Nothing…" It's a lie, and he knows it and doesn't like it. But not even Jakob's disapproving eyes can distract me.

Eyes, I think, remembering Jackson's eyes. How the parasites moved inside his head and stared out at me. *I'll never sleep without Ambien*, I think. But Jackson died right before McAfee—

"Oh shit," I say. "McAfee!"

"What?" Willem says, stopping just a few steps from the main beach.

"McAfee is still running loose. We never killed him." I look at Jakob. "Did you?"

He shakes his head slowly, offering a solemn, "No."

"Stop!" The voice is different, and new, and very human. But it sounds angry and maybe afraid.

I slide out from under Jakob's arm and leave father and son behind as I charge out onto the beach.

I should be surprised by what I see. I should be terrified and fall back before running away. But I don't.

Instead, I charge toward the bloated form of McAfee as he lopes to the red Greenland Coast Guard Zodiac and three terrified-looking crewman. One of them has a 9 mm pistol aimed at McAfee's chest.

"Stop or I'll shoot!" The words are spoken with a thick accent but would have as little effect in any language. When McAfee is just a few feet from the raft, and reaching out for the crewman, three shots ring out. When McAfee isn't fazed by the bullets, the man empties his clip. But it does no good. You can't kill the undead by shooting them in the heart.

"You have to aim for the head!" I shout, drawing the .45 Glock. The man and McAfee both turn toward me.

"It's okay," McAfee says, sounding like he's got a mouth full of steak. "We're friends."

Ignoring everything my father taught me about how to shoot, I charge forward, take aim, and just ten feet from McAfee, I pull the trigger.

A divot with a hole in the center appears on McAfee's already ruined forehead. An explosion of brain, blood, and white parasites blossoms from the back of his head. He falls back, hitting the sand with a wet thud. The last of the Draugar is dead, and none of them deserved it more than McAfee, who was more of a monster in life than he was undead.

The crewman points his 9mm at me. Eyes wide and face pale, he says, "Who are you?"

"Jane Harper," I say. "You're expecting us."

Willem and Jakob hobble up behind me.

The crewman points his gun at them. "Who are they!"

"You know you're out of ammo, right?" I say.

The man looks at the gun and then lowers it.

Jakob extends his hand. "Captain Jakob Olavson of the *Bliksem.*"

Relief floods the man's face. He points to McAfee. "What the hell was that?"

"Long story," I say. "Help us on board."

As the three-man crew help Jakob on board, the crewman says, "I thought there were four?"

I feel sad for a moment, thinking about Chase and the way he died. But I still feel proud of him. He overcame a lot and became a better man. I'll remember him differently than I would have a few days ago. "He died," I say. "Well."

And the strangest thing about this moment isn't that I said, "He died well," like I'm some sort of Klingon. It's that the five Greenlander sailors listening to me nod like that's good enough for them.

Then we're all on the boat, launched and zipping over the waves. The air feels much colder as we cruise over the ocean, but my tension and fear are already slipping away. We survived. We made it.

Fifteen minutes later, we climb off the Zodiac and onto the deck of a bright white coast guard cutter. It looks a lot like the coast guard ships in the United States except that it has a green stripe instead of a red one. We're given dry blankets and cups of hot cocoa.

The captain greets us with a wave and offers his hand to Jakob. Before either man can introduce himself, there's a dull thud beneath our feet. The captain only looks mildly concerned. "Iceberg?" he asks a crewman as he looks over the side rail.

There is no doubt that this vessel is an icebreaker, and I'm maybe a little desensitized to fearing for my life, so the issue barely registers. That is, until the crewman flinches away from the rail and shouts, "Captain!"

As we all rush toward the rail, the crewman points to the ocean below and shouts, "They're killing each other!"

You'd think that nothing would surprise me now, but this… This is horrible. The sea is red with blood. Sleek black bodies slide up and out of the water, moving fast. I count at least twenty dorsal fins. The orcas. But they're not alone. Scores of large walruses are in the water with them, and they're not running away. As the orcas swim in to attack, the walruses fight back, thrusting their tusks into the whales' skin. An orca breeches, its body writhing. The thirty-foot mammal strikes the side of the cutter, shaking the vessel.

The captain storms away, shouting orders in Greenlandic.

The battle continues as we get underway. And that's when I notice it. The whales aren't attacking the walruses; the walruses are attacking the whales.

These are the walruses that the polar bear attacked.

Like walruses, and people, orcas are mammals. They're warm-blooded.

And the perfect home for the parasites.

The Draugar have survived, too.

Water churns behind the boat, as its two powerful screws propel us away from the horrible scene. *Someone needs to come up here and kill them*, I think, but then I realize it's too late. There were at least a hundred walruses on the beach, and there are maybe fifty in the water. If the orcas are infected, they could be halfway around the world before someone returns to this island. And they'll likely infect any mammal they come across on the way.

As though to prove my worst fears valid, a herd of ten walruses breaks away from the battle and follows the cutter.

Willem and Jakob stand on either side of me, watching the Draugr walruses give chase. As I lean my head on Willem's shoulder and he puts his arm around me, Jakob turns to me and says, "We must tell the world about this, Raven." He turns his gaze back toward the island that nearly claimed our lives. "*We* are the sentinels now."

EPILOGUE

A week after escaping from the island, I find myself under guard at a hospital. Willem and Jakob are both here too, in the room across the hall. We communicate mostly by shouting back and forth, because we're not allowed to leave our rooms. "So you can heal," the doctors say about our confinement, but the policeman outside the door says otherwise. Of course, an armed cop is far better than a parasite-controlled Draugr, so I don't complain.

Our wounds are healing. Our spirits are lifting. We're happy to be alive. We're prisoners, I suppose, for now, but it's not bad actually. The food is good, and I feel safe. Really safe. The problem is that no one seems to be taking our story seriously. We've been interviewed by a number of government agencies, some from Greenland, some from the United States, and despite our stories matching, the investigators' noses crinkle every time like they've just smelled a corpse.

Having just finished a chocolate pudding, I lean back in my bed and look at the TV, which is muted. It's a local news show, but it's happily in English. I see a photo of the *Sentinel* and sit up straight. This is the first time I've seen any mention of the shipwrecks or our rescue. As I turn up the volume, the image changes to my face, and the pretty newscaster smiles as she says my name.

"Our sources say that Jane Harper, one of three survivors of last week's tragic collision between the whaling ship *Bliksem* and the antiwhaling vessel *Sentinel*, has come forward with a claim that sounds like it's straight out of a Hollywood zombie movie. There are parasites, she claims, that are able to take over the mind of the host and turn them into killers. The parasites mature inside one victim and are spread to the next through a bite. Harper went on to describe, in graphic detail, how several other survivors were killed due to encounters with these parasites.

"Though Harper was once a champion of the antiwhaling community, she now believes that Greenland's local walrus and whale populations should be exterminated due to parasitical infection. The antiwhaling community has cut all ties with Harper, who will be undergoing a psychological evaluation, along with her fellow survivors, Jakob and Willem Olavson, who support her claims.

"Authorities believe it is likely that all three survivors might be suffering from shared hallucinations brought on by the cold, starvation, and dehydration, but they haven't ruled out other possibilities, such as contaminated food and water or a natural toxin of some kind. But they are also looking into the possibility of foul play. A team of forensic investigators will be returning to the island next week to search for bodies and any evidence that might indicate a crime had been committed.

"While Greenland's Oceanographic Institute confirms that whale populations are migrating differently this year, they blame the behavior on global warming, which, it seems, is a much more urgent, and real, matter than parasitic zombies."

The newswoman giggles, regains her composure, and says, "In related news, an orca off of Nuuk attacked a man today. This attack is the first on a human outside of captivity. Experts say that the whale likely became confused in the murky waters of Nuuk Bay, where it accidentally struck the man's small fishing boat. If the man fell atop the whale, it's likely the creature acted instinctually to defend itself. They say that the whale merely bit the man's leg and then pulled him to shore, showing the orca realized its mistake and then saved the man's life. The victim was seen leaving the scene on foot and has not yet been identified."

"Orcas don't bite people," says Charlie, the officer stationed at my door. He's a nice enough guy, serious about his job but friendly. He must have heard the volume come up and peeked in. "Not ever."

I turn to Charlie, frowning, and say, "No, Charlie. They don't."

———

ACKNOWLEDGMENTS

The Sentinel couldn't have been written without the stalwart support of a few individuals who have generously given their time and energy. Kane Gilmour, my personal editor and sometimes coauthor, Stan Tremblay, who formatted the original self-published edition, and Roger Brodeur for proofreading just about everything I write, I offer you a hearty "Thank you!"

To Scott Miller, my agent at Trident Media Group, thank you for your resolve, commitment and hard work. At 47North, I must thank Alex Carr for not resisting the siren call of Jane Harper and for taking a chance on relaunching a self-published novel, and its sequel. May there be many more to come. Also at 47North, thanks to Katy Ball, Patrick Magee and Justin Golenbock. Your support means a lot and I'm looking forward to knocking this one out of the park with your help.

Last, but never least, my dear family. Hilaree, my wife, and Aquila, Solomon and Norah, my wildly creative and fun children—I love you guys and am thrilled to be sharing the adventure of life with you.

ABOUT THE AUTHOR

 Jeremy Bishop began his career as an artist and comic book illustrator, before turning to screenwriting, and eventually fiction. His first horror novel, the post-apocalyptic zombie epic *Torment*—a #1 bestseller in Horror on Amazon.com, was a self-publishing success story. In addition, as bestselling author Jeremy Robinson, he has written more than thirty sci-fi, thriller and action/adventure novels and novellas, five of which are published by Thomas Dunne Books/St. Martin's Press. His novels have been translated into eleven languages. He lives in New Hampshire with his family.

Made in the USA
Charleston, SC
11 July 2013